ALL HALLOWS NIGHT

SICK
AND
TWISTED
BOOK 1

LEIGH KELSEY

www.leighkelsey.co.uk

Join my mailing list here https://bit.ly/LeighKelseyNL

Or chat with me in my Facebook group: Leigh Kelsey's Paranormal Den

Ebook and standard paperback cover by Temptation Creations

Foiled paperback cover by Artscandare

Ebook header by Leigh Designs

Paperback chapter design by Cat Cover Designs

❀ Created with Vellum

BLURB

It was a normal Halloween party until the cult crashed it.

I expected beer kegs and douche-bros trying to grind on me. I *didn't* expect blood, chanting, and a twisted ritual.

It turns out our college is home to the Cult of Nightmare—that's Night*mare*, the living embodiment of traumatic dreams. The goddess herself transformed fifty college students into our Halloween costumes ... and bound us to her command.

Now, our little town of Ford's End is overrun with witches, ghosts, sexy nuns—and me, the bride of death.

See, Nightmare has a bone to pick with the other gods, and she's using us to do her dirty work.

There's just one problem: Death, who shows up with his two lieutenants, Misery and Torment, to claim what's theirs.

Their bride. Me.

PLAYLIST

TWICE - Cactus

(Sorry, Cat, I had to…)

For every spooky little weirdo that grew up obsessed with gothic horror books and murder mystery shows.

This book is exactly like those, but with more dicks.

NOTE

THIS SERIES CONTAINS THE FOLLOWING:

- Polyamory (everyone loves everyone in this series!)
- Mild somno
- Ddlg dynamic
- Hate fucking
- Felching
- Dubcon
- Jealousy
- Stalking
- Murder
- Threats
- Secrets
- And a super cute prairie dog

THE END OF THE BEGINNING

*H*e watched from the shadows as the woman he loved wept in the arms of one best friend while the other was lowered into the earth. Both of them were like shadows in long, black coats, their ink-dark umbrellas held aloft to keep the rain away. The coffin made a hollow wooden clang as the pallbearers made a pitiful job of placing it in its final resting place. Another coffin, another innocent person twisted by Nightmare into deceit, manipulation, and betrayal. Exactly as *he* had been.

Maybe he ought to be in his own coffin for what he'd done to the girl weeping, unaware he stood watching. Unable to stand the sight of her pain, or the home it had carved inside his own chest.

He rubbed his breastbone where a permanent ache had struck up and wondered how long it would be until his burial. He'd been alive for so long; would Nightmare's games finally lead to his true death? Once, he'd hoped to find peace in life, but he knew peace in death was his only option now.

His eyes never wavered from the tall woman standing

straight-backed by the open grave, her hands white-knuckled around the umbrella as she cast a fistful of dirt onto the coffin. Her quiet, straining sobs cut right into his heart until a tear burned a hot trail down his cheek, too.

She'd lost one of her closest friends, and he would never forgive himself for his part in it. For his own deception and betrayal. He did this, put those tears in her eyes, placed that haunted look in her eye. She deserved light and happiness and the best things in life, and all he ever did was crush those until not even a glimmer existed in the world.

He watched her the whole time she stood by the grave, speaking softly, and then as she traced the winding path through the graveyard, now alone. He wanted to approach, wanted to wrap his arms around her and swear his loyalty to her, only her. But that was impossible, as it always had been.

He watched her leave and couldn't imagine a worse pain than having the woman he loved so close, and yet impossible to reach.

What had he done?

CHAPTER ONE

CAT

*T*wo Months Earlier

Rain glided down the car windows, teardrops zigzagging in a frantic, senseless pattern I identified with a little too closely. I'd been frantic all morning, my anxiety at a hundred percent, and it had only grown as we'd driven two hundred miles from Harrogate to a Scottish village whose name I'd only learned last week when the acceptance letter dropped through my letterbox.

I felt sick by the time we drove onto the ferry and sailed from Portpatrick to another village so tiny even a google search didn't bring up results: Ford's End, home of the prestigious Ford School of Medicine—our end destination. It was an island halfway between Scotland and Ireland and every bit as grey, dismal, and wet as I'd expected. You'd think the university being as prominent—and wealthy—as it was, it'd have constructed a bridge so we didn't have to travel by ferry. Apparently not.

I sighed, watching the downpour, my stomach winding tighter. Weren't rainstorms supposed to be bad omens? Every horrific event in every book I'd read seemed to begin with a rainstorm. At least it wasn't a thunderstorm. In gothic books, thunder and lightning meant a dark stranger would appear at your window, or you'd hear a mysterious tapping at your bedroom door. And then get haunted, turned into a vampire, or murdered. Or all three rolled into one delightful package.

"I'm getting out," Honey, my eternally optimistic best friend said, her blue eyes wide with excitement and a near-permanent smile curving her cheeks. "I want to explore."

I gave her a strange look, making sure she saw me look from her, to the rain outside, then to her, and back to the rain.

"Don't wander too far. We should be close to Ford's End," my dad, Orwell Wallison, warned from the driver's seat. He had one hand on the steering wheel while another adjusted the gaudy feathered hat he insisted on wearing because it added an *air of prestige.*

"Do take an umbrella if you're getting out, Honey," my mum, Clarissa, said, turning in her seat to give my friend a warm look. Mum's name was one everyone in the medical field would recognise. Hell, she wrote one of the books on our syllabus. She was *thrilled* I was going to Ford, where she herself studied medicine, but less pleased I was getting a medical degree to become a vet. "And consider doing a little rain dance to keep the gods happy."

I could have pointed out rain dances were to summon rain but I just tucked a smile between my cheeeks and watched Mum fondly. Both she and Dad had been raised in conservative, rich families, and when they met in their late twenties they entered a delayed rebellious phase where they both adopted a hippie lifestyle. It had lasted just long enough for them to have me and my brothers before Dad cut his long hair and moved on from the bohemian lifestyle. Mum very much had not moved on.

"Sure, Mrs. W," Honey said with a double thumbs up. Knowing Honey, she might actually dance in the rain just to avoid letting Mum down. We joked we were sisters separated at birth, with the same love of making people happy, the same fear of rejection and failure—but she was the extrovert version to my introvert.

Honey might not have been Mum and Dad's biological child, but we'd all grown up together—me, Honey, and Byron, my as-yet-silent best friend who stared gloomily out the window beside me—and they were every bit their children as me, Virgil, and Zoltan.[1]

"I'm getting out, too," I said impulsively when Honey cracked the door open, rain driving its way across the leather seats onto the dark-wash jeans I'd worn with a soft cream jumper. Comfort clothes, because today was going to be a nightmare of anxious proportions. I needed fresh air, needed to walk, to do *something* to burn off my nerves. Mum opened her mouth, but I smiled knowingly and said, "I've got an umbrella in my bag."

I also had pepper spray and a rape alarm, because I'd read far too many horror stories that took place at college or university, and just because Ford was full of medical students whose workload could only be described as insanity, that didn't mean they wouldn't find time for hobbies. Some people took up cardmaking, some people hit the gym, others were serial rapists in their spare time.

Mum called me disillusioned, her cynical sunshine. I couldn't fathom why.

"We're gonna be fine, Cat," Honey said brightly, slinging her arm around my shoulders when I stepped onto the unsteady ground of the ferry and shut the door behind me.

7

Byron wasn't budging; he rested his chin on his fist and stared at the frothing sea. He was supposed to be flown into Ford's End by helicopter, but he'd shown up at our house in the middle of the night with his bags packed and sadness in his eyes. He'd argued with his parents again. Dicks. Honey and I had tried everything to get him to talk for the five hours we'd been in the car, but his reticence was here to stay.

I'd win him around, though. I just had to find some popcorn on this island.[2]

"Define *fine*," I murmured, giving Honey a sideways glance as she wrangled me around the car and towards the railing. There were five other cars making the crossing, full of medical students or Ford staff. A broad-shouldered blonde guy leant against the railing a few paces away, staring into the churning sea. His clothing screamed *I have more money than God*, but who didn't? There were no scholarships to Ford, and God forbid anyone's family be struggling for money behind closed doors. If the students found out, they'd be ripped apart.

Honey squeezed me closer, her cerulean eyes glowing with excitement. "We're gonna nail school, get the highest grades in all our classes, have a butterfly-worthy social life on the weekends, and graduate in three years as total medical badasses."

I couldn't hold back a snort, a smile curving my lips even as rain sluiced down my long brown hair, the frizz it summoned out of control. "Butterfly-worthy?"

"Butterfly-worthy," Honey confirmed fiercely, her face splitting in a beaming grin when the fog on the sea parted, for just a second, to expose the island we were sailing towards—towering and rocky, with a sprawling village that followed the curve of its roads, a dense woods that hugged the edge of the island and swept up to the top where several bigger buildings clustered, a spire currently attempting to puncture a heavy grey cloud. "We're in our social pupae stage right now, but by the time we graduate, we're going to be beautiful social butterflies."

"I'm going to take pupae as a compliment and not punch you in the tit," I said sweetly.

"Hey, pupae *is* a compliment. Have you ever seen them? Wriggly little cuties."

I wrinkled my nose. Nope. Definitely not. "I feel like we're about to get shipwrecked on the Island of Dr. Moreau."

"Ooh, that's appropriate," said Honey, who'd never read the book where the mad doctor cut apart animals and humans to make twisted mutants. She threw me a wink. "Maybe this doctor will be one of our professors."

"Looking at the place," I drawled as the fog swallowed the view again, "I would not be surprised."

NOW WE'D FOUND SOLID GROUND, THE ISLAND WAS GROWING on me and the adventure of it all was starting to hit, making my stomach flutter with giddiness. The nerves were still there, but my curiosity took over when we landed on a jetty at the base of Ford's End and drove onto a beach road ringed with heavy, dark green trees. I peered out the window at the woodland we passed, Dad's car taking a small, winding road through the village to the top of the island, where Ford School of Medicine hulked at the top.

Byron hovered by my side as I climbed out and surveyed the school grounds.

It still gave me *haunted island where we're going to be vivisected* energy, but there was something a little Indiana

Jonesy about it with the trees around us, like we'd travel into the woods and find a secret cavern with a priceless golden statue.

Ford was split into seven different buildings, all arranged in a rectangle around a park that boasted not one but *two* fountains for reasons that weren't quite apparent at first glance. Benches and old oak trees were dotted around the park, and there were already people sitting on them, presumably second and third years. Topiaries had been carved to resemble Ford's sea serpent mascot, the newest thing about this place—everything else had a history and weight to it.

"She certainly didn't waste any time," Byron said with his first smile of the day, his blue eyes warm as he watched Honey where she stood off to the side, flirting with the broad-shouldered blonde guy from the ferry.

"We're social pupae-ing," I told him, and patted his arm when horror crossed his tanned face, his understanding far quicker than mine had been. "We're going to evolve into beautiful social butterflies—yes, you too," I insisted when he began to object. "We'll be talking to people, going to parties, making friends—you should make your peace with it now," I told him sympathetically.

"Good god," he breathed, only half joking.

I snorted, bumping my shoulder into his. "We'll get through it. Introverts unite." I held up my fist and he bumped his against it.

"Safety in numbers, I like the way you think, Cat. What are we waiting here for anyway?"

Dad appeared out of nowhere and slung his arms around both our shoulders. "Patience, children. Someone's coming to take your bags from the car and show you to your new digs. Did I use that correctly? Tannie taught me it."

"Flawless usage of the word digs, Dad," I assured him, excitement and curiosity beating my nerves even deeper into submission as I smiled. Dad always had a way of making the worst problems feel like nothing to worry about, and I needed that comfort right now. Because looking at the historic grey buildings around me, their windows watchful and contents unknowable, the largest building spearing the sky with its spire, the university sprawling and wide... I was a little daunted.

"Did I slay the house down boots?" Dad asked, ultra seriously.

"You slayed, Dad," I agreed, and wondered if he'd continue to watch *RuPaul's Drag Race* now I'd left home and Zoltan—Tannie—had returned to his own uni.

Byron suppressed a smile despite his grumpy mood, but then his attention snagged on something in the distance. He assaulted my arm with rapid taps. "Oh my God, it's Lurch from the Addams Family."

"Byron, don't be unkind," Dad chided, and then choked on a laugh at the same time my eyes flew wide. Shit, By was right—it really did look like Lurch. Walking out of the massive double doors of the biggest building was a man who had to be nearing seven feet tall, with papery-white skin, a square face, and massive shoulders that made the blonde guy Honey was flirting with look like a stick drawing. He wore a black coat almost to the floor and a blocky hat, like he'd stepped out of a Victorian novel.

"Staff and students stay in different buildings, right?" I asked, probably being unkind but unable to shake the prickle of unease that formed behind my shoulder blades.

"He's just a very tall man," Dad said, shaking his head and squeezing my shoulder. "No need to be frightened. Besides, the bigger a man, the more luggage he can carry. Remember that when you're shopping for husbands, Cat."

I rolled my eyes but despite the hulking giant making his way across the park towards us, I couldn't keep a smile off my face. "I'm here to study, Dad, not to find a husband."

He wasn't deterred. "Good place to find husbands, a medical school."

"Mum found you at a charity gala," I drawled, giving him a snarky look.

"And Honey's mum found Godfrey at Cambridge," he pointed out.

I smiled, remembering the stories Honey's parents told, of her *heir to a Fortune 500 company* father getting the shock of his life when the wild child he'd fallen in love with at college went on to become a vicar.

"Chances of me attracting a billionaire are dismally low, so don't get your hopes up," I drawled. They tended to go for glamorous women with flawless blonde hair, tanned skin, and petite bodies to die for. Not tall, almost-too-curvy girls with dull brunette hair, lips bitten red, glasses, a permanent wince, and fingers that wouldn't stop spinning a ring around and around and around my finger.[3]

We fell silent when the hulking man reached us, his shadow cast far.

"Where are your bags?" he asked in a deep voice like a rockslide. Chills went down my arms, but I kept in mind what Dad had said. *He's just a tall man, nothing to be afraid of.*

"Over here in the car," Dad replied, overly friendly to make up for Byron and I not quite managing to avoid staring at the man. "Orwell Wallison, nice to meet you, old boy."

"Doyle," the massive man replied in a grunt, following Dad back to the car.

"He's cheerful," Byron remarked quietly, leaning his shoulder into mine. "Chances of him murdering us in our sleep?"

"High," I murmured. "Oh, look who's deigned to grace us with her presence again."

Honey stuck her tongue out at us, jogging back to our side. "Don't be sulky. I only left you for ten minutes."

Byron slid a canny look at her. "Did you get his number, at least?"

Honey wiggled her phone at him, her face lighting up. "Of course I did. What kinda girl do you take me for?"

"A chatty one."

She reached across to poke his shoulder.

Mum appeared out of nowhere, making us all jump.

"Jesus," Byron hissed, earning another poke from the vicar's daughter. "I didn't know you could teleport, Mrs. W."

Mum smiled sneakily, wind batting her dark hair around her face. "There's a lot you kids don't know about me. I could be a secret superhero. Dr. Strange eat your heart out." She touched my shoulder. "Ready to go inside?"

I sucked in a slow breath and nodded, trying to hold onto my curiosity when nerves spiked. The faster I went into my new room, the faster I could get the lay of the land, and the less scary it would be. The unknown was terrifying; I'd learned a long time ago that not knowing was what scared me. Once I'd been to a place, met a person, accomplished a task—whatever gave my anxiety power—it lost its control over me.

I turned my ring around and around my finger.

I'd been terrified of going to high school, but after a few weeks it was as ordinary as primary school. This would be no different. Even if it was bigger. On an island in the middle of the Irish Sea. Completely isolated. With a dozen times more pressure and families rooted in old money and new technology. Sure. No different.

I glanced down at my ring, a spiky gold crown encircling it to remind me of my inner bad bitch, and that I could rule anything like a queen, even my own panic. Tannie's words, not mine.

You're not anxious, you're a queen and a bad bitch.

"I'm ready," I lied, and followed Mum, Dad, Honey, Byron, and Lurch—sorry, Doyle—into a three-storey grey building to our right.

The back of my neck tingled, and I could have sworn someone was watching us, but when I glanced back to the park no one was looking our way.

I shook my head and let the door fall shut behind me.

CHAPTER TWO

CAT

I really shouldn't have counted my lucky stars about the lack of a thunderstorm. I shoved the sleep mask off my eyes and squint-glared at my new bedroom as thunder rumbled and rain battered the old window above the bed. The shapes of the wardrobe, desk, and shelves on the wall were still unfamiliar and my heart-beat quickened, but sudden lightning illuminated the sky, bright enough to drive through the brocade curtains, and I settled as I saw where I was and that I was alone. No bogeymen. No scary, six-foot-tall porter who'd broken into my room while I tried to sleep. For *five hours,* and counting.

"Ugh," I groaned, and let my mask fall back over my eyes, rolling over and hissing when cold sliced across my back as the covers rode up. I yanked them back down, shivering. This room was freezing, not at all helped by wind that drove through gaps in the aged window frame.

The first thing I'd buy when I got down to the village—unimaginatively called Ford's End like the island—was a heater.

I wanted, very suddenly, to go home. But that was easier said than done when there were only two ferries a day until term began, when the boats would drop to one *a week*. Also, it was the middle of the night.

I was here to stay, and I had no choice but to live with it.

I sighed, relaxing into the bed as it began to warm again, and then jumped at a sudden crash of thunder and a rush of wind so severe that it sounded like a screaming woman. My body tensed instantly, and there went any chance of sleep.

I groaned. Why didn't I go to med school somewhere warm and temperate? I could have taken a gap year, or could have been studying medicine in Australia like Virgil right now.

Virgil...

I pushed up my mask again and fumbled under the cold pillow for my phone, light blinding my eyes as I stabbed what I thought was the clock app, closed the calculator app, and eventually found the world clock. It was just after two p.m. in Sydney. *Thank fuck.* I didn't stop to wonder if he'd be in class; I swiped clumsily at my phone until it began to ring, then mashed it to my ear.

"Prickly," he answered instantly, annoyingly upbeat. Maybe the Aussie sun was giving my serious oldest brother a sunny disposition.

"Poet," I replied, my voice rough. "I hate it here. Come rescue me."

He snorted, which was more like him, and said, "No chance. You got yourself into this mess, wanting to follow in Mum's footsteps. I tried to tell you the creepy island in the middle of the ocean wasn't your best option, but would you listen?"

"You don't need to gloat," I grumbled, rubbing my eyes and staring at my room as another flash of lightning lit the unfamiliar walls, followed by the distant rumble of thunder. "It's freezing, and stormy. I'm in bed like a fucking ice cube."

"So get another blanket." I could hear his signature dismissive shrug.

"Sure, Virgil, let me just go get another blanket at three a.m. in the damn morning. Good idea. Capital."

"God, don't say capital. You sound like Uncle Edgar."

I snorted, smiling despite myself. "Was it like this when you moved away? The homesickness?"

Virgil sighed. "It gets easier. You get used to your new home, settle into your new life. Then when you go home, you feel out of place there. Fun, huh?"

"Your definition of fun needs some work."

He laughed. "You'll be fine. The first few nights are the worst. You're in one of those ancient dorms, right?"

"They're private rooms now, but yeah," I agreed, rubbing my eyes.

"There's gotta be a supply closet somewhere. Go explore, raid it."

"What has Australia *done* to you?" I asked with mock horror. "Explore? Raid? Who *are* you?"

"I'm you but better."

"Alright, asshole, don't quote memes at me. Go study or whatever you should be doing."

"You were the one who called me, Prickly."

"A lapse of judgement," I assured him sweetly, and then sobered. "It's not been the same at home without you."

"I'll be back at Christmas," he reminded me. "That's less than two months away."

"If you think that sounds optimistic, I have some very bad news for you," I drawled, my chest tightening. Two months until I could go home, until I saw Mum and Dad again, until I was in the same room as Virgil and Tannie. I didn't know how I would do it.

Families were only allowed on the island to help us settle in, and only for a single day. After that, they weren't permitted. I was completely cut off. If I hadn't had my phone, I wouldn't have heard from them for two months.

"You'll be fine, Cat," Virgil promised more seriously. "You got through what happened in—"

"I know," I cut off, a shiver moving down my body, memories sinking teeth into me. "I'd rather not remember. Thanks."

"I'm here if you need me."

"I know," I repeated, darkness closing in around me until I couldn't breathe. "I've gotta go find a blanket. Talk soon."

I put the phone down before he could reply, and flattened my hands over my ears like it would drown out the noise, the voice. But it was inside my head, my own memory weaponised, and there was no escaping.

I hadn't really meant to go hunt down a utility closet, but I couldn't lay here alone with my thoughts. So I threw off the covers, replaced them in the hopes they might hold onto the scrap of heat my body had left, and grabbed slippers and a velvet dressing gown I'd unpacked only hours ago.

It was silent in the hallway outside my room, but a silence I didn't trust, like the building was holding its breath.

I knew memories were getting to me, encouraging my paranoia when this was literally just a building full of med students, but I couldn't help but flinch at the shadows created by trees dancing outside the windows, gasping at a sudden glare of lightning. I hated storms.

The wind sounded like piercing screams, as if someone was wailing in grief in the Rosalind Woods.

It's his mother, a dark voice whispered in my mind. *She's come to claim revenge for what you did to her son. You should make her pay, too. Make her regret raising a son like that.*

I shuddered and walked faster, eyeing the numbered doors around me until I found one that wasn't. I held my breath, skin prickling as I prepared for someone to jump out and find me doing something I shouldn't. I opened the door slowly, wary of squeaking hinges.

Great. It was only cleaning solutions, mops, and buckets. I closed it carefully and moved on, goosebumps all down my arms and my breaths coming faster. The memories were too loud, history too close. I felt it like a shadow rearing over me, wanting to drag me down into the depths of Hell. Felt it reach out cold, clawed fingers, and I quickened my steps to outrun them, my chest closed off so I could only gasp.

I glanced down at my ring, but I didn't feel queenly enough to rule my own mind right now, let alone anything else.

I wanted to keep going and run off the island, but I stopped at the next unmarked door, and exhaled a hard breath of relief, a tiny weight falling off my chest so I could gasp down air. There were towels and blankets and spare sheets here. I grabbed two blankets and a sheet for good measure, closed the door, and hurried back to my room.

I was no safer from my thoughts here than out in the hallway, but I felt better with a door between me and the outside world.

I cocooned myself in the blankets, added another pair

of socks on my feet, and forced myself to breathe, to relax, to forget.

I slept fitfully, and woke to the tinkling xylophone of my phone's alarm. Before I could even tell the alarm to fuck off, I jerked upright, blinking bleary eyes. Someone was standing across my room, watching while I slept and—

It was the coat I'd hung on my wardrobe door.

I slumped back onto the mattress with a groan.

This school was going to be the death of me.

CHAPTER THREE

CAT

$\mathcal{I}$ wasted all my allotted time before orientation slapping concealer over my dark circles, adding blush to my sallow cheeks, and painting a sharp black wing on both eyes, because there was very little that winged liner couldn't solve. I had just enough time to grab a slice of toast and an iced coffee from the dining room downstairs before I met Byron and Honey outside. Honey was as bright and excited as ever, a massive grin on her face and her dress a bright yellow to match her mood. Byron hid under a massive hoodie with the hood up and sunglasses over his eyes, his arms wrapped around his middle. It was a very relatable look, and one I regretted not copying. All that time wasted on concealer and I could have just hidden behind shades.

"Gimme," he groaned, lurching towards my coffee.

"Hey." I held it out of reach. "Get your own."

Honey caught his hood before he could duck back

inside the building and do just that. "We're gonna be late already. Let's go, let's go!"

"I couldn't brave the breakfast room alone," Byron muttered to me. "There were too many people in it when I got there."

And it was blissfully empty just now. I tipped my straw towards my best friend in pity, and he slurped up a quarter of my iced latte before I wrenched it away.

"Thief," I hissed.

I'd been friends with Byron long enough that I didn't worry about catching cooties from using the same straw. I followed his example and drank enough coffee that my eyes glazed. Oh shit yeah, I dumped three pumps of vanilla in it. That was the best thing about coming to a school where no expense was spared—we had amazing coffee and the best food.

In the main building, the ground floor had a cafeteria, a pasta bar, a restaurant, a Costa Coffee, a bubble tea shop, and a Japanese ramen place that didn't even franchise in the UK. My stomach was looking forward to the tour part of orientation.

"Hurry up," Honey urged on the path ahead of us, her satchel bouncing on her shoulder.

"Motherfuck," Byron hissed when we walked under a stretch of trees still covered in last night's rainwater, and leaves divested themselves of their burdens.

I sped up to avoid the same fate, but a fat drop splashed on the top of my head, as cold as ice water. "I hate rain," I announced. "I know it's the only reason we have plants and flowers and a thriving ecosystem but—"

"It's far too early for the word ecosystem," Byron grumbled, but there was warmth in his blue eyes when he threw me a smirk. "Can I have more coffee?"

"Sure," I agreed. "There's a coffee shop in the main building."

The look he levelled on me was so flat and annoyed it reminded me of an exasperated cat, and I burst out laughing.

"By, stop being grumpy and walk faster," Honey called. "You too, Cat. Exercise will wake you both up."

She said that like I didn't usually start my day with a jog, but I didn't point that out. I was too drained after a night of restless sleep, and too keyed up with nerves about, well, everything. The orientation, meeting our classmates, meeting professors, memorising my schedule, learning the layout of the university—and that was just what was on my anxiety agenda for *today*.

But Honey was right. If we got there late, it would be so much worse. Everyone would stare, already huddled into their groups and cliques. Whoever was guiding us through the school today would scowl with disapproval. I hated disapproval. My stomach knotted and I quickened my steps.

"Lend me some of your optimism," I said to Honey. "I need it more than you."

She laughed, about to reply when we reached the end of the path and spotted the group of people hovering awkwardly at the bottom of the steps to the biggest building—which I'd learned the name of the second we were given our welcome packs.

Unlike most schools, they didn't send out any information to students before we got here and enrolled. No class list, no syllabus or staff list, not even a map of the place. It was weird and a *tad* alarming, but Ford was a school with old traditions and this mystique was one of them.

I only knew about the food places because of gossip Honey had picked up last night. Mum said the secrets were

23

necessary since so many students were from high profile families—children of billionaires and business moguls and celebrities and even royals sometimes—and it was a security risk to send out maps, or even upload them to a website that anyone could browse.

Which I understood, but it was frustrating for someone to whom arming themselves with knowledge and information in advance wasn't just smart preparation but a survival instinct.

I ran my thumb over my crown ring and dragged air into my lungs. The last thing I needed was to make a fool of myself by passing out. Instead, I waited for Byron to catch up to us and then pulled my lips into a smile—not too wide, not too small. Friendly but not smirking, not stretched and psycho either. It was the smile I'd mastered years ago that said *I'm completely normal and just like you.*

Judging by the looks of it, our guide wasn't here yet. Would they be a member of staff or a senior student? I knew good behaviour was rewarded with positions of power among students—Mum had told me that much. She was strangely secretive about parts of her time here, citing security issues. If she told me too much, it would put others in danger. Even though she knew full well I wasn't going to tell anyone, and neither was I an axe murderer who'd use that information to go on a killing spree.

That's not quite true is it? A dark whisper spilled through my mind, tightening my smile until it was harder to maintain. I took a long drink of coffee just for something to do, and thankfully a tall girl a couple years older than us jogged down the path towards us, her body clad in a heavy woollen skirt perfect for this dreary weather—even though it *had* finally stopped raining, wonders will never cease—and a purple tartan jacket. Her cornsilk hair was pulled into a tight bun that spoke of strictness, but was streaked with a single line of baby pink rebellion. She pushed up wire-frame glasses and gave us all a big smile, meeting each of our eyes.

"Sorry to keep you waiting," she said, her voice strong and clear like a bell. "I'm Erika, your guide for orientation. Can I ask everyone, give me your names one by one, and I'll check we've got everyone we're waiting for. Then I'll show you around Ford and get your schedule and ID cards."

A weight fell off my shoulders and I inhaled a longer breath. It was good to know what to expect, and even better that Erika seemed genuinely friendly. I'd been so scared to make a bad impression on a professor, and knowing my luck it'd be the strictest one.

Byron bumped his shoulder into mine, his eyes soft. "Breathe, Cat."

"I am breathing," I muttered. Now, at least.

"He's here, he's here," Honey whispered suddenly, turning to us with massive baby blue eyes, a grin dimpling her cheeks.

"Ooh," Byron teased, "loverboy?"

"Not so loud!" Honey hissed.

I allowed a smirk even as I focused on listening for our names, nudging Byron when his was called.

Golden-haired loverboy of the broad shoulders turned out to be Alastor Carmichael, which earned a low laugh from Byron. The Carmichaels were rivals to his family's company, Everett Corp, with decidedly different approaches to providing the market with insulin. Everett Corp saved lives by lowering the cost, since insulin was insanely marked up for no reason other than profit. Carmine was the company driving the price higher, presumably for fun.

"By," Honey whispered, her azure eyes big and pleading. "Please don't start shit with him."

"Me?" Byron flattened a hand to his chest. "Start shit? I have never once—"

"Here!" I said emphatically when my name was called. My cheeks burned when more than one student turned to look at me. A dark-haired guy in a white T-shirt and jeans smirked. I held his gaze, my stomach a mess of nerves and panic, but I didn't look away until he did. I knew what he thought, but it wasn't that I was a total nerd brimming with excitement to start school. If I didn't register my attendance, I would literally *die.* I rubbed my thumb over my ring and talked myself down from the ledge of panic.

I was *fine.* It was just scary because it was the first day and I was in the middle of nowhere, and it was a little weird how school began in November instead of September. But I was a bad bitch and a queen and this wouldn't break me, like everything else hadn't broken me.

"Here," Honey said and held out her fist.

Bewildered but compliant, I fist-bumped her. "What's that for?"

"You asked for some of my optimism. Fist bumps are part of the transference process."

I snorted.

Erika raised her voice. "We're missing Mason Lindgren. Does anyone know him?"

"Lindgren?" the model-esque dark-haired guy in the white T-shirt asked. I didn't catch his first name, but his surname was pretty easy to remember—Ford. Like the university. The guy beside him, smaller, with chestnut hair instead of ink-dark, was also a Ford. Brother? Cousin? "As in, the Lindgrens of Munich?"

Erika shrugged with a carefree smile. "Not a clue. And you'll find families and names don't matter as much after a few months at Ford. Well, unless Mason turns up in the next minute, we'll start without—"

"I'm here, I'm here," a short, dumpy white guy in a windbreaker and jeans ran across the lawn. "Fuck, sorry I'm late, damn alarm didn't—"

"You're here now," Erika cut in with a forgiving smile. "And my advice? Less swearing unless you're in the student areas. If professors hear you, they'll make an example of you, even outside classes."

"Yay," I whispered to Honey and Byron. "Another thing to worry about."

Byron smirked, but Honey chewed her bottom lip.

"Question," Loverboy, AKA Alastor Carmichael said, crossing his arms over his big chest as he drew Erika's attention. "Is it true there's no fresher's week at Ford?"

"It is," she confirmed. "There's no letting you settle in gently here. Classes will start the day after tomorrow, so if you didn't already bring your own books and supplies you'd better pick those up from the library or bookshop. *But,*" she said with a secretive smile, "I heard there'll be a party tomorrow on Halloween. Pure rumour, of course."

"Of course," White T-Shirt Ford agreed with a matching smile. It made sense that a Ford would know everything that happened here, *or* he was the one hosting the party.

"You're having a Halloween party? At Ford?" Mason, the latecomer, let out a low whistle. "That's brave. Isn't the school built on an old burial ground? I heard there was a pagan cult here before Ford was built."

I rolled my eyes. *Sure.* People scoffed, but others exchanged shifty glances like they believed it.

Erika shook her blonde head, laughing. "Don't believe everything you hear. We might be med students who deal

27

with science and facts, but that doesn't mean we won't make up a ghost story just to mess with people."

She marked something on her tablet and tucked it away. "Right. Follow me and I'll lead you to coffee and welcome packs."

More beautiful words had never been spoken.

CHAPTER FOUR

CAT

*D*espite my body being convinced the end was nigh, we got through the rest of orientation with zero casualties. We even made a couple friends with fellow students in our year, and then gorged on tonkatsu ramen for dinner in Honey's room while we memorised the campus layout and compared our timetables.

By the time I went back to my room, via the shower room that had blessedly private cubicles, I was feeling more optimistic and the spectres of my past were very far away. My bed was even warmer thanks to my pilfered blankets, so I didn't shiver when I climbed in and opened Youtube to watch videos of cute ducklings and decompress from the day.

I survived. I did it. Tannie was right—I could accomplish anything.

I let out a deep sigh and relaxed into the mattress, relieved it was actually plush and comfortable unlike most dorm beds, but I leapt out of my skin when a terrifying scraping came from my door.

I jumped onto the bed with a yelp, climbing to my feet, expecting rats or ghosts of old pagans and—

I frowned at the envelope that had been pushed under my door. With a soft *what the fuck?* I climbed down to investigate, grabbed the envelope—heavy and made of quality cream paper—and opened the door, scanning the hall to see who'd left it.

Was this a threat? Had someone singled me out as easy prey already?

There was no one out in the hall, but across from me the door opened and a black guy I'd seen at orientation poked his shaved head out, doing the same as me.

"You got one, too," I realised, the words blurting out when I saw the envelope he held.

"Yeah," he agreed, frowning. "What the hell is it?"

Down the hallway, other doors opened until we all hovered—me, Byron, Honey, my adjacent neighbour, a redhead girl I thought was called Rhona, and a Pakistani girl named Milani Hussain. We all held an identical envelope.

"This is weird as fuck," Byron remarked, glancing from Honey to me.

I cracked open the wax seal on my envelope but before I could read the contents, Rhona—or whatever her name actually was—let out a squeal. "We've been invited to the party."

Oh, joy.

I sighed, wilting against the doorframe and praying to every introvert god in existence that I could get out of this. No such luck. One look at Honey's face and I knew she'd make us go. Besides, I didn't want to stand out as being miserly so soon after getting to Ford. Blending in was the wisest course of action.

I read the invitation and suppressed a groan. Even better. It was a *costume* party, and I hadn't brought a costume to med school because I wasn't insane.

"I'm not going shopping with you," Byron said before Honey had even opened her mouth. He glanced at me and added, "You're on your own with this one, Cat."

Charming.

Luckily for Byron, shopping was one thing I'd never complain about. When we all disappeared back in our rooms, despite the threat to my introvert ways, my optimism returned.

Tomorrow was going to be a good day.

TONIGHT WAS GOING TO BE HELL.

Honey and I had spent the day vying for elbow room in the single shop in the village of Ford's End that sold costumes—a dizzying collection of rooms that seemed to go on forever and contained everything from shovels and rope to wind chimes, wholesale Pepsi, pet supplies, friendship bracelets, and all manner of vaguely useful junk.

Despite being our designated extrovert, Honey still struggled to fight through the cramped rooms to the costume section where Ford students were already packed like sardines. They behaved like vultures, swooping on the carcases of clothing rails, snatching up whatever entrails were left and clutching them possessively to their chest. Oh, did I say *they*? I meant *we*, because I did the exact same thing.

The only costume left in my size that wasn't hellishly boobaceous was a floor-length, silk-adjacent dress covered in detailed albeit scratchy lace. I snatched it up desperately, and only realised the strange ruffle of lace hanging down the back wasn't a ruffle but a *veil* when I joined the cluster of people near the single, well-used checkout. Great. I was going to my first med school party as a bride.

"Ooooh," Honey said, joining me with excitement dancing in her eyes and a brand new friend trailing in her wake.[1] "A wedding dress. Your dad will be thrilled."

I gave her a deadpan look. "I'm going as the bride of death."

It was that or the bride of Frankenstein, and I didn't have enough green eyeshadow to cover my entire face.

"Creepy, I love it," said Honey's new friend, a squat bronze-skinned woman with bright amber eyes behind heavy rectangular-framed glasses, long brunette hair, and a violently red coat, scarf, and hat combo. Her lipstick was the same pillarbox shade. "I'm going as a zombie." She held up her costume on its wire hanger and gave the decayed green dress a wiggle. "But with massive cleavage obviously, because I'm a *woman* and I couldn't *possibly* wear a costume without both nipples poking people in their eyes."

I snorted. I liked her.

I'd just begun to smile when a shoulder rammed into mine, throwing me aside, and I hit a shelf full of porcelain teddy bears fishing in a koi pond so hard that pain exploded down my side and I gasped a cry.

"Hey, watch it!" Honey snapped, instantly at my side. I was surprised to find a hand with violently red fingernails helping me back to my feet, sweeping dust off my coat where I'd slammed into stock that definitely hadn't been rotated in the past six months.

"Are you alright?" she murmured, peering into my eyes.

I nodded. "Thanks…"

"Darya," she supplied. "You're Cat, right? And the guy

32

you were with at breakfast is Byron? Honey was talking about you."

"That's us," I agreed, and snapped around to face Honey when a rough male voice raised in volume.

"Do you know who you're talking to, worm? I'm Orwell *Ford.* As in, I own this island. So when I want to get past, you move out of the fucking way."

Honey squared her shoulders, but she didn't fight him. She just muttered, "Asshole."

Without a word, Darya and I flanked Honey, and I kept none of my emotions off my face when I faced the arrogant bastard. He probably got everything he wanted because he was from a family with a fancy name and endless money and he had passable looks. Not the tall, dark, handsome vibe of his cousin, and the sneer made him uglier, but I knew the type. Entitled, superior, cruel.

Make him regret sneering at your friend. You know his type. You know the damage boys like him can do if left unchecked.

"There's a thing you might not have heard of," I said before I could stop my mouth, anger overriding any anxiety that might have hit if I'd actually thought before acting. "It's called a queue. Do you need a moment to Google it? I'll wait."

Orwell laughed, somehow still managing to sneer. "And who the fuck are you?"

"Someone standing in the queue who won't be walked all over." I had a fancy name and money too, and I was so fucking *sick* of men like him, who thought they could bully their way through the world. Memories flashed, but I shoved them away, angry enough to battle my mind into submission for once.

A long arm slung over Orwell's shoulder, and Duncan Ford appeared like a movie star stepping out of the shadows, his megawatt smile making my stomach curdle.

"Let's not make enemies before term's even started, shall we, Orly?" Ford threw a beatific smile at me, Honey, and Darya. "Nice to meet you ladies."

His smile lingered a little too long before he guided Orwell away, his eyes staying on me a beat too long for comfort. And I didn't miss the fact they'd both made their way to the front of the line anyway. Duncan was just a pro at doing what Orwell had clumsily tried to achieve.

And I got the sense that neither of them would forget us talking back despite Orwell being the ass the shoved *me* into a fucking shelf.

"Great," I muttered, checking my wedding dress was still intact. "I've pissed off the guy hosting the damn party. Tonight is going to be great."

CHAPTER FIVE

CAT

"*S*tand still," Byron huffed, doing my makeup but under protest and complaining the whole time. Honey had expressly refused to help because she needed to straighten her hair, slick it back, and spray it black to fully achieve her black cat Halloween costume. Which left me and Byron trying to figure out how to paint a skull on my face.

"I *am* standing still," I retorted, adjusting my weight. The rustle of not-silk brushed my legs as Byron painted a long stroke of white paint down the hollow of my cheek, mirroring it on the other side.

"There," he said, standing back to admire his work. "No wait, one sec." His tongue stuck out as he narrowed his eyes and swiped more white paint on my neck, down to my chest. "*Now* you're done. You look badass, Cat."

I peered into the mirror I'd hung above my desk and grinned. Hey, I did look badass. He'd done a really good job with shadows and highlights, bringing out the gaunt-ness of my cheeks so I looked skeletal, the white paint adding details until I didn't look creepy—just scary and pretty, all at once.

"I legitimately love you, By," I told him, grabbing him into a fierce hug. "Now where did you put your wig? I'll help you style it."

Between us, we were a very fetching trio of black cat (sexy), male vampire (grumpy), and bride of death (scowling as I tried to walk in the platforms Honey made me wear instead of my Converse.)

The party was being held in the grey-brick building directly across the park from ours, where third-years had their own house with massive, luxe bedrooms instead of small dorm rooms. And where, I discovered, the Ford family were given the special privilege of living even in first year. It was called Ford House, so I supposed it made sense. Entitled bastards.

"Last chance to back out," Byron sighed, skulking along the path at my side like a vampire who'd been mourning his lost love for a century. "We can go back to our rooms, no one will ever notice."

"Someone will," Honey disagreed. "This is our best chance to make a good first impression. Going home will make us look like snobs."

"She's right," I said begrudgingly. I held out my hand, pinky finger extended. *Introverts unite.* His face softened and he hooked his pinky with mine, eyeing the three-storey house with less hostility.

It was a lovely building, all mullioned windows, pointed arches, and heavy Gothic architecture. I was surprised there wasn't a gargoyle crouched on the roof, watching us walk down the path to the stained-glass front door.

Byron yelped, grabbing my arm when lightning shot

across the sky in a violent arc, throwing Ford House into stark, merciless light for a split second. It caught on the empty plastic cups left on the doorstep and the topiary bush someone had already fallen into and left in a pitifully crooked state. It looked like the party got started before we arrived. That was good—drunk people paid less attention —and bad—drunk people were drunk and also people and I disliked both.

"There, there." I stroked his back. "I'll protect you."

He grumbled, letting go of me and casting a sullen look at the sky. "Why is it always fucking raining?"

"We're on an island between Ireland and Scotland," Honey pointed out, the whiskers painted on her cheeks curving as she smiled.

Her smile dialled up a few degrees when the bone-cream door opened and spat out Alastor Carmichael dressed as the Donne Darko rabbit with his bunny head dangling from a nonchalant hand.

I stopped dead on the path when Alastor sprayed vomit across the lawn and the lopsided bush, clearly already trashed. Poor little topiary. It was a comfort to know something was having a worse day than I was.

"Lovely," Byron said, wrinkling his nose.

I eyed the panelled hallway through the open door, the music that had been muffled moments earlier now blazing and unapologetic, the thumping bass of the Dua Lipa remix making my blood jump in a matching rhythm. Music I loved, but parties less so. Luckily, alcohol fixed most things and there was guaranteed to be an endless flow of it in a frat party thrown by a guy whose family owned a fucking *island*.

Walking into the grey brick house and voluntarily entering the miasma of booze, perfume, and vomit was a whole assault on my senses. What the hell was I doing here, dressed in a flowing white dress with a long ivory wig smeared with Honey's pink hair chalk?[1]

Byron and I came to an abrupt stop when Honey rushed past us, vanishing into the kitchen at the end of the hall.

"She's not...?" I murmured, a furrow in my brow.

"Oh, she is," Byron argued when our eternally sunny friend reappeared with a glass of water and brushed past us back outside.

"She hardly knows the guy," I huffed. "By, promise me if I ever lose my mind over broad shoulders and a nice smile, shake some sense into me."

"I promise to shake you back to sanity," he vowed, laying a hand over his heart as we entered the kitchen and made a beeline for a keg of beer beside an impressive tower of plastic cups.

"Holy shit, Cactus," a raucous male voice shouted down the hall. "You've got tits."

"Do *not* call me Cactus." I gave the dick who'd spoken— Mason Lindgren, the German guy, dressed as a ghost-buster—a fierce scowl, then turned to scout the kitchen for food. It was best not to encourage them with attention. The same techniques used in dog training could be applied to college boys, but no fucking chance was I rewarding anyone for good behaviour with a treat.

Cactus Bengal-Tiger Wallison. It was one hell of a name. And *joy*, it looked like someone here had access to student records. Not surprising in this uni, with these students.

Break his face so he can never speak your name again, a dark impulse whispered to me, chills shaking over my bare shoulders. *Make him swallow his own teeth. Don't stop until his face turns blue.*

I bit back unease and ignored it like I always ignored that voice.

Except for June three years ago. Only three people knew. No one else could ever know.

"Cat," Byron said with the note of someone repeating something they'd already said.

"Sorry," I sighed, accepting the cup and taking a long drink. I expected to wince at its cheap taste but damn it was the good stuff.

"Don't worry," By soothed, squeezing my shoulder. "They're not out *that* much."

Great, now I was painfully aware of the off-shoulder neckline of the dress, which turned out to be more booba-ceous than I initially expected. I didn't even need to glance down. They were *right there*, plump and curvy and on full horrific display.

"Because you love me, please tell the truth," I said, glancing around the kitchen and only recognising a few people.

"They're right in front of me and I can't stop staring at them," Byron blurted. "And I don't even like girls. You're about to make a crazy amount of friends tonight."

I groaned, wilting against a marble countertop. "I have two friends, and that's more than enough."

"Hey." A tall, redhead guy who clearly didn't hear my last remark gave me a winning smile. "I'm Eddard. I *love* your outfit. Skeleton bride. Hot."

I had a split second to make a choice, and I decided to throw my best friend under the bus and hope he didn't exact revenge later.

"Aw, thanks!" I said in a sweet voice that was nothing close to natural. "My husband helped me pick it." I batted my lashes at Byron, reaching over to entwine our hands.

Eddard made himself very quickly scarce. He didn't even make an excuse. I snorted.

"I've just decided I'm keeping a fuckboy tally. How many do you think I'll thwart by the end of the night?"

Byron raised an eyebrow, lifting our joined hands. "Can you thwart them *without* the use of a husband? I would like to talk to some people tonight, thank you."

I stared at him like he'd grown a second head.

"Only if they're hot," he added.

"Obviously." It went without saying.

"And to answer your question, at least ten, maybe twenty." Byron winked. "And look, here's your next one."

I groaned, glancing at the short, blonde 'wizard' eyeing me up from across the room. By the time I glanced back, Byron had disappeared. Sneaky bastard.

So much for introverts unite.

CHAPTER SIX

DEATH

*T*here was a disturbance, like a tremor along a violin string usually still. A soft humming sound in a place of eternal silence.

I squinted out the bay window at the castle grounds and strained my hearing for anything out of place. There was nothing except Misery's prairie dog *yahooing* in her freshly cleaned gilded enclosure.

Sometimes I fantasised about touching that creature a little too long, letting slip a little death magic, and freeing myself of the yowling that woke me every morning when I'd slept poorly. It was an empty threat; I loved Miz too much to hurt him. Besides some days she was the only thing keeping his sanity patched together when Tor and I couldn't reach him.

I rubbed my eyes and wondered if I was hallucinating the disturbance. Maybe the role of Death had finally driven me to madness. Or perhaps insomnia and exhaustion had. But I could still *feel* it—the tremor, the thrum, the alarm.

Something was happening right now, in another place, far above. And for some unfathomable reason its thread reached all the way here, into the domain of the death gods.

I rose from the padded window seat, sending my magic out through the world, searching, searching—and paused.

Upstairs, Misery's prairie dog was yahooing again, but ` at the end of the tether someone was screaming. Multiple people.

And many were going to die.

CHAPTER SEVEN

CAT

I was up to seven fuckboys thwarted, but the last one was kinda hot in a Cillian Murphy way so I'd taken his number. I wasn't going to call him, but he didn't need to know that.[1]

Honey was chatting up Mr Broad Shoulders 2024, so I found a spot against the living room wall to lean and people watch. Dylan Ford was the centre of attention, naturally. With his good looks and excessive money, he had both men and women clinging to him, throwing seductive smiles in an attempt to hook a future billionaire. I couldn't blame them. He was a powerful ally to have at Ford's End Medical School for Stuck Up Twats, Alarmingly Social Best Friends, and Introverts Who'd Rather Be In The Local Animal Shelter Than At A Frat Party.[2]

Better a friend than an enemy, anyway. I shouldn't have spoken up with the Fords earlier, but I couldn't bring myself to regret it either. I was tired of being walked all over by powerful men from powerful families. I just hoped I hadn't made myself a target—or worse, made Honey and By targets by association.

I sipped from a red cup of fruity vodka and fuck knows what else—the beer ran out an hour ago—and kept an eye on Honey and Alastor. He seemed okay, but didn't all creeps seem okay at first? I glanced away when they decided to stick their tongues down each other's throats on the sofa. Good for Honey. I was bored.

The shop of many rooms where we got our costumes must have sold out their entire stock, because in the last ten minutes alone I'd seen four people in the same long, black cloak with their hoods up. Maybe they'd all come as grim reapers and tragically misplaced their scythes. Maybe they were dressed as the creepy cult from Hot Fuzz.[3]

"Cat," Byron greeted with a sage nod as he came to splay across the wall beside me, a half-empty cup in his hand. "I see your boobs are still there."

"They are," I agreed. "Fortunately all the stares have not burned them from my body."

"I'm happy for you."

I gave *him* a sage nod this time. We both jumped in surprise when the music shot up several decibels.

"Sorry, sorry!" someone shouted. Mason Lindgren. "Wrong fucking way."

"Tell me he isn't about to..." Byron laughed, his eyes a little glossy, cheeks a little red. There was also a smudge of lipstick on his jaw I very graciously did not point out.

A hollow clang of wood came from the foyer and then Lindgren was crossing the room with a guitar in his hand. A laugh burst out of me, loud with inebriation. "He is. He really is."

Byron wiped a tear from the corner of his eye. "Please

be Wonderwall. Please be a meme come to life. Universe, I never ask much of you, just give me this one thing."

"There's no way." I shook my head, the long white wig clinging to my cheeks, staticky. My head was itchy underneath; another drink and I'd probably rip out the pins and throw the damn thing off just to let my scalp breathe.

Byron and I held our breaths when Mason began to play, and disappointment was instantaneous when it wasn't the initial chords of Wonderwall but...

"It's *Don't Look Back In Anger*," I cried, grabbing Byron's hand, unable to contain my glee. "Oh my god, oh my god."

"It's real," he laughed, crying. He grabbed my arm and for some unknowable drunk reason we both sank to the floor, gasping for air as we laughed too hard. "The ancient frat party lore is *real*."

I dropped my head onto his warm shoulder and laughed until my belly ached, and it felt good. All the stress and worries of starting over somewhere new, where I didn't know the rules and expectations and patterns... it all swept behind laughter.

Another black cloak swept past, brushing my ankles as the tall, hooded person—either a dude or Gwendoline Christie—walked around the coffee table to look out the window. Something buzzed against my hip and I jumped.

"Did you bring a vibrator to a party?" I asked Byron, a furrow between my brows.

"It's my phone," he said between hiccupping laughter. "*Move*, I can't get to it with your shoulder in the way."

I giggle-snorted. "That's not my shoulder, By."

"Oh, god. It's so soft. Why is it soft?"

"Moisturiser," I informed him, leaning back so he could fish his phone from his pocket as Lindgren belted out the final chorus.

"Keep your moisturised bosom to yourself, Wallison."

Byron glanced at his phone, squinted at the text, and the smile fell off his face, comically fast.

"What's wrong?" I asked, sobering at the dread I watched spill through Byron's dark blue eyes.

His phone rang, a shrill tone that briefly drowned out Lindgren's crooning, and my friend flinched.

"By," I breathed. "You're freaking me out. What's wrong?"

His throat bobbed. He angled the phone away from me, rushing to his feet. His hands shook. "It's Sterling."

His sister. "Is everything okay?"

"No." He bolted to his feet, grabbed the wall when he swayed, and I followed in a rush, reaching for him. "I need to talk to her. I'll tell you everything when I come back. Stay here, watch Honey and make sure that guy doesn't take advantage of her."

"By," I complained weakly, but I didn't protest when he fled the room, shoulder-checking another black-robed figure. "Great outfit," I drawled to the robe, my pissy mood and worry spilling out. *"Very* imaginative."

The hood turned, too dark inside to glimpse any features, but chances were they looked at me a moment too long because they were ogling the Heaving Bosom.

"My eyes are alllll the way up here," I said, slurring a little. The fruity vodka packed a stronger punch than beer it turned out.

The robe didn't reply, which was fine if a little rude. I gave them my middle finger behind their back, watching the cloaked jerk stride across the room to grab Mason Lindgren's shoulders like they were about to hug. Instead, my heart jumped against my ribs when *more* hooded figures emerged from the many doorways that connected this room to the rest of the house. There were *five* of them now, every one I'd seen tonight gathered in one room.

"Honey," I called in warning, my heartbeat tripling for a reason I wasn't entirely sure of. But I'd seen enough horror films to know how this ended, and I wasn't keen to stick around for whatever fucked up initiation was about to play out. Clearly Ford was one of those universities where animal sacrifice and chanting was all the rage, but I was going to pass.

I skirted the group of robed figures and made a beeline for Honey.

"Weird shit," I told her, grabbing Alastor's shoulder and pulling him off my friend.

"What the fuck?" he spat, a mean look crossing his face.

"Creepy fucking cult." I pointed emphatically and grabbed Honey's arm, heaving her off the sofa and wincing when she swayed into me. Goosebumps covered my arms when Lindgren's wailing cut off suddenly, replaced by a low, repetitive chanting. "We're going," I told my friend, "say goodbye to Carmichael."

"Bye, babe," Honey said agreeably, batting her lashes at Alastor.

I hurried us towards the door, but before we could reach it—or before the three other people sober enough to realise this was about to be an initiation of fucked up proportions could get there, too—every door slammed shut.

The chants rose in volume.

Fuck. Was I completely pissed, or was blood dripping down the walls?

"Honey, tell me you see that," I whispered, going cold all over. We hovered, frozen as I panicked, processing the fact the doors had closed on their own.

"What the fuck?" someone shouted, loud with both inebriation and panic. "The walls are bleeding."

Great. Wonderful. I wasn't hallucinating. The walls

really were overflowing with thick, viscous blood, dripping from the ceiling towards us.

Cold sluiced down my back as I stared around the room, my arms trembling where I gripped Honey desperately tight. In the middle of the room, a red circle burned itself into the parquet floor, not just branding the wood but flickering higher. Flames. This was so much worse than an initiation.

How were they doing this? It had to be SFX. Was someone's parent working on a film set, and they'd stolen supplies? How were the walls *bleeding*?

I took another step back, unable to stifle a whimper when the coffee table erupted in fire. One moment it was fine, the next it was ablaze, no flame bar visible. Like it was … like it was magic. But magic didn't exist. Bleeding walls didn't exist. This was a huge, elaborate prank. It had to be.

Sprawled out on the expensive rug next to the coffee table, his eyes wide and face tight in horror, was Mason Lindgren. He looked ten years older. Looked petrified, his skin bleached with terror. What had he seen? What had the robed figures *done*?

"What are you doing to him?" someone else yelled— Rone, whose room was across the hall from mine, and whose name was emphatically *not* Rhona. My eyes shot to her now as she lurched forward dressed as a sexy pirate, anger in her eyes. "Hey, cult assholes. What the fuck are you doing—"

She fell back with a cry when one of the robed figures reached out a single pale fingertip to her. Rone splayed against the unlit fireplace with her hand pressed to her head and horror flashing through her eyes.

"Stop," she panted. "Please stop. I'm sorry, fuck, don't— don't do this—"

I tightened my grip on Honey who was too drunk to

understand how screwed we were, and spun for the door. There were already people there, wrenching on the handle. As I watched, Duncan Ford hauled himself into it, shoulder first, but it held fast. Whoever closed it must be outside, making sure it remained locked. Even though all the doors had slammed shut at the same time. There had to be a rational explanation for this. It was a prank. It wasn't—

We all flinched, drunk, sober, and everything in between, when Mason began to scream.

CHAPTER EIGHT

CAT

There were five robed psychopaths and twenty one of us in the room, but any hope of fighting the bastards died with whatever they did to make Rone and Lindgren scream. It was horrific, their screams high and piercing, reaching right into my chest and making my heart skip. Behind us, Duncan Ford threw himself at the door, over and over, his desperation mounting.

"Now, listen here!" his cousin said, staring towards the five cloaks arranged in a circle around the fiery circle burning the rug—and Mason in the middle of it, screaming harrowingly, his eyes staring at nothing.

A different robed figure lifted a hand, pointing a tanned finger at Orwell as he strode at them with a shocking amount of purpose for someone dressed as the aubergine emoji.[1] I could have sworn I could see straight through the cloak to the bay window, but in another blink they were solid. A stunned hush fell over the room when

Orwell dropped to his knees with a blood-curdling scream.

"Orly!" Ford yelled, vaulting across the room to his cousin's side, and glaring murderously at the robed figures who resumed their chanting, this time fiercer, louder.

"We have to find a way out of here," I whispered to Honey. Duncan glanced up, hearing me, and a strange understanding passed between us. We likely hated each other, but right now we were two of very few sober-ish people in the room, which made us allies. "This is your fucking party," I hissed at him.

"Not this." His handsome face was contorted in anger—and fear, barely concealed beneath. "Come on, Orly, get up." He hooked his hands under his cousin's arms but Orwell threw his head back and screamed louder.

I swallowed hard, my whole body icy. Duncan had thrown himself at the door over and over, and it hadn't budged. And not six steps away, five robed nutjobs were chanting louder, shouting shit that sounded like Latin, like a curse, like every horror film I'd ever had nightmares after watching.

Someone stumbled into me and I flinched so hard Honey nearly slipped from my arms. A red-faced guy in a clown costume swayed on his feet, his eyes glazed. "Woah, shit, boobs."

"Woah, shit, *sacrificial cult shit*," I hissed at him, shoving him away with my shoulder, pulling Honey closer like a shield against me. I didn't know what to do, how to get out.

"Open the doors, you freaks," a girl called Milani Hussain yelled, throwing her wine glass at the circle of robed figures. It hit the shoulder of the tallest one and crashed to the floor, shattering on impact. "Save your cosplay bullshit for comic con."

This time the figures didn't turn, no one pointed a menacing finger at her, and she didn't drop to the floor. Because they were shouting at the top of their lungs, Latin flowing in a rapid, frantic stream that made me icy cold. Duncan had propped Orwell against the wall and threw himself at the door again, Alastor Carmichael right there with him, and three other guys whose names I didn't know —we'll call them Batman, Mario, and Vagina after their costumes.

Please, please open...

My heart tripled, until it beat fast enough to thump its way out of my ribs, but I kept my eyes on the door, hoping, praying...

I was about to set Honey beside Orwell Ford and throw myself at the door, too, when Batman lurched forward, momentum carrying him to the foyer floor as the door opened all at once.

I flew towards it, arms and elbows brushing mine as twenty-one panicked people moved at once for the exit— but we never even reached the door.

The scent of blood rose, and another voice joined the chanting, impossible to place in all the chaos. It wasn't any of the people close to me, but it had to be one of the med students with us. What the fuck...?

Duncan skittered back, his face especially pale, his eyes wide. His face had lost all its life as he recoiled from the doorway, bumping into Honey but undeterred as he fled—*her.*

My breath caught. I became very aware of the silence, of the sudden absence of chanting, as a wall of cool, solid air pushed us back. My feet skidded across the polished floor, Honey's too.

And into the room walked a tall, imposing woman of remarkable beauty, her footsteps resounding loudly. I could only look at her for three seconds before my head exploded into pain, my eyes watered, and I was forced to look away, but it was enough to glimpse golden skin, elegant features, waist-length hair in a shade of red so dark it was like dried blood, and eyes in two different colours— bone-white and ink-black. From the iris of her white eye, blood poured down her cheek, the single stain on her staggering beauty.

I gasped down air, drowning, suffocating. My eyes fixed on the floor where black lace trailed behind the woman's dark dress like a gothic train. I clutched Honey as close as my shaking arms would allow. It was so cold, so quiet, so still. Instinct told me to run and never stop running.

"Oh, god," Honey began to chant, "Oh god, oh god."

"God*dess*, darling," the red-haired woman said with a mild smile that did nothing to mask the power trembling in her voice. Power unlike anything I'd felt before. It was the same power that made the walls bleed, that had pushed us back from the door, that covered the strange woman like a miasma. Power that didn't exist. That couldn't be real. It wasn't something that could be explained by natural forces, wasn't even ley lines or thin veils or whatever else caused a rash of hauntings on Halloween night. This was… it was…

"Magic," Duncan Ford breathed.

The woman smiled at him, the sharp edges of her lips curling deeper into her cheeks. At once, Rone, Mason, and Orwell stopped screaming, and I sucked in a sharp breath of relief, shushing Honey who still gasped panicked words under her breath.

The power, the undeniable *magic* in the room, swelled, like a single heartbeat. As if in answer, a loud, dull thud resounded through the room. I flinched when the blonde wizard who tried to get my number exhaled a curse and knelt where—where Rone had collapsed. She no longer leaned against the fireplace but splayed on the floor, her mouth slack.

"She's—" He shook his head, the bleached horror on his face comical paired with the long silver wig and star-spangled cloak he wore.

"Dead," the terrifying woman finished for him. "Of course she is. How do you think I'm here?" She laughed softly, a tinkling sound. "Where is my disciple? Come forward."

I froze, digging my fingernails into Honey's arm when she whimpered and flinched into me, the redhead's stare passing over all of us, searching, probing. I swore the coppery scent of blood became stronger, forcing down my nose into my throat until I choked on it.

Why was no one running at this woman, trying to stop her doing—whatever it was she was doing? People had tried to take down the robed psychos. They failed, but still —why was everyone rooted to the spot, just *staring* as she swept around the room, heads lowered like subjects before a queen?

She surveyed us before gliding through the circle of fire with a contemplative sound. The flames didn't burn her, didn't even eat through the delicate black lace of her train. The sight of that unburned lace hit me like a blow. It was— magic was real. I was watching it, right in front of me, and it could have been flame retardant fabric but deep down I knew it wasn't. Like I knew this wasn't a creepy initiation for med school. It was bigger. More.

What the hell had we got ourselves twisted up in? My breathing fractured and sped.

"We have to get out of here," Milani Hussain breathed, grabbing my arm in apparent desperation as the red-haired woman stood in the heart of the burning circle beside Mason Lindgren. Was he—like Rone was he dead?

"You," the woman—goddess?— breathed, excitement lighting her face as she regarded Milani. I kept my attention on her chin, not daring to look higher, primal terror warning me away from those mismatched, bleeding eyes. "There is terror in your blood. Whose line do you hail from?"

"I don't know what you mean," Milani gasped, digging her nails into my arm. "I don't know who you are or what's going on, but I'm not part of this. I only came to this party to fuck Duncan, so count me out of—this. Whatever it even is."

"Are you my disciple?" the terrifying woman asked, the air quivering with the power in her voice. It pressed on my chest, crushed my lungs until I wheezed.

"No," Milani whispered, shrieking when the red-haired woman lifted a hand, like the robed figures—who were conspicuously still and silent now—had earlier. Milani was ripped away from my side, the toes of her high heels dragging across the floor like she was possessed. With power thumping, alive in the air, I wasn't sure possession was wrong. "Let me go," she hissed. "Please, I won't tell anyone—"

"It would have been useful to have a child of terror as my disciple," the woman said, her head tilting as she watched Milani float across the floor. Sharp breaths were taken around the room. If people could speak, they used their voices to swear, to plead, to pray. My lips were sealed together. I was frozen, silent.

"Alas, you are too useful to my enemies."

"Who the fuck *are* you?" Milani demanded shrilly, wrenching against the force dragging her to the terrifying woman.

"Nightmare, darling. I am Nightmare."

A hush fell over the bleeding room before pleas and prayers renewed at twice the volume. Nightmare didn't seem like a cool name two goth parents had given their kid; it felt like a title, like a warning. As if every night terror and traumatising dream originated from this beautiful woman from whom power thumped like a heartbeat.

Milani was finally close enough to fight the woman. Nightmare. But her arms were locked at her sides with invisible bindings, and she could only thrash uselessly as Nightmare lifted a finger, pressed it to Milani's forehead, and a dissonant, howling scream tore from the girl, drowning out all other noise.

When Nightmare pulled back, Milani's eyes rolled back into her forehead and her legs fell from under her. I gasped frantically when another thump went through the air, through the atmosphere of the world, like it had before. And I understood. When Milani hit the ground, I knew that the thump meant she was dead, and that Nightmare's power grew with each death.

Dead. Of course she is. How do you think I'm here?

And there was only one reason we would all be surrounded by her power, too: she planned to murder every last one of us.

CHAPTER NINE

CAT

*N*ightmare stepped over Milani's body and toed the line of fire around her, giving the gathered students a curious look. "Where is the bride of death?"

My stomach sank to my feet.

I clutched Honey with shaking hands and irrationally hoped that line of fire somehow trapped Nightmare, even if she'd willingly walked into it.

Not me, not me, I'm not the bride of death, please mean someone else.

"There you are," Nightmare said, a smile in her voice. I darted the world's quickest glance at her and couldn't trap a whimper when I found her eerie eyes on me. "It was pure chance, you realise? Whoever chose the dress and veil would become his bride. But he'll like you—a scared little rabbit with fire in her eyes. Yes, he'll like you very much."

I shook my head and realised I wasn't frozen in place at

all, I was just terrified. *No,* I wanted to say. *No. I'm no one's bride, no one will like me, no thank you very much.*

I got the sense she was smiling at me but I couldn't breathe, couldn't lift my head, couldn't do anything except shake and cling to Honey who lunged forward suddenly and said, "Hey, my bitch'snot marrying anyone. *Even* if they've got a giant schlong."

Terror had me shivering, my hands snapping out to grab her. Like our movement had shocked them out of their frozen terror, everyone in the room erupted into a sudden flurry of motion, racing for the door.

"Yes, my terrors, run. Run so I can chase." Nightmare scuffed her shoe against the line of fire again and flames shot so high they obscured her face. A wall of heat hit us. The five robed figures started chanting again.

I didn't stick around to see what happened next. I grabbed Honey, shoved her out of the bloodstained room, and ran as fast as my legs would carry me through the hall, under the obnoxious chandelier, and out into the garden. I sucked down air like I'd been drowning. My ears buzzed. I could still feel the horrid weight of Nightmare's power, could still taste blood.

"That was a joke, right?" someone gasped behind us. "That wasn't real."

An asshole shoved past us so forcefully that I splayed into the topiary beside the door, and I was so afraid, so shaken, that I didn't care that vomit smeared on my white dress. Or that Alastor Carmichael was the dick who shoved me out of the way in his frantic attempt to get free.

Honey pulled me back to my feet, her blue eyes wide and glassy. "Are you alright?"

"No," I breathed, but I guided us back onto the path and down it towards the gate. The only way out was through, and I didn't dare hesitate. Nightmare would chase us, would hunt us down. I choked back a cry.

Whoever chose the dress and veil would become his bride. But he'll like you—a scared little rabbit with fire in her eyes.

A chill tripped down my spine. I clutched Honey tightly as my numb feet carried me away, scanning the garden for Byron, needing my friend's stability and reassurance. I wanted a hug so suddenly that my eyes burned.

"We need to—get out of here," I rasped, ignoring the fracturing of my breathing, the adrenaline shaking through my system until my legs were jelly. I grabbed the fence post and then we were through the gate, surrounded by jesters and grim reapers and sexy nurses.

"What the fuck *was* that?" Justin Merchant demanded, grabbing Duncan by the front of his plague doctor outfit and wrenching him close. Justin's fist collided with Duncan's nose in the next moment, cartilage crunching. I glanced away at the gushing blood, too reminiscent of the walls in that room.

"I know you're her disciple," Justin snarled in his face. "It was your party, all your idea, because you were going *to fucking sacrifice us.*"

The word sacrifice sent a chill down my spine and I shuddered, holding Honey tighter to my side as we cut across the path in front of Ford House, aiming for the park that would take us home. But Nightmare, whoever she even was, just did all that on Ford grounds. Was anywhere safe?

Oh, god, she killed Mason Lindgren. And Rone. And Orwell. And Milani.

"If anyone's her disciple, it's *you*, Merchant," Duncan Ford spat, his voice thick with blood. "Everyone knows you're obsessed with the devil and all that shit—"

"Look!" someone shrieked, and despite every instinct in

my body I couldn't help but turn back towards Ford House. My stare went to the windows, the glass gleaming blood-red, but snagged on the sheer amount of people milling in the street around the building. Far more than the twenty-one of us who'd been trapped in that room. Vultures, dying for a story to tell their friends, or just other people like us who'd got caught up in whatever the fuck was happening tonight.

"What is that...?" the guy in the clown costume breathed. "Why is it... breathing?"

The crimson light *throbbed*, every bit as alive as the power was around Nightmare. I backed up towards the park, grabbing Honey's hand and squeezing so tight I must have rearranged her bones. I couldn't feel the cold of the sea wind on my skin, couldn't hear the shouts of alarm and speculating murmurs anymore. I felt the caress of that red light across my skin, like a tangible touch, and judging by the way Honey stiffened she felt it too.

"Run!" someone yelled. Duncan, maybe, his voice garbled by his broken nose.

I stumbled back a step but too late. Sanguine light exploded from Ford House, bursting through every window, through the door. It cast everything it touched in shades of vermillion blood. And it touched all of us, splashed over part of Milton Hall and the park. No one was spared its bloody glow, and I knew deep in my bones it was far more than light, like that woman had been far more than human.

As the crimson light swept over me, I heard Nightmare's sultry voice again.

Yes, he'll like you very much.

CHAPTER TEN

CAT

*M*y hands shook, my arms trembled uncontrollably, and my teeth threatened to chatter as I hammered on Byron's door. Honey had stumbled wordlessly to her room, her eyes glassy and afraid, and collapsed on her bed to sleep off the alcohol in her system and whatever Nightmare *did* with that red light. I felt... different. Wrong. Like I'd been taken apart and put back together almost perfectly, but with a slight misalignment that would always gnaw at me like the jagged spires of a broken tooth.

"Byron, please open up," I choked out, knocking harder, staring at my pale hand. I should have been covered in blood after what I saw tonight, should have borne some signs of that red light touching me, but my hand was as normal as before I went to the party.

"What?" Byron demanded after a few seconds, wrenching open the door with a fierce scowl on his face.

I wanted to burst into tears.

"It's four a.m. Cat, I'm trying to sleep," he snapped, and I flinched back at the roughness of his voice, the lack of its usual care.

"I'm sorry," I mumbled, too fragile and freaked out to find even a spark of fire in my blood. I should have snapped right back at him but I didn't have the energy.

How was it four a.m.? Classes started at twelve tomorrow. I was exhausted by the mere thought of them.

"Something happened tonight, after you left the party," I said weakly, pressing my lips thin when they wobbled.

"Yeah, for me too," Byron muttered, his eyes dark and faraway. "And I have enough of my own shit to deal with, Cat. Can this wait until tomorrow?"

I recoiled another step in the hall. "What...?"

What was wrong with him? Where was my grumpy but loving Byron? I *needed* him, needed a fucking hug, but he was glaring, furious, and stressed, and I didn't understand why he was taking it out on me. Tears burned the backs of my eyes, the tip of my nose tingling.

"Sterling's pregnant," he sighed, pinching the bridge of his nose. "Sorry for snapping, Cat, I've just—got a fucking lot on my mind."

"Right," I said in a small voice, dimly registering that their parents would disown Sterling for getting pregnant at sixteen.

I didn't know what else to say, didn't have the energy for this, and he'd been a dick so it freed me up to be one too. I turned and walked away without even a goodbye and slumped into my room, feeling more alone than I remembered feeling before. So much more alone than even last night, when it felt like my world was ending.

I closed the door, made sure the lock was engaged, and

let out the sob that swelled behind my solar plexus, the sound clamorous in the silence. I hated this room, hated this university, hated this whole damn island.

I scrubbed my tear-streaked face and stumbled to the dresser, frantically ripping out a makeup wipe, desperate to erase any sign of the Halloween party. I knocked a tube of lipstick and a pot of liner off the table and did not care. I didn't care if I destroyed this entire room. My hands shook, Nightmare's voice still in my head, sensually soft even as she *killed people.* I couldn't stop seeing them—Rone, Milani, Orwell, and Mason Lindgren. They were dead, and even though I was still clinging to the idea of an elaborate prank, I couldn't escape how *real* it felt. And if it was real, they were dead. Really, finally dead. Killed without a stab wound, gunshot, or even poison. Killed by the mere presence of Nightmare.

And I couldn't understand that.

So I shut it out, locked it away in a vault in my mind, and scrubbed the makeup off my—off my face—off—

I *scrubbed—*

"Oh god," I sobbed, throwing aside the pristine wipe and reaching for another, violently dragging it over the skull makeup on my face. Again and again I tried to scrape the paint off my face, but it didn't budge, not even a smear left on each wipe.

It was—I—I couldn't breathe.

I backed away, shaking, and curled up on my bed, gasping helplessly. My head spun violently. Pain and pressure pounded through my chest like a wrecking ball. I ripped at the dress clinging to my body and cried in relief when the zip tugged down, when I managed to crawl out of it. But a single glance in the mirror showed the makeup was still there. As if whatever Nightmare had done tonight, with the fire and blood and glowing crimson light... had made it permanent.

And staring at myself, I couldn't deny it.

Magic was real.

CHAPTER ELEVEN

MISERY

I felt it like a thousand wounds, a thousand miniature blades stabbing my skin over and over. I expected blood to bloom over the ice-white skin of my arms, to cut apart the stories I painstakingly inked on my body—each mark spinning tales of failures. So I would never repeat the mistakes again.

But the ink remained, my skin was whole and pale and unbloodied. And yet... the prickling, the warning, the awareness deep in my bones that my worst dreams had finally come true.

I burst into Death's office, relieved to find Tor here too, although slightly irritated that his mouth was wrapped around Death's cock and I hadn't been invited.

"She's back," I blurted, my voice guttural and low, nothing like the silken poetry it had been compared to for the centuries I'd been alive. As if having a pretty voice made the misery I inflicted any less ugly.

"Come here," Death said calmly, his eyes the colour of storm clouds—grey and full of depth—but lacking the churning violence of a storm. They were striking eyes when put in a face like his: excessively handsome, all stern planes and smooth brown skin, his mouth wide and full and always graced with a suggestive smirk or a gentle smile.

"She's back!" I gnashed my teeth, storming across the fine rug of his office to the desk he sat behind, splayed luxuriously in his chair while Torment knelt at his feet. "Did you not hear me?"

"I heard," Death replied, those calm-storm eyes unwavering from my face.

"You knew," I accused, my body tightening, tension in every line and limb. My hands curled into fists. I wanted to swing them at the gilded globes in six alcoves around the room, each the map of a domain. I wanted to shatter them, then rip every leather-spined book off his shelves, and unleash my anger on the windows until glass shattered and his precious office screamed as loudly as I screamed on the inside. "You *knew* Nightmare was back and you're here getting your *dick sucked?* We should be out there, killing her! Or fucking running or—"

Death stroked a hand over Torment's shaved head, pushing him away with a gentleness that made my heart ache, and then he stood. Before I could blink, Death was across the room, grabbing a fistful of my hair, long white strands balled up in his fist.

"Take a breath," he ordered, steely but with unwavering patience.

I bared my teeth. Forced a breath. "Your dick's out."

"I'm mortified," he drawled. "Breathe, Miz."

I shook my head, not caring that some strands of hair ripped out. I dragged down another breath. I was distantly aware of Torment shoving to his feet, pulling his trade-mark worn leather jacket over a black vest that bared his heavily inked arms. Unlike my self-inflicted tattoos, his were sentient and appeared of their own will with every major torment in his life.

"We killed her once," Tor reminded me in a gravelly, low voice I'd always envied. Mine was honeyed and feminine, nothing like the rough masculine voice Tor possessed. "We'll do it again."

"We need to find out how she came back in the first place," Death said, his lush mouth pressing thin. He held my stare, not breaking eye contact until I felt the first trickle of calm hit my panic, disrupting the automatic response.

"She'll come back," I said, curling my hands into tighter fists. "Even if we kill her again, she'll come back."

Tor shrugged. "So we keep killing her over and over." He snorted. "Actually, that sounds fun."

Yeah, it would. For him. For me it sounded like hell, and for a death god to experience hell that was saying something.

Death let go of me long enough to tuck his cock away, then took my face between both hands, his skin warm against my panic-iced cheeks. "There's a complication, but I need you to remain calm, Miz."

Even the word complication made my blood boil, my breathing escalating.

"Do you need me to get your therapy rat?" Tor asked, so dryly I wasn't sure if he was serious or joking.

"She's a prairie dog. And yes," I bit out.

He disappeared the same second I spoke, winking from existence like he'd never been here, only a glimmer of dark smoke on the air.

"We won last time," Death reminded me, easing the

glare from my face with slow, gentle caresses of his thumbs. "We'll find out how she returned and win this time, too."

Tor winked back into existence with Peach clutched between his olive-gold hands, her black eyes gleaming with love and excitement. Tor tolerated Peach, meanwhile she was infatuated with him. She probably liked his rough voice, too.

"Here, take your child," Tor huffed, wrinkling his nose in a way that brought a smile to my face. I cradled Peach in my arms, the thrum of her heartbeat and the warmth of her against my chest immediately settling me.

"What complication?" I asked, eyeing Death as he leaned against the back of one of the green leather chairs arrayed around the fireplace.

"I felt a tremor four hours ago, something linking this realm to the mortal realm."

I stiffened, breath catching in my throat. I hadn't been to the mortal realm since... since it all ended. I didn't want to go back.

"Wait for the good part," Tor said, his brown eyes bright with amusement, excitement, or scorn—it was hard to discern which.

"I went to investigate," Death continued, sliding his hands into the pockets of his trousers, casual and relaxed. I didn't buy it. I knew Death when he was languid and at peace and this wasn't it. "And I found four dead teenagers, a burned ritual site, and—"

"What?" I demanded when his words hovered, unfinished. Peach made a startled sound; I relaxed my breath, dragging air into my lungs. *Calm, calm.*

"Nightmare has risen again, her cult likely involved."

I knew it. I could *feel* her, feel the ripples of her poison brushing my skin, roiling against the inside of my skull.

"And she used the deaths of those teenagers to not only restore herself to the realm of the living, but to curse anyone in the vicinity of her ritual site. Fifty-one of them to be exact."

"Cursed how?" I asked tightly, jumping when Peach nibbled at my finger in a request for snacks; I stroked her in a compromise, distracted by the pressure gathering in my chest, the dread hovering over us like a dark cloud.

"From what I could tell in a brief examination," Death said, turning around one of the many golden rings he wore, "it was during a Halloween party that Nightmare returned. The students of Ford medical school were in costume to celebrate the occasion."

I flinched at the name. *Ford.* So she was still on Ford's End after all these years.

"Nightmare's curse turned them from costume to reality. They're cursed to become whatever appearance they took last night."

"So werewolves will howl at the moon," Tor explained with great amusement, "reapers will hunt souls, and vampires will want a little blood snack."

"And the bride of death..." Death trailed off.

I jerked forward a step. My ears went fuzzy, muffled. The bride *of Death?* "What?" I breathed, faint.

Death spun his ring faster. He didn't look at either of us. Oh god, it was over. After hundreds of years, we were over, just like that. Nightmare had finally done it, finally found a way to truly break me.

He said, "One of the mortals was dressed as Death's bride, and since costumes have become reality..."

"You... have a wife," I breathed, staring at my oldest friend, my oldest love.

"Which brings us to the important question," Tor said, giving us an unusually sombre look, his mischievous eyes newly grave. "Death, if you had to pick one of us, me or Miz, who'd be your best man?"

I tried to shape my lips into a smile. But Nightmare was back—on Ford's End, where it had all ended. Or not ended at all. And I couldn't ignore the pull in my soul, wrenching me all the way back there.

"You're not coming out of this well," Death told Tor with some amusement. I couldn't understand how they could joke and fuck around in his office like the world wasn't ending all over—

Tor's arm hooked my neck, dragging me into a hard hug. His lips mashed to my temple. "Don't worry. We'll come out of this fine, you'll see."

But not only was Nightmare back, she'd created a link, either accidentally or intentionally, between a costumed mortal and Death. Between her and us. And I couldn't shake the feeling that a trap was closing around us, its edges sharp and eager for blood.

"You're wrong anyway, Miz," Death said with a strange mix of calm and humour. My heart skipped when I met his eyes. "We've done everything as a team for hundreds of years, so *I* don't have a wife. *We* have a wife."

CHAPTER TWELVE

CAT

I didn't sleep, which turned out to be good luck because it took me three hours to work up the courage to grab the door handle, let alone step out of my room. I didn't take my thumb off the crown ring on my finger, spinning it over and over and over, my chest so tight I couldn't choke down a single scrap of air.

But I made it out. I made it to class, with Honey silent beside me and Byron... absent. I didn't know where he was, but we were in a different class today so maybe he wasn't avoiding me. Maybe he didn't hate me. Or maybe he *did* hate me, he'd realised there were a thousand better friends in the universe, and he'd decided he needed nothing to do with an anxiety-ridden burden like me.

My makeup never washed off, even when I showered with the water at igneous temperatures, but no one commented about it. I asked Honey about it but she shrugged and said she couldn't see anything; I performed the same check when she asked if her cat nose and whiskers were still there. Everyone else was distracted and jumpy too, like something was off with them, like they couldn't forget what had happened in Ford House last night, either.

By the time the lecture ended, I'd taken in nothing of the information, made no notes on my laptop, and I was ready to explode. I kept trying to find the positive in the situation and coming up blank. What was the positive about witnessing murder? Worse—unexplainable murder that had no rational explanation.

Honey yawned so wide her jaw cracked, her eyes hazy. "God, I'm exhausted," she said as we left the ancient lecture theatre, an air of history and gravity hanging over Milton Hall, the spire-topped building where most classes were held. The grey skies made it bleary and miserable outside; it threatened to rain again. It always threatened to rain on Ford's End. "I need a twelve-hour nap."

I needed the opposite. I was drained and my body desperately begged for rest, but I dreaded it. My whole waking day had been a nightmare, but if I slept? We'd been tormented by a woman literally called *Nightmare*. What would she do while we slept?

I briefly leaned my head on her shoulder. "I need coffee. I'm gonna drive down to the village. You coming?"

"Pass," Honey groaned, pulling her black beret further over her head like it could block out the dull light as we crossed campus. Her azure eyes narrowed balefully at the sky. "Do you see rain, Cat? I see rain. I hate rain."

I gave her a strange look, pulling my bag higher on my shoulder and wincing at its book-induced weight. I shouldn't have carried two romance books with me today but I needed the reassurance of having them, like I needed my crown ring.

"You didn't hate rain when we made the crossing," I reminded her as we reached a fork in the path, where one way led to Lawrence Hall and our rooms and the other veered past the laboratory to the garage where Bugattis, Aston Martins, and Maseratis now sat beside my beloved lime-green Lamborghini Urus, delivered this morning to the island by a one-time ferry.

Honey gave me a horrified look. "Shit. I remember standing out in the storm. What was I thinking? My fur must have been soaked." She shook her head and laughed at her past self, coaxing a weak smile from me. "I'll see you when you get back. If you want to earn my eternal love, you could pick me up an iced latte."

"Consider your eternal love earned," I replied with a slightly stronger smile. Because of everything that had happened, and how fucking terrified I was just to exist, to breathe, to walk, to be outside, I grabbed my friend into a hug and squeezed tight. "Go straight to your room, okay? Be careful."

"I will if you will," she agreed, squeezing me just as hard.

It pained me to release her, but comfort coffee and comfort books didn't come without risk and effort.[1] At the very least, they didn't come without driving down to the village that sold them. So I forced my arms to drop and took a step away from Honey, dragging my stare away from her when we parted.

I couldn't fight the feeling I'd never see her again, like Nightmare would swoop in and take her from me like she took Mason Lindgren and Milani Hussain.

But nightmares only happened after dark, and it was barely four p.m. I twisted the ring around my finger, my thumb worrying the spikes, and followed the path, giving Ford House a very wide berth but unable to stop staring at it. It looked completely normal. No blood, no glowing windows, no cult ritual. I shuddered and kept walking.

Byron's words from last night followed me all the way to the low-slung garage building on the edge of campus, where the forest hugged the edge of the cliff. The sea's choppy wind was stronger here, lifting hair off my shoulders and throwing pink-tinged strands into my face.

That was another thing I did *not* want to think about, along with the people Nightmare murdered, the makeup that wouldn't wash off my face, and Byron snapping—my hair wasn't dark brown anymore. It was the same white as the wig I wore last night, complete with pink where Honey used hair chalk to colour the nylon. Only this wasn't nylon —it was real hair, as if I'd always been this colour.

Honey's was permanently smeared black, too. No magic hid those marks; the changes were there for all to see. We didn't talk about it.

I batted the hair away and walked on, my stomach clenching. I was lucky the dress had allowed me to remove it, or it'd end up yellowed like Miss Havisham's wedding gown. There—I'd found it, the single silver lining. I wasn't forced to wear a piss-stained dress.

I got out my keys and the remote fob dangling from it, relieved when the huge metal door slid into the wall and the garage proved to be empty. I couldn't handle socialising right now; even asking for my coffee order was skirting impossibility. I was dangling over the edge of a breakdown, clinging to the tiniest scrap of composure, the handhold narrow while my body dangled over a perilous drop.

Hopefully *an iced caramel latte with oat milk and an iced latte, please* didn't send me over the edge.

It took me two minutes to locate my car's bay, another two to find where my keys had fallen to the bottom of my heavy bag, and then I was sliding into the soft leather seat. Enclosing myself in the familiar scent and a sense of safety nothing else had given me on the island.

I exhaled a sigh, a weight falling off my shoulders when the car purred to life. It was only when I peeled out of the garage, closed the big metal door with the fob, and was driving down the hill away from Ford that I realised what Honey had said.

I remember standing out in it. What was I thinking? My fur must have been soaked.

Fur?

CHAPTER THIRTEEN

CAT

I survived asking for coffee, thanking the barista when she handed them to me, and even got through checking for stock on the book I needed more than air in a tiny, hole-in-the-wall bookshop I found tucked between a tea room and florist. I emerged half an hour later with two lattes, three slices of Victoria sponge in a white cardboard box, and a book about a vampire who marries her werewolf enemy.

In my car, I took a long sip of my coffee and hoped I could buy Byron's love with a cake slice. Life was completely off kilter with him mad at me, and I didn't like it.

I flicked on the radio to fill the silence as I drove up the winding hillside road to Ford, unsurprised when the clouds burst. It was strangely comforting, the drumming of rain on the car's roof, the swish of windscreen wipers clearing my view, though the landscape around the road was far prettier when it wasn't drenched in grey and misery.

I groaned when the radio station skipped, *I Should Be So Lucky*—my mum's favourite—jumping until Kylie sounded like a robot speaking in morse code. I didn't dare take both hands off the wheel to fix the radio with how winding and narrow the road was. I doubted Ford's End picked up more than one radio station anyway, being in the middle of the Irish Sea.

The morse code music cut out entirely, fading in a swirl of unsettling gibberish until silence filled the car. Great. So much for that. I eyed the dark clouds, knowing they were to blame for the loss of signal, and kept both hands on the wheel as I guided the car smoothly around a bend in the road, scaling the mountain Ford was built atop.

Why did people build castles and manor houses on the top of hills anyway? I knew they were defensible from a height but god, the distance from the bottom was killer. Or was that the idea? Their enemies would get halfway up the hill, wheezing, crawling on hands and knees, and decide to slide back to their ships?

In the silence, my mind wandered. I wondered who had lived at Ford before it became a med school, wondered if this island had been something else before it belonged to the Ford family. Mostly I wondered about what Mason Lindgren said at orientation.

Isn't the school built on an old burial ground? I heard there was a pagan cult here before Ford was built.

I'd dismissed that as paranoia and hearsay, but after last night it was harder to roll my eyes at. I watched Mason splay in the middle of a ring of fire, scream like he was being tortured, and then *die*. Mason was dead. Who would tell his parents, his siblings? Would they ever know, or would they wait for a call, a letter, a visit from their son, only to find out he never made it to classes on his first day?

Music blasted abruptly from my car speakers, far louder than it had been before, and I jumped hard enough that my hands jerked the wheel before I regained control and straightened the car's path. Shit. Shit!

"I love you, Taylor, but now is bad timing," I panted, my heart beating in my throat, as fast as a bird's. *Blank Space* played at full volume.

I exhaled a rough breath when the road's tight curve expanded through a long stretch of moorland that would, eventually, become the woods around Ford. Fog crept across the moor's rolling grasses, purple heather poking through the spectral mist every now and then. *Almost home.* If Ford could be called home.

The engine coughed a sudden plume of exhaust fumes, and a chill went down my spine. There was no way. No fucking way I was having car troubles right now, in the middle of a desolated road, surrounded by fields and nothing else. Taylor's voice morphed like something out of a twisted fairy tale. *But you'll come back each time you leave 'cause, darling, I'm a nightmare dressed like a daydream.*

I flinched at the word nightmare, and then my car stuttered, inexplicably, to a halt.

I froze, my breathing coming fast. Was this Nightmare? Was she here?

I twisted, staring out the windows, searching the fog for her long red hair, her black lace dress, but I didn't see anything except mist and grass and, in the far distance, the beginnings of the Rosalind Woods.

My heart quickened. I turned the keys in the ignition, over and over, but my beloved car didn't even choke out an attempt to start. Well, I wasn't getting out of the fucking car. If Nightmare was out there, I was staying in here.

I slid my phone from my pocket and hissed a curse when it slipped out of my shaky hands. Fine hairs rose on the back of my neck when I bent to retrieve it, convinced when I sat back up Nightmare would be in front of the car. My heart skipped, but when I shot back into my seat there was no psychopath in front of me, nothing but the fog and the moors. Or... was the fog darker? Thicker?

I shook my head hard. "You're seeing things, Cat. You're going mad, and that's completely reasonable given you saw four people murdered last night and no one would ever—"

Believe you.

I was being watched. The back of my neck burned with the knowledge. My hands shook harder. I was being watched, and I couldn't see anyone in the moorland, but I knew it was her, knew she was out there. The wind picked up, a whispering howl that shook the grasses, swirled the fog and—oh god.

It wasn't Nightmare racing towards my car, vulnerable and small in the middle of the moor road. It was three riders on horseback, their steeds pitch black with dark smoke flowing from their hooves. The riders' bodies were cloaked in flowing dark fabric, faces hidden behind onyx helmets so sharp and terrifying that a squeak left me. The tall rider in the middle raced faster than the others, their helmet topped with a wicked metal spike. I forgot how to breathe. Forgot to remind my heart to beat. Forgot—

My hand reached for the car door.

"What the fuck are you doing?" I screamed at myself.

I felt my fingers curve, heard the soft click of the door opening, and couldn't stop it.

"Do you want to die?" I demanded, like I wasn't screaming at my own hand.

Cold rushed into the car, wind catching strands of white and pink hair, tugging on them like the wind had turned against me, encouraging the madness that gripped my body.

I was going to die. Like Mason and Milani and Orwell and Rone died—I was going to die, right now, because my legs swung over the edge of the buttery leather seat and I *stood*. My head turned of its own will, eyes fixing on the rider with the spiked helm, my heart sprinting faster.

I needed to run, run away—

I didn't even slam the door shut before I took off, feet pounding the tarmacked road, carrying me *towards* the riders.

"No!" I snarled at myself, barely able to breathe. I wrenched so hard at my arms that they jolted, and then I did it again and again. The thunderous sound of hooves filled my ears, filled my heartbeat until it skipped in sync with them. Fear gave me enough control to twist around and propel myself into a sprint *away* from Nightmare's terrifying riders.

But a knot tightened around my heart, like a fist gripping it, tighter and tighter with every step I ran away. Nightmare controlled me right now, I knew she did. She'd sent these horrifying riders, like Nazgul dispatched to find the one ring, and she was in control of my body, tugging me towards them like gravity to the ground.

"You can run," one of the riders taunted, gravely and rough, and I flinched, catching the toe of my shoe on the ground. On the flat, poreless tarmac. Had Nightmare made me trip, too, or was I going mad? "We love to chase."

"Tor," someone hissed—smooth, elegant, and cold enough to send chills skittering down my spine.

I ran faster, staggering along the curving road, each breath dragging a panicked whimper from my throat. My eyes blurred with panicked tears. Legs turned to jelly. And that fist squeezed tighter around my heart until I wasn't sure blood flowed.

Nightmare wanted me to stop running, to turn back, to embrace the hellish riders with open arms. Since I didn't have a death wish, I kept fighting, kept my weak legs stumbling forward.

Maybe I could run down to the village and plead for help. But hooves pounded so loud, so close, and I knew I wouldn't reach it in time. I wouldn't get anywhere remotely close to Ford's End. Heat kissed the back of my neck from the dark horses, the cloaked, helmed riders, the—

I screamed when hands grasped my shoulders, and I was suddenly airborne. Tears of fear streamed from my eyes, my whole body locked and frozen until I—slammed into place on the back of an enormous horse that wasn't entirely solid under me.

"Nightmare is following you," a warm voice said against my nape, the words brushing my skin, stirring my hair until I shuddered hard. "But she can't have you. You're ours, little bride."

CHAPTER FOURTEEN

CAT

*L*ittle bride. The words rang in my head, slicing through soft brain matter until they were all I could hear. All I felt was warmth and solid muscle against my back, the violent rocking of the horse under me, and the press of arms on either side of me, keeping me from falling off. My entire body shook.

Little bride. So Nightmare had sent them to kill me, or to do something worse. I couldn't think what that something worse might be right now—other than the obvious *worse* three men could to do a woman alone and vulnerable —but my mind was flitting from ideas of torture and threats to dismemberment and—

"You're not breathing," the rider said, his voice masculine and gentle. I flinched despite its softness.

Little Bride. I was trapped. If I threw myself off the horse's back, the fall could break my arm. Or my neck. So I froze, and shook, and waited to see what they'd do.

"Breathe, little bride," that warm voice commanded, coloured by worry as if he cared about me, as if we weren't complete strangers and he hadn't been sent by Nightmare to kill me. *"Now."*

His hand met my stomach and pressed, forcing my mouth open on a desperate gasp. I took an involuntary breath and started to shake. The numbness and shock was waning, and in its place was truth. I'd been kidnapped.

"Please don't—don't hurt me," I rasped even though it was pointless. Either they would or wouldn't and nothing I said would change it. I shook harder, gasping air, the purple moors blurring past as the horse rode feverishly fast, the other two riders pressing closer on either side.

I froze when pressure brushed my head, then my shoulder, and I was so wild with panic that I didn't realise at first what they were. Kisses. Nightmare's rider had kissed my head and my shoulder, and if he was doing that—

"Peace," the rider with the gravelly voice spoke beside us, loud enough to make me flinch. "We're not going to hurt you. I can feel your torment and fear. It's unnecessary."

"Thanks, that helps *so* much, I'm definitely calm now," I snapped breathlessly.

A laugh stirred my hair. Glad I was so amusing to them.

The third rider gasped sharply. "She's here. She's hunting the bride."

My blood turned arctic, and I forgot how to breathe again. "I thought *you* were hunting me."

"Rescuing you," the rider who held me disagreed, making my head spin when he placed another kiss in my hair. "Tighten your legs around Mort, and here, hold onto the reins."

I was like a doll as he placed my hands where he

wanted them, soft leather meeting my palms, my fingers curling numbly around the reins.

"Rescuing me," I echoed, my temperature somehow dropping lower. I shuddered, and could have sworn the fog rolling over the moors stretched towards us like ghostly hands.

"We're not Nightmare's mindless followers," the one with the gravelly voice said, as if I'd asked a question. "We're her sworn fucking enemies, so anyone she wants dead or hurt is our ally."

"Tor," the rider holding me warned softly. It was a softness full of threat, somehow more dangerous than a shout. I stiffened, grasping the reins in white-knuckled fists as the horse leapt faster under us. Fog and shadow kicked up under its hooves. Mort's hooves?

A soft hand swept the fog-damp strands of hair away from my neck, and my breathing stopped as a careful kiss found my throat. Warm breath feathered over my skin, and somehow I was a thousand times more sensitive, goosebumps rippling down my neck and across my chest.

"You're going to be very afraid," he said, "but you're safe with us. Close your eyes, my bride."

I went as still as the dead, my eyes wide open. Like hell was I closing them in the company of three strangers, especially when they said Nightmare was following us. That, I believed. Them rescuing me? Not so much.

My bride this time. Not little bride.

I was mad, right? I was completely and utterly insane to be thinking what I was thinking. Because Nightmare had said *where is the bride of death* and *he'll like you—a scared little rabbit with fire in her eyes. Yes, he'll like you very much.*

Was this rider the *he* she spoke of? I sucked air in sharp, painful breaths. Had I been given to him like a toy, something to play with and break? *We're her sworn fucking enemies.* I didn't buy it. This was fucked up and four people were dead and I felt *wrong* down in my bones, like my skin didn't fit right over them.

"I can't take this," the third rider spoke, quiet and serious. *She's here,* he'd said, as if he could feel Nightmare closing in on us, feel her sinister power reaching out like it had that night and—

The horse on our left nudged closer, the rider leaned across the distance, and cool fingers circled my wrist. All my anxiety, all my stress, my suffering, *vanished,* swept away at sea, the tide returning only measured calm to me.

The rider released my wrist but I didn't move, didn't know how to react. I'd never felt this before, not for as long as I could remember. It was... empty. Strange. The place inside me that was *always* heavy and tight with stress was hollowed out. No, unburdened. Cleared, like my chest was a cluttered room and he'd tidied everything until there was logic and sense and *space.*

Air rushed into that space, and all I could do was freeze and blink. I'd never known my lungs could take in so much air. Never known I'd been living on rations.

"Fuck," I breathed, staring absently at the road, the moorland cloaked in grey fog on either side of us. "What did you—*how* did you do that?"

He didn't answer, only nudged his horse away.

"Questions and answers later," the rider holding me said, something final and decisive in his voice. "Close your eyes, bride, or don't blame me if you see something you wish you hadn't."

I shrugged. I wasn't closing them.

"So be it," he murmured, and kissed the shell of my ear. Cold shivers flashed down my body, turning rapidly hot.

But I knew what they planned and I hated it. I *seethed.* More men who felt entitled to shit they didn't deserve, just like June those years ago. My nostrils flared with my next breath, darkness and rage gathering inside me.

Kill them. Kill them now before they can hurt you.

The rider behind me jolted like he heard the voice too. I hoped he did, hoped he knew what would happen the second his kisses wandered below my neckline.

I was so distracted by thoughts of violence they could inflict on me, and violence I could unleash on *them,* that I missed the moment when our surroundings changed. My eyes focused back on the road when the rider's arm tightened around me, and I sucked in a whimpering breath at the sight of a dark castle rising above us where the village had been.

"Oh god, how—?"

The castle towered over us, twice as tall as Milton Hall, a black, gothic conflagration of towers, spires, bridges, flying buttresses, beautiful tracery, and windows of stained glass but in shades of colourless grey instead of jewel tones.

"Death is everywhere, and can be found in any place," the rider behind me murmured, feathering a kiss across the sensitive spot behind my ear. "Now, it will answer to you. You can access my domain whenever you wish."

I swallowed. Ignored the tingling in my neck and held onto the unease rapidly rushing into the empty place in my chest where my anxiety lived. "Your domain."

I knew. I didn't want to. I *really* didn't want to. But I knew who held me, who spoke with such care and tenderness, who was warm and solid and kissing my skin like I was precious to him.

Where is the bride of death?

Little bride, he'd called me. And then *my bride.* And now here was a dark castle in the middle of Ford's End where it hadn't existed a minute ago, and the horses weren't exactly solid or *living* under us and—magic. Again. Undeniable and real.

"My domain," he confirmed, fingers stroking my stomach. "The realm of Death."

CHAPTER FIFTEEN

TORMENT

I loved wearing a helmet. No one knew when you were grinning your head off, an uncontrollable smile curving your cheeks until they literally hurt. She was so fucking cute. The bride. Our bride. Cute and sexy and afraid and a little dangerous. An aura of death clung to her, a whisper of violence, and it made me hard in a damn instant. Swathed in the dark cloak of death, no one could see my hard-on.

I was rarely jealous, but I wanted to be the one holding her, feeling her body against mine. Would she be soft? Curvy? Warm? God, I could almost feel her in my arms and the imagined sensation had me biting back a groan. I hadn't been with a woman in... fuck, over seven hundred years. When I'd been alive, before I became Torment.

It wasn't that no woman had ever caught my eye, but they never held my interest the way Death and Miz did. No one else truly understood what it meant to be a god linked to death, to be in torment every second of every day. Well, maybe the other gods, but they were conceited dicks. Plus, women tended to lose interest in me when they realised with a single touch, I could give them the most unbearable pain, drag them through every unspeakable memory and fear they'd ever had, and intensify those emotions until there were only two results—madness and death.

That was a pretty rapid mood killer.

But this woman, this brave, beguiling mortal, was my bride. She could run, but I would always find her. And I'd prove she had nothing to fear with me. I'd sooner burn down the world than inflict that acute kind of torture on an innocent person.[1]

I couldn't take my eyes off the bride as we rode into the shadow of the castle, close enough that its familiar scent washed over me, soothing the torment that made me want to scream, cry, and rip my heart out for a split second before it all roared back. I was always surprised there was space for it inside me, that so much pain actually fit in one living body. Well. Not living, I supposed. I'd been dead seven hundred years.

I needed to know her name. The bride. I watched her go still, watched her knuckles whiten where she gripped Mort's reins, watched her eyes widen—a pale grey like the silver veil of souls, like ominous mist, like spectres and hauntings. I needed her name. Needed everything. Her favourite colour. Her favourite food. What brought her joy, what made her sad, what drove her to pure rage. I wanted a list of her enemies numbered in the order of who'd harmed her the worst, with itemised bullet points of exactly what they'd done, so I could decide how I might kill them.

She was mine. My bride.

I hadn't had anyone as mine since I joined Death and Misery, hadn't entertained the thought that someone else might be mine to keep, mine to love, mine to—

She tore herself away from Death with an abrupt wrench, so sudden that he couldn't anticipate the move. Before any of us could stop her, she rolled off Mort's back and dropped to the ground, landing with a rough cry.

The sound of the impact went through me like the clang of a bell and I leapt off Lanai's dark back, releasing my grip on her spectral mane as I swung to the ground. I landed beside the bride, reaching for her before I could stop myself. And why should I stop? She was our bride, my girl.

"Are you insane?" I demanded, scanning her body with frantic eyes. I caught her face, my hand moulded to her pale cheek. "Are you hurt?"

"I'm fine," she snapped, recoiling from me. "Leave me alone."

"You're obviously not fine. Fine people don't hurl themselves from the back of a shadow shire."

A furrow knitted her brow, and for a single moment I had all her attention. It was heady. I couldn't look away. "Shadow shire?"

"The horse," I clarified, reaching for her again, sliding my fingers along her cheek and marvelling at the softness, the *heat*. "Tell me if this hurts," I said and forced my hand away from her face to grasp her leg, rotating her foot. When she didn't hiss in pain, I repeated the motion on her other foot.

"It's fine," she said quietly, still frowning. "Why do you care if I'm hurt?"

Because I know torment, my bride, and I don't want you well acquainted with it, too.

"We'll explain inside." I wrapped my hand around hers,

guiding her to her feet and glancing at Miz and Death who'd climbed off their steeds and hovered, watching through the slits in their helmets. Speaking of... When the bride was steady on her feet, and I was sure she wasn't going to run, I reached up and pulled off my helmet, dropping it into a pool of shadow until I needed it next.

"Oh, you're..." she said, her grey eyes wide on my face.

My chest swelled. I lifted my head, a smile pulling at my mouth. "Striking? Devastatingly handsome?"

"Normal," she corrected, swiftly popping the inflated balloon of my ego.

"Were you expecting a monster?" I drawled, wrapping my hand around her elbow, unable to resist touching her. My thumb caressed the fragile skin above her forearm through her shirt. She really ought to be wearing a coat; a chill like this could make mortals seriously ill.

She swallowed, biting the inside of her lip. My cock throbbed viciously at the sight. "Well, you were wearing the helmet and cloak, riding a huge shadow horse..."

I smiled, and barely swallowed a remark about her riding my huge shadow horse instead.

"Tor," Death warned, as if sensing the words on the tip of my tongue.

The bride glanced over my shoulder and froze. I glared. The beautiful bastard had removed his helm—and so had Miz. Pretty fuckers, both of them, Miz icy and elegant, Death rendered in warm browns and rich golds, his features not as delicate as Misery's but no less arresting.

"Who are you?" she breathed, her pulse thrumming in her throat. It called to me like a siren song, whispering promises of comfort and affection. I shook the feeling away.

"We'll tell you inside the castle," Death replied, ever-calm. "But until we're inside, Nightmare can still find us."

"Us," she echoed, a knot in her brow. "She's hunting you, too?"

Misery flinched. The bride didn't notice.

"Unfortunately," Death agreed, sweeping his arm at the castle towering above us, onyx and glossy and threatening. "Will you join us inside?"

She laughed softly, the sound full of fear. "Yeah, sure, I'll join you in your ominous Transylvanian castle."

I smirked, trailing my eyes over her in a different way to when I assessed her for injuries. The royal blue shirt she wore was scuffed with dirt from the fall, but no less alluring; the way it hugged her chest and waist made me want to fall at her feet and beg her to keep me for all eternity. Even her denim cargo pants enticed me; what did she keep in her pockets, what secrets did she have tucked away? And god, *her face*. Sweet and round, her skin pink and flushed darker at her cheeks, her eyebrows strong. There was an innocence in her beauty, but one look in her steely eyes and I saw suffering, a delicate language I was fluent in.

My fingers brushed her jaw before I'd given them permission to move, and her breath caught, her eyes flaring with fear, hands trembling.

"There's an illusion here," I murmured, tracing the edge of where it sewed to her face then flowed down her neck to her chest. "What are you hiding, little bride?"

Fear changed to terror and she stumbled away from me, lifting a hand to ward me away.

"I'm not a threat to you," I promised her. "I'd rather my ribcage be cut apart and my heart ripped out than cause you harm."

She froze in surprise but the fear remained. "If you're not a threat, why did you fuck with my car and kidnap me? And don't give me lies about protecting me."

"We'll explain in the castle," Misery said, edging closer,

wind catching long strands of his pale hair. "We need to go inside. She's almost here."

The bride held her hand between us, her only weapon, her only shield. My heart ached. I would give her a dozen weapons, cover her beautiful body with them until she rattled with steel and iron.

"I'm not hiding anything," she said breathlessly, her attention returning to me. "I don't know what the illusion is, but I can guess who put it there. There's—there's makeup on my face I can't wash away. The makeup I wore on Halloween, when she did... whatever she did." Her throat bobbed. "Nightmare."

Miz flinched and this time she caught it, confusion muddying her grey eyes. "She's listening," he said. "Mind your words."

"Inside," Death ordered, iron entering his words. "Now."

He started towards our bride. Idiot. I was ready to lunge after her, unsurprised when she ran.

It was worrying easy to catch her, my arms wrapping around her waist, pulling her back into me. "Sorry about this, little bride, but if we stay out here, not only will Nightmare get her hands on you, she'll also gain access to the domain of death, and I can't allow that."

I threw her over my shoulder, my hands secure against the backs of her thighs, and hurried to the gate with Death and Misery flanking us. Fuck, the *heat* of her, the softness of her chest and stomach.

"Put me down!" she raged, breathless with fright.

"Terror," a sultry feminine voice called on the wind. "My terror, come to me."

I tightened my grip on our bride, rage making my entire body bristle.

"She's not your anything," Death argued, his voice low and ominous in a way I so rarely heard.

"Oh god," the bride choked out, trembling harder against my shoulder, her teeth knocking together. "Oh, god, oh god."

I sprinted, faster than I'd had any cause to run in years, and skidded into the expansive courtyard before the castle that was the domain of death. An entire realm contained in a single building.

"Miz, gates," I hissed, spinning around to stare at the winding Ford's End road, the moor entirely covered in fog now. I realised why our bride had taken up her panicked chant at once; Nightmare had taken form, and floated down the road towards us, her red hair like a flag of blood behind her, her poisoned, beautiful face smiling, hand stretched out in entreaty.

I only breathed again when Misery slammed the iron gates shut and Death stood behind them, a dark force gathering around him. His power was a cloud of darkness and silver, souls pressing their faces from the inside of it, horrific and gruesome. They spread out across the gates in a shield Nightmare could never cross.

She yowled in fury, like a pissed off cat, and I exhaled a long sigh, letting down the bride from my shoulder. I settled her with hands curled around her slim biceps, not quite able to stop touching her. My heart stuttered when I saw her teary grey eyes.

"I hope you weren't attached to your car. I'm afraid it might be the victim of Nightmare's little tantrum."

I tried to coax her down from her fear with a smile, but it had no effect. Shit. Death and Miz hovered, their eyes on her.

I tucked a pink lock of hair behind her ear, my touch lingering, and gentled my voice. "Let's go inside, shall we?"

CHAPTER SIXTEEN

CAT

$\mathcal{I}$ froze on the road outside the castle, forced to choose between being murdered by these three men or being caught in the crimson glow of Nightmare's magic again. In the end, the gravelly-voiced man threw me over his shoulder and took the choice out of my hands, and thank fuck he had. Any longer and Nightmare would have reached me.

I didn't know what she wanted, but it couldn't be good. Cold trickled down my arms, lifting fine hairs as I help-lessly followed the riders through a massive wooden door into an endless warren of hallways and rooms. Their horses had gone up in smoke, *literally*. One second they were there, the next gone.

The gentle man who'd held me as we rode was nothing like I'd expected. He was tall and broad and so unfairly handsome that it was hard to keep my eyes off him. He'd just kidnapped me, kind of, and the last thing I should be doing was tracing my eyes over the planes of smooth, brown skin, the mouth curved into a patient smile, the eyes watching me with an endless well of kindness I wasn't sure was a lie. I definitely did not look at his wide shoulders, his powerful biceps, or the way the sleeveless, embroidered tunic he wore stretched across his chest.

I jumped when his hand skimmed my forearm, and panic at getting caught looking held me in place as his touch travelled down, fingers intertwining with mine. I remembered the reverent kisses he placed on my body while we rode, though I tried very hard not to. It was the most intimate I'd been with someone in months, and I didn't know how to feel about wanting more of it.

"What's your name, my bride?" he asked, his voice like caramel—sweet, rich, and addictive. I bit my bottom lip.

I swallowed, nerves making my pulse race. They'd just ostensibly saved me from Nightmare, and my paranoia suggested it could all be one big set-up to get me to trust them, but... I didn't have Nightmare's sharp eyes on me right now, didn't have her soft taunts in my ears, didn't feel the heavy thump of her power, and I was so grateful for that.

"Cat," I answered quietly.

"Like a pussy cat?" he asked, his smile deepening, making him even *more* handsome. Ugh.

"Yeah," I said too quickly. "Like a pussy cat."

"That was an obvious lie," the man with the gravelly voice said, spinning to face us where he walked ahead, like he'd been waiting for an excuse to look at me. He kept doing that. Looking at me. Touching me. "What secrets are you keeping, Cat?"

I scowled at the floor, looking away from his face— equally handsome as the others' but different, harsher. His features were soft but sharpened by his shaved head and tattoos, his mouth set in what appeared to be a perpetual smirk. His golden skin and glittering soft-brown eyes, made me think of Central America. He was also far closer to my five-foot-seven height, which would make kissing him easier and *why was I thinking about kissing him?* It was similar to the force that had propelled me out of the car, Nightmare's magic brushing my soul but... I wasn't compelled. Not completely. And—oh god, he was right in front of me.

I slammed to a halt in the middle of a dark corridor lit by green lamps and jumped back with a shriek, his face exceptionally close. I could see the flecks in his eyes, his irises the colour of milky coffee and—*my latte!* Fuck, I abandoned it in the middle of the road with my car. And my book![1]

"What's your name really?" he asked with an intensity that made me break out in goosebumps.

"Cat," I answered, my breath a little short. "Cat Wallison."

"Mm." He flicked out his tongue, *so* close to brushing my lips. A shot of heat laced my blood. "No, I still taste the lie."

"You can't taste lies, don't bullshit," the pale, long-haired man said with a sneer that made me instantly dislike him.

"My name's Tor," said the man two inches away from my face with the shaved head and sexy intensity.[2] "This is Miz. And um—"

He glanced at the six-foot-three man towering over us, all beauty and sincerity.

"Death," I finished for him, gratified by their shock. "Yeah, I figured that out by you all calling me your bride. I was dressed as the bride of death the night Nightmare... well, I'd rather not talk about what happened. It doesn't take a genius to put two and two together and get Death."

"We already know what happened," Death said gently, squeezing my hand. I jumped. I'd forgotten he was even holding it; the sensation was so natural, so right. I glanced at him from the corner of my eye. He wasn't what I'd expected of Death. The spiked helmet and horror horse or whatever Tor called them was more accurate. But this softness was ... strange.

"Let's get you a drink, and we'll explain who we are to you," he suggested kindly, dropping a kiss on my forehead that stunned me into compliance.

The pale-haired man said nothing throughout this, only speared me with disapproving glances as we moved through the castle that was surprisingly ordinary and solid brick, not shadowy or smoky like the horses. I avoided his stares, barely keeping my breathing under control without getting into a staring match with a man who obviously hated me.

But... were these actually *men,* or something else, something more sinister like Nightmare? The man beside me was Death. *The* Death. I wasn't sure what that meant, but I knew it meant I was his bride and he was my... husband? Fuck, I didn't know. I wished Honey and Byron were here with a fierceness that made my chest hurt.

I saw what Death did to the gates to stop Nightmare following us. The dark magic, like a veil of ink stretched across the iron, with people inside fighting to get out, hands and faces pressed to the surface. I shuddered, and gasped when Death stroked a hand across my shoulder blades, a weight settling over me.

Fear made my throat tighten. I glanced down at the cloak of feathers that flowed from my shoulders to the floor, warm and reassuring despite its terrifying origin.

"Thanks," I mumbled automatically. Shit, should I be thanking these people? Were they like the fae where expressing gratitude implied a debt I'd have to pay?

"Don't worry so much, Cat," he murmured, fingers stroking down my hair next. No feathers or darkness gathered around me this time, the gesture simple. Comforting in a way I didn't want it to be, and entirely blamed on Nightmare's fucked up magic tying us together. "You're safe here. You have my word no one will hurt you."

I glanced at him quickly, looking for signs of deceit and really struggling to find any. Maybe he believed what he was saying. Maybe Nightmare was playing a game with all of us, and had tricked them into caring about me. Her face formed in my mind, unnaturally beautiful, her eyes mismatched, the pale one bleeding down her flawless cheek as she smiled. I shuddered and pulled the cloak of black feathers tighter around me.

"Here we are, Cat," Tor said, my name soft and lingering in his mouth. He guided us through a stone archway and into a warm sitting room decorated in shades of amber and red, a fire roaring in a huge gothic fireplace across the room. Above it hung a portrait of the three of them. In the portrait, Miz was smiling at Death, his eyes a bright, piercing gold, his cheeks curved, one arm slung around Tor's waist.

Oh. I blinked, looking quickly away from the painting, like I'd glimpsed something private I wasn't supposed to. They were all *together,* intimate and clearly possessing a deep affection. What did that make me, as Death's bride? A homewrecker? No wonder Miz hated me.

But why didn't Tor? His latte eyes still shone with an intensity I hesitantly labelled interest as he swept me away from Death, the tall, gentle man holding onto my hand until he was forced to surrender it. I was bundled onto one of the plush, amber-coloured sofas, my taut body immediately swallowed into comfort and luxury. Tor plopped down beside me and—*stared* at me, his elbow propped on his knee, chin propped on his hand.

Uh. Okay.

"What's it short for, beautiful bride?"

I glanced away, my cheeks hot at his constant attention, nervousness tightening my chest. "Cactus," I begrudgingly admitted.

Miz snorted, sinking onto a sofa opposite us and watching as Death approached a drinks trolley shaped like St. Paul's Cathedral, opening the dome to draw out a bottle of gold liquid the same colour as Miz's eyes. At least in the painting. I daren't look at the actual man long enough to see if they were the same in real life.

"My cute little succulent," Tor breathed with something like fascination. I stared at him in surprise and a little like he was insane.[3]

"Here, Cat," Death murmured, catching my hand to place a glass in it, handing another to Miz when he sat beside the pale, stiff-backed man. I watched him thaw, surprised to see it at all, when Death rested his broad hand on his knee. "So," he said, watching me, "you know I'm Death. But you might not know what that means."

"Probably that you can kill me," I muttered, then took a quick drink when it came out a little louder than planned.

"I can kill *anyone* with a single touch and a flicker of magic," Death agreed with a smile that struck me as sad. "I don't kill everyone, obviously, or there'd be no one left in the world. Most die naturally, and arrive in my domain of their own will. But it's my job to kill those who stubbornly cling to life when their time is up. To maintain the balance of life and death in the world. A balance," he added, "that Nightmare has thrown into chaos."

I swallowed, then drank more of the burning golden liquid. It wasn't pleasant, but I needed the warmth when this conversation made me so cold inside. "Did you kill the people at the party?"

"No," Death replied with clear irritation. "And neither did their souls arrive here. She consumed them."

"Consumed," I echoed, the cold spreading further inside me. "I think I—felt it. Like a sick heartbeat. They died and then it was all I could hear, feel…"

Tor slid closer to me. I jumped when his arm came around me, holding tight to my body, my new feathered cloak trapped between us.

"How do you tie into this?" I asked, looking at each of them. "I'm not an idiot; Nightmare turns up, kills people, and suddenly you're here racing to my rescue."

Tor held me tighter, like he was trying to hold off the inevitable and stop me pulling away from him.

"We're here because of what Nightmare did," Death said gently, his grey eyes heavy, sad. "Nightmare is consumed with a thirst for power, and she'll stop at nothing to get it. This isn't the first time she's gathered a cult, enacted a ritual, and killed people. I'm so sorry you were caught up in it."

"She said it could have been anyone," I murmured, turning the glass in my hand. "It just happened to be me because I picked the bride of death costume."

"It's all a twisted game to her," Miz said with a low laugh, throwing back the contents of his glass and pushing off the sofa to get more. "She likes playing with people, pushing them to the edge of their limits and seeing what happens when they break."

"Miz…" Tor murmured, watching him.

"She cursed you," Miz said harshly, pinning me with a look that made my heart quicken, my whole body prickling with warning. "Everyone who was there that night is *cursed*. That's why you're wearing an illusion—you look normal on the surface, but deep down you are *hers* and your face shows the truth."

"Misery," Death said, soft and steely at once. "This is not the way to tell her."

Miz—Misery—laughed high and sharp. "She'll find out either way. It's better that she knows the truth instead of you dancing around it." He looked me in the eye. "Nightmare caught you up in her ritual, bound you to be the bride of Death—which means you are the bride of all three of us—and now she can find you anywhere and do whatever the fuck she wants with you. She owns you, Cactus."

For the first time, I didn't cringe from my name. I was too afraid to even feel embarrassment over it. "How do I undo it?" I breathed, shaking.

Misery shook his head, his beautiful face cold. "You don't."

CHAPTER SEVENTEEN

CAT

*T*or—which I discovered was short for Torment—rode me back to Ford and deposited me on the road before the scrolling iron gates, sea serpents coiling around the latch. It was dark, only a few lights twinkling in the village at the base of the hill, but more lights blazed from the buildings deep inside Ford.

Death. Torment. Misery.

Three men who embodied those traits, who were responsible for inflicting them on the world. Death gods.

Hearing those words together—*death* and *gods*—was my final straw. I'd jumped off the sofa and strode for the door, meaning to run out the gates and back up the winding road to Ford. But when I flung open the heavy black door, it was a whole other city I looked out on, the sky tinged as red as blood, the buildings all formed of blackened stone and of a style I'd never seen before, angular and sharp, with flat roofs. I wasn't anywhere near Ford's End—the village *or* the island.

Magic, again, clear and undeniable. A chill rippled down my arms.

"I'll take you back," Tor had offered, following me the instant I leapt off the sofa.

I spun my crown ring around and around my finger, staring at the unfamiliar city. The unfamiliar *world?* My domain, death had said. I wasn't sure what that meant.

"This isn't Ford's End," I breathed, my ears ringing.

"No, Cat," Tor confirmed gently. "It isn't."

Now, I strode through Ford's gates, not entirely sure how his massive, black horse—Lanai, he'd called her—had ridden out of the domain of death and into the world of the living, let alone how she'd ended up depositing me at Ford's gates.

I wrapped my arms around myself as I walked towards campus, Death's feathered cloak still draped over my shoulders even though it seemed like the sort of thing that should have dissolved the second I was away from him. I felt eyes on me as I walked down the tree-lined path, but it was a relief to know it was probably Torment watching me and not Nightmare.

Those names... they didn't exactly inspire confidence. Tor and Death kept insisting I was safe, but unless I was losing my entire fucking mind, they were like Nightmare. Powerful. So much more than human. Literal embodiments of the worst traits in humanity.[1]

Wind slashed through the trees and caught my hair, and I shuddered, huddling further into the heavy cloak, the weather not helping my mood. My head was a mess. Either the death gods had fucked with my car and sprung a trap, or Nightmare had been messing with me, chasing me.

Probably pushing me to have a mental breakdown like Miz said she would.

Strangely, Misery was the only one I trusted to be honest with me. He didn't soften any blows, didn't skirt around the truth. When he said I was cursed on Halloween by the chanting, the robes, the murders, that crimson light... I believed him. I didn't want to, but I believed him.

"Cursed," I murmured, swallowing the knot in my throat and shaking harder. I blamed it on the cold and knew that was a lie. Nightmare cursed us that night. There had been fifty people around Ford House when red lights exploded from the windows. Were they *all* cursed?

If I was now the bride of Death, what did that make clowns and ghosts and the guy dressed as a fucking pussy?[2]

"One problem at a time," I told myself, the wind stealing my words until I barely heard them. My car was still broken down on the road; Tor rode us past it even though I tried to get him to stop. It wasn't safe, he said, as if it was any safer in the campus where I'd been cursed in the first place.

I didn't have my phone; in the chaos of the death gods chasing me on their shadow shires, I'd dropped it, which meant I couldn't call a garage to come tow my car. I needed to get back to Lawrence Hall and borrow Honey's phone or Byron's. Byron... I'd abandoned the apology cake slice. Fuck. That was supposed to make it harder to stay mad at me, and now I didn't have a peace offering.

I rubbed my eyes with cold fingers, feathers brushing my cheek like Death's featherlight kisses had. I pushed back any thoughts relating to the way they'd looked at me, touched me, kissed me. I was touch starved and greedy for affection, so my judgement was clouded. Any normal person would have punched them in the dick and run away.

Fear had frozen me, but so had the sight of the horses, the cloaks, the helmets, and the inescapable fact that they weren't *human*. There were two Cats now—before and after Halloween. Three days ago, I'd have run at the sight of the riders, but now? I couldn't escape it. Magic, darkness, danger—it was everywhere. I choked on it now, crossing campus in the dark.

Even now, there was a fist clenched around my heart, urging me back out the gates and down to the hill where I'd first met the death gods. Nightmare's curse at work, forcing us together. I sank my teeth into my bottom lip and ignored it. At least it hadn't taken over my body this time. At least I walked the curving road toward Ford instead of being compelled away.

Lights grew brighter, closer, their glow diffused by the fine rain that hung in the air around me, drenching the feathers of my cloak. Relief choked off my air at the sight of it, but I was still wound so tightly, anticipating Nightmare's attack, that I flinched when a soft voice called,

"Cat Wallison? Is that you?"

I halted abruptly, my breathing racing, cold spreading through my body. I wished I had the same power as Nightmare, as the death gods. But I was a cursed human against gods. I was easy prey.

I tensed, one second away from running like I should have when the riders came towards me like a scene from a horror film, but I paused at the figure who emerged from the mist and rain.

"I thought that was you," Carmilla Poppy, my microbiology professor said, a smile curving her eyes behind pillar-box-red glasses as she hurried closer. "What are you doing out in this awful weather?"

"My car broke down," I explained, relieved to see a

living, breathing person and not a hellish god. "On the road up from Ford's End."

Carmilla Poppy was a short, petite, forty-something woman with a cropped bob of reddish-brown hair, freckles scattered across a pale, kind face, and an energy that instantly calmed me. It had earlier when I took her first class, and it did now. Her kindness was palpable, and fuck did I need some reassuring kindness right now.

"Have you had to walk up the hill in this rain?" she asked, eyes widening as she reached me. "Of course you have, look at you, you're soaked through. Typical that cars never break down when it's sunny and fair."

I laughed softly, the sound expelling some of my dread and leaving a smile on my face. "It could be worse. At least it's not snowing."

"Yet," Poppy added before I could. "Go on inside. Have you called a tow for your car?"

"Not yet. My phone's dead." And left somewhere between the car and the road because an inexplicable force propelled me towards three horrifying horses with even more horrifying riders, but I didn't say that part out loud.

"The garage won't open until nine tomorrow." Poppy frowned, fishing out her own mobile from the pocket of the pastel blue blazer she wore, an enamel poppy pinned to the lapel. "Tell you what, I'll give Edgar Doyle a call and see if he'll come out to pick up your car. He's an old family friend so I should be able to sweet talk him."

Another knot unwound from my chest. "That'd be amazing. Thank you, Professor Poppy."

She waved a hand. "Carmilla, please. I'm not one of those stuffy professors that demands formalities as a sign of respect from day one. I'll *buy* that respect with a box of pain au chocolat," she said with a wink.

"I'll hold you to that," I replied, glad there was at least one professor who wasn't, in her words, stuffy.

"Emerson Radclyffe's the one you want to watch out for," she told me, glancing up from her phone—red with poppies all over the case—to give me a wry look. "He's a stickler for rules, tradition, and excessive formalities. And I did *not* tell you his name is Emerson."

I winced at the thought of the stern, grey-haired white man I'd glimpsed during orientation. "That secret is safe with me. I'm not chancing risking his wrath."

"Smart girl. Now go on inside, get dry and warm. I'll have your car brought in."

"Thank you," I said profusely. "You're a life saver. I don't know what I'd have done without you."

She batted me away with a smile. "Flattery will get you everywhere."

I hurried up the path towards Lawrence Hall, where my room was dry and semi-warm, and was immensely glad I hadn't run into Emerson Radclyffe instead of Carmilla. I got the sense he wouldn't be helping me tow my car so much as getting me written up for disorderly behaviour.

Lawrence Hall wasn't home yet, but relief still hit me when I pushed open the heavy door and made my way past the breakfast hall—empty—and winced at the clock on the wall that must have been wrong because there was no way it was past eleven.

No wonder I was hungry.

With no distractions, my mind wandered back to the party, to Nightmare and the curse and the death gods I was apparently bound to. Married to? I'd been too big a coward to ask how exactly they defined the word bride. Was I engaged to be married, or had the curse already signed the certificate?

They'd been equally sweet and cagy, upfront and secretive. They knew Nightmare—I saw Miz flinch at her name, at her proximity. No way had they told me the full truth, but maybe I should have been glad of that. The bit of truth they *had* told me was horrifying.

I was cursed.

We were *all* cursed—Honey, Duncan, Alastor, Darya, and everyone else who'd been there. Byron ran out because his sister called, and I prayed that meant he was spared. Otherwise he'd, what, become a vampire? Hunger for blood?

This is so fucked up.

I might have dismissed it all as bullshit if I hadn't *felt* the change, the discord within me. And if Honey's words didn't ring, over and over, through my head.

My fur must have been soaked. Her fur, like she was already thinking like the cat she'd dressed as for Halloween.

"Fuck," I hissed, because I needed to say it out loud, because the truth was so bad I couldn't keep the expletive in my head.

I trudged up the steps to our floor, my chest so tight it was like Miz had never wiped out all my anxiety on the ride to Death's domain.

Instead of continuing to my room, I hovered outside Honey's, my hand curled in a fist to knock. But my courage deserted me. I had to tell her. She needed to know. But I didn't want to speak any of it out loud. She'd think I was mad. All the things the gods had told me...

But they still hadn't told me where *they* tied into Nightmare's plan, why they were interested in me in the first place. Because I was their bride? Or because they were in league with Nightmare?

The answer seemed obvious.

I lifted my hand and knocked softly on Honey's door.

CHAPTER EIGHTEEN

CAT

*T*he irony wasn't lost on me. My name was Cat, and yet Honey was the one curled up in a pile of fleece blankets on her bed, kneading the fluffiest blanket while she purred.

Purred.

I froze in the doorway, just staring.

"So, uh, this is a thing," I said, blinking. I quickly shut the door behind me, unable to take my eyes off my best friend. She was *purring,* kneading the fleece like cats made their little biscuits, and when she lifted her head to look at me, not only did the purring ramp up in volume, but her eyes changed. Her slit pupils widened, and a big grin crossed her face.

"Cat!" she cried happily, arching off the bed in a decidedly feline stretch before rushing across the room to head bump my shoulder. I staggered back. "Where did you go? I tried to find you, but your scent was faded so I knew you hadn't been back. And—you're all wet." She made a face and let go of me, shaking out her hand to try and get the droplets off.

"I…" I looked at her, at her slit-pupiled eyes, and burst into horrible, gut-wrenching tears.

Between sobs, I told her everything, from what happened while she was drunk at the party to just now, Tor bringing me home via his massive, shadow-dark horse.

By the time I finished, she was no longer purring and her eyes were so wide I saw myself reflected in them. She didn't have whiskers, fur, or claws, but her mannerisms and behaviour screamed *cat*.

"So," she said, plopping back into her pile of fluffy blankets. "I'm a cat, you're a bride of death. What about By?"

"I don't know," I admitted, perching on her desk, my feathered cloak thrown over the chair to dry. "He left before everything happened, and I don't remember seeing him when the house started to glow. I think… he might have escaped it."

"Good. That's good."

"Except we're cursed and he's not and it's a pretty big secret to keep from him." I rubbed my eyes, tired.

"We could just tell him," she suggested, flexing her fingers like a cat extending and retracting their claws.

I shook my head swiftly. "No. He's got enough to worry about. You know Sterling's pregnant?"

"Shit! He didn't tell me that." Her eyes were impossibly wide.

"That's why he ran out of the party. He got a call from her. He told me when I got home after… after everything happened." I shrugged, still hurt by the way he looked at me, snapped at me. "He's freaking out about their parents finding out. I don't think we should make him even more stressed with this curse shit."

Honey sighed and climbed off the bed again, wrapping her arms around me and squeezing until I grunted. "We'll figure this out, Cat. I know it's scary, and we don't really know what it means to be a cat or death's bride, but curses can be broken, right?"

"Right," I agreed weakly.

She hadn't felt the full force of Nightmare's power. I wished I'd drunk more that night so my memories were muddied too, wished I couldn't recall the exact way the air throbbed when people died. I swallowed hard, squeezing her back.

"And hey," she said, pulling back but giving me a reassuring smile. "I've always loved cats. Dad never let me get one. He said they smell because of all the litter trays and —*oh god*, am I gonna need a litter tray?"

Her eyes were very wide, her mouth hanging open.

"I reckon you can keep using the toilet as normal," I assured her, squeezing her shoulder.

She deflated with a sigh. "Thank fuck for that. My legs muscles aren't strong enough for all that squatting."

I snorted. She grinned, a laugh bubbling up from her stomach, and then we were both laughing for no reason at all, expelling stress and panic and traumatic memories in wild laughter.

Honey fell back on her bed, laughing until she calmed and gave me a sly look. "Are they hot? Your three husbands."

"They're not my three husbands," I instantly argued, my face hot.

She waggled her eyebrows. "I think that's a yes."

"Fine, yes, they're insanely, unfairly hot. But it's not like they're interested in me. The only reason they know I exist is because of the curse."

"They call that a meet cute."

"Pretty sure a curse is not a meet cute," I drawled, but I was smiling again. "And anyway, one of them hates me and one of them is wayyy too intense."

Her smile hooked deeper. "That's only two. What about the third?"

I scowled, but the expression softened when my memories went to the way Death held me, his kisses travelling over my neck, my shoulder, his voice steady and warm, his smoky eyes patient and kind.

"He's terrifying," I sighed, leaning back against the dresser. "Beyond scary. He'd make even serial killers run screaming. But he's kind."

Honey nodded. "And kindness is your kink."

"Hey," I protested. "I have more kinky kinks than that."

"Oh yeah?" She grinned, sprawling out on the bed as she watched me. "Like what?"

"I immediately regret protesting. I have no kinky kinks. Perfectly ordinary, thank you very much."

"I know you like older guys, so I guess that's a kink?"

"More a preference." I'd burned out on guys my age after a single one, and I had no interest in going back to immature, cheating assholes. I supposed that was one thing the gods had going for them. They were all older than me. Probably very, *very* old.

"Let me guess. You're scared of rejection like me and eager to please—"

"I know it's true, but I'd rather you didn't say it out loud, it just sounds sad—"

"So my guess is praise kink."

I rolled my eyes, pretending to scowl. "I suspect the pot is calling the kettle black."

She laughed "You suspect correctly. Okay, what else? We're in uni now, Cat. Sex talk and kinky shit is what med school is *for.*"

"And here I thought it was for learning medicine."

She deployed the Stare, and said nothing, knowing full well I would break.

I crossed my arms over my chest and looking at the floor I said, "Fine. Dom/sub, dirty talk, some bondage, breath play, primal play, Ddlg, degradation, and CNC. What's yours?"

Honey's eyes were wide. "Damn, you've got a whole list."

My ears burned. "Yeah…"

"I just like getting my hair pulled and being called a good girl."

I stared at her. She stared back, then grinned.

"Shit, I need to be more adventurous," she laughed, blue eyes crinkled. "Learn more about myself. A great sexual awakening. How did you learn all this stuff anyway? You've had like, one boyfriend and I really doubt he could find the clit."

"Internet," I answered, "and no he could not."

"Waste of space," she muttered, then grinned at me. "Do you think your new husbands will do all that primal bondage stuff?"

I groaned. "It's not an actual marriage, and they're not my actual husbands."

"But they're hot, and you *liiike* them," she teased.

"Nightmare will kill me before I get a chance," I muttered, only half joking.

"All the more reason not to waste time. Go listen to Jason Derulo's *Pony* and bite those men, Cat." At my look, she snorted and said, "I have no idea what primal stuff means, and I'm happy in my innocent little bubble. Just promise me something, Cat."

"Anything," I agreed seriously.

"If you find another hot, six-foot-something god, send him my way."

A laugh burst up my throat, and then we were both giggling again.

"You've got first dibs," I promised her, my smile fading.

"We'll end the curse, Cat. First thing tomorrow, we'll go to the library and start finding ways to do it. The gods said Nightmare did this before, right?"

"Yeah."

"So someone must have been in our exact position before. All we need to do is find an ancient tome or a very worn journal, and we'll be back to normal in no time."

I forced a nod and wished I agreed with her.

CHAPTER NINETEEN

DEATH

*S*he was sleeping in my cloak. I froze at the foot of her bed, concealed in a veil of shadow, and stared at the beautiful woman curled up in bed, her hands tucked under her chin, eyes hidden behind a sleep mask with ducks embroidered all over it. She slept in my cloak. In the feathered cloak I conjured and draped around her shoulders. She was *sleeping* in it. I tried not to read too much into that and failed.

Her lips were parted, visible in the soft moonlight sifting through the curtains, her skin like alabaster in its glow. When a soft, fearful cry left her mouth, I rushed across the distance, my blood running cold.

"Hush, little bride," I soothed, sitting on the bed beside her, indulging the need to touch her, running my fingers over her hair. "I'll watch over you while you sleep. Nightmare won't get anywhere near your dreams."

She made another of those breathy, frightened noises

that stabbed right through my ribs into my heart—dead but still beating thanks to the half-life I had as a god. Still beating and now hers.

"My beautiful wife," I murmured, stroking her hair and relieved when she settled. "I vanquished Nightmare once, and I will do it again. You have my word and my promise."

I smoothed the wrinkle in her forehead with my thumb and cast off the last tendrils of shadow and smoke concealing me when she sighed, a sound of peace and relief. A sound that told me, deep down in her soul, she felt safe with me. Because she knew me, because she recognised my presence from when we met three years ago? Or simply because Nightmare had bound her to me, and the curse compelled her to feel so?

"We'll solve this problem, Cat, you'll see." I feathered a kiss over her forehead and, drunk on the taste of her skin, the peaches and cream scent of her filling my lungs, I lavished more feather-light kisses across her face, even the places hidden by the duck-embroidered mask she wore.

My lungs were so full of her scent I knew I'd never get it out. It was the same with the amber and sandalwood of Tor's scent, the violets and fresh snow of Misery's. They were mine as I was theirs, and I would stop at nothing to keep them safe.

Nightmare was the clear threat, but there were others. Her cult of mindlessly violent followers. And whichever disciple had conducted the ritual that brought her back—a hopeful who wished to join her cult. I'd find them all eventually, but would it before Miz or Cat were harmed? Both were burdened by what they'd been through at the hands of Nightmare, and I knew Nightmare's tactics well enough to know she'd take advantage of their trauma.

"But I won't let her," I promised my wife softly,

brushing a stand of white hair from her beautiful face. "I would die before I let her touch you."

Her sleep seemed more restful now, and pride that I'd given her that made my chest swell. I stayed beside her all through the night, indulging in gentle touches and butterfly kisses, letting her presence wrap around me like an embrace until I knew I would find her anywhere, hear her voice no matter where I was.

"You are in my blood and bones, little bride," I told her as the sun began to rise. She'd turned towards me in her sleep, her hands still folded under her chin, her mouth parted. I bowed over her to brush a kiss to those tempting lips and whispered, "I'll be back tonight."

I'd watch over her every night until I knew Nightmare was vanquished again.

I forced myself to rise, to cloak myself in shadow and smoke again, but I only left her room when I'd procured breakfast for my wife from the banquet downstairs— grapes and strawberries and croissants and cream-filled breads—and withdrew a tulip I'd snipped from my garden, cultivated in the domain of the dead so it would never wither. It was the same violent green as her car and, I hoped, her favourite colour.

I left the offerings on the table opposite her bed and, sensing another shadow of death hovering, desperate for his own time with our wife, I faded into darkness and returned home.

But part of my soul tugged me back, to my bride, to my wife.

CHAPTER TWENTY

CAT

A slow-curling warmth woke me, and I let out a deep sigh, feeling well rested for the first time since I got to Ford. I kept my eyes closed, just appreciating the peace, the lack of chest-cinching anxiety. It would return, but in these first few moments before my mind remembered how to think, I was gifted quietude and calm.

My clit throbbed, a wave of pleasure and need moving through me, and there were no prizes for guessing what kind of dream I'd been having, even if I couldn't quite remember dreaming. Oh god, did I dream of Death and Miz and—

My clit pulsed again and—and—oh god, that was a *tongue*—

I ripped my eye mask off, my breath catching in a panicked gasp as I stared down my body. The covers had been pulled down, the bottoms of my fuzzy cartoon pyjamas removed and *Tor* lay between my legs, his gold hands splayed over my inner thighs as he ate my pussy.

In the hysterical moment between me *seeing* him and speaking, Honey's words came back to me. *You've had like, one boyfriend and I really doubt he could find the clit.*

But Tor had no problems finding it, and made my eyes roll back by circling it over and over.

"What—" I gasped, pleasure making my hips jerk, "the fuck do you think you're doing?"

He brushed a reverent kiss to my throbbing clit and said, "Waking my wife."

Wife. God. Okay, that answered the question of what *bride* meant to them. My hands shook, and I swear I lifted them to push him away, but Tor's tongue traced those euphoric circles around my aching nerves again and—god.

"You taste fucking amazing," he told me between sloppy licks, and I realised I was soaking wet when he flicked over my entrance to devour every drop that dripped from me. How long had he been doing this while I slept…?

"This is so fucked up," I groaned, covering my face. Partly because I knew it was inflamed and not my sexiest look[1] but also so he couldn't see me bite my lip.

"I thought of you all night," he said against my pussy, making me shudder at the sensation of his breath on my heated, sensitive skin. "I couldn't get you out of my head. My bride. Mine."

Tingles rushed down my legs. I bit my lip harder, unable to stop my hips bucking up into Tor when he groaned and devoured me with wild, ravenous curls of his tongue.

"Look at me, my cute little succulent."

"I can't," I said, ignoring the name.

"Not even if I do this?" he asked and—sealed his lips around my clit, flicking with his tongue. A grunt drew out of me before I could stop it. I had to release my lip from my teeth or I'd draw blood.

"Why are you—? I'm not really—you don't want me, this is just the curse messing with you."

"Look at me," Torment said again, and his tone was so different, the madness and obsession replaced with a grave seriousness.

I swallowed, dropped my hands, and met his feverish brown eyes. He was every bit as handsome as I remembered, his face soft and sharp at once, his head shaved in a way that only enhanced his vicious beauty, and his mouth —his mouth shone with my arousal. I couldn't look away even if shyness and my crumbling self-esteem made me want to.

"I don't give a shit about the curse, Cat. It only made you our bride—it hasn't made me feel what I do. I want to be here, with your fucking irresistible taste on my tongue, with your body in my hands, because you are sexy as fuck, and brave, and I love those little quips you throw my way when your fear dips. I'm enthralled by you. *You* are what has me aching and desperate for you, not anything that bitch did."

It was a pretty convincing speech as far as speeches went. The fierce way he spoke, not letting a single iota of doubt form, helped. He meant every word, and it was baffling but flattering as hell.

"Oh," I breathed.

"And," he added, hands gliding up the outside of my naked thighs, "everything I uncover about you, every scowl and gasp and frown, just makes me even more desperate for you. You are my wife. Mine to keep. So lay back, Beautiful, and take as many orgasms as you want from me."

My eyes were wide. I had reservations—a whole stack of them—but it was a little hard to remember them with a hot as fuck man between my thighs, willing to give me *as many orgasms as I wanted.*

"Do you really like the way I taste?" I asked after a moment, propped up on my elbows but relaxing, bit by bit, as he scattered open-mouthed kisses up my thighs to my centre.

"I'm *obsessed* with the way you taste," he corrected, his light brown eyes filled with fire. "You don't mind if I keep you in bed for the rest of your life so I can keep my tongue buried in your pussy, do you?"

"Um. I have classes."

Tor's response was a sulky sound that made me smile. "Fucking school."

I laughed, the sound bursting out of its own will, and Tor's eyes flashed up to me, lingering, *staring.* "What?" I asked self-consciously, my face burning.

"You are... beyond beautiful," he breathed, hands skimming up my thighs to spread them wider. He kept his eyes on me as he lowered his head, kissing my clit. "My Cat. My wife."

I scraped my teeth over my lip, nerves tangling my belly, but I asked, "Does that make you mine, then?"

"Oh fuck yeah," Tor groaned, his eyes going heavy lidded. "I am entirely and completely yours." He dove back into my pussy, stroking all the sensitive places, like he'd already learned exactly what made me gasp and my hips jolt. "You have to share me with Death and Miz, though," he said against my entrance, catching all my arousal on his tongue like it was the finest wine and he couldn't bear to miss a single drop.

"Won't that—" A whimper ate my words when he tightened his grip on my thighs and dragged me closer, his mouth finding my clit, wrapping it in heat and blissful pressure. "Oh, god. I don't want to—to—"

Get between them.[2]

Tor groaned, the vibrations making my eyes cross, ripping a guttural sound from me before he released my throbbing clit. "There's a place for you among us. Don't worry so much, my wife. You won't cause conflict."

Miz already hates me, I wanted to say, but I dropped back against the bed, my elbows collapsing under me when his tongue swirled *inside* me, finding places I hadn't realised were quite so sensitive.

"God, Tor," I groaned, and ignored the fact I barely knew him, and he was only here because of a curse. People grabbed random men and hooked up all the time. This didn't have to be more complicated than that.

Except he kept calling me his, and his wife, and looking at me like *that.*

"That's it, Cat," he murmured, watching me. "You lay back and let your husband take care of you. Tell me when you're close. I want to watch you come. No, I *need* to watch you. I'll die unless you come all over my tongue."

"Seems—dramatic," I gasped, a deep throb going through my pussy as his motions turned frantic, edged with that same intensity I'd first noticed in him. Like a predator who'd sighted prey and refused to let it escape.

"It's fucking essential," he groaned against me, fingers biting deeper into my thighs, his breath quickening as mine did. I should have felt the icy bite of my room's temperature but I caught fire beneath him, every flick and suck and stroke pushing me higher, until I was so hot I couldn't bear it.

"Mine," he gasped. "Mine, all mine."

And the secret part of me that longed to be held, loved, protected, *claimed* filled with relief and satisfaction, and deep, fulfilling pleasure. As my body wound tighter, my soul seemed to exhale a breath of relief, and the combination of the two was ruinous.

"Oh fuck. Tor!"

"That's my girl," he groaned, tongue lashing my clit. "That's my wife."

"I'm close," I gasped, grabbing fistfuls of the sheets so I didn't grab his head and keep his mouth where I needed it. "Fuck, I'm gonna—"

Tor's next exhale was deep and growling and so sexy that my back arched. "That's it, Cat. Come for your husband. Come all over my tongue, sear your taste into my tongue so I'll taste your pussy all day."

I couldn't take the dirty talk. I screwed my eyes shut, my breathing rupturing as pleasure drove into me. My hips slammed up into him, and butterflies filled my belly when his arm pressed to my stomach, keeping my ass to the bed so he could keep eating me. Hot little breaths left him, each one a groan, a growl, perfectly synced with every bolt of pleasure that clenched my pussy, throbbed in my clit.

I squirmed as he kept licking me, my skin as hot as fire, the sheets rasping every sensitive inch of it and the places where our bodies met fucking bliss. I loved his hands on me, loved the feeling of him pinning me down, and it was that edge of control that made me come harder than I ever had before.

When pleasure's chokehold released me, I melted into the bed with a groan. "Fuck."

"Mm." Tor kissed my clit, the seam of my thigh, my hip bone. "I think my wife likes being held down."

My inner muscles throbbed, a deep clench of pleasure that squeezed a whimper from me. It was answer in itself.

Warm hands glided up my waist and under my fuzzy pyjama top. Kisses graced every bit of skin he bared—the curve of my stomach, the plain of my ribs, the lace trim of my cotton bra.

He made a soft sound of protest. "I'm mortally offended that you sleep in a bra."

"Sorry," I said, but I was smiling. "My boobs have a mind of their own while I sleep; they're too big so they flop around all over the place."

Oh, god.

My face burned. *Why did I say that?* What the hell was wrong with me? Here I was with the hottest man I'd ever been in bed with, and I was talking about boob flops!

But Tor wasn't looking at me like I was insane. His eyes shone with insanity. "I want them to flop all over me," he groaned.

I blinked. I wasn't used to my weirdness being a turn-on. In the next moment, I grinned. "That could be arranged."

He groaned again, deeper, louder, and pulled himself up my body as his hands wandered higher. Hot lips met my own, and I opened for him, his tongue greedily stroking mine, filling my mouth with my own sweet, smoky taste.

"Fuck," he moaned, and kissed me harder. One hand ripped from under my shirt so he could cradle my face, turning me to kiss deeper, fiercer, while his other hand dove under my bra. The heat and rasp of his fingers over my delicate skin made me groan into his mouth, and he turned feral at the sound of it.

I'd never been kissed like this—like Tor was starving for me, like he would die without another taste. His powerful body shuddered against me, and he sucked my tongue into his mouth in a desperate plea I answered by memorising the contours of his mouth, crushing my lips into his between rough, impassioned strokes.

"Oh, *god*," he cried, his dark-jean-clad hips driving into

me, the friction and texture of it against my bare thighs making me kiss him harder. Tor gasped between each rough press of our lips, his thumb and forefinger catching my nipple and pinching until I arched up into him with an answering cry.

"This is madness," he groaned, his eyes especially dark when he tore away from my mouth only to kiss my jaw, my throat, the hollow at the base of my neck. "This is addiction. This is everything."

"Tor," I gasped when he returned to my mouth, taking control of me until I was arching up into him, greedy for more pleasure. He indulged my desperate need, but a glimmer of bright, out-of-place colour caught my eye and I dragged my lips away.

There was a lime-green tulip sitting on my desk, beside a plate full of fruit and pastries. My heart melted. "You brought me a tulip...?"

He kissed my cheek. "Not me. Death."

I startled, giving Tor a wide-eyed look. "Death was here?"

"He was," he confirmed with a kiss to my opposite cheek. "He's every bit as in love with you as I am."

"Love," I echoed, laughing a little hysterically. "You've known me a day, Tor."

"More than long enough to know you have my heart," he agreed, scattering a bridge of kisses across my nose. "And I'm sorry I didn't bring you a beautiful flower, but I did bring a better gift."

Cold rushed into my body as he climbed off me, my skin pulsing where he'd left kisses and touches. He approached the desk, where his gift had been laid flat beside the rose, and—I startled, sitting up in a rush when he came at me with a knife.

"Here, my cute little succulent."

Oh. He wasn't going to stab me, especially after he just made me come. I felt stupid for the initial panic and accepted the dagger he held out, flushing with warmth.

"I realised you don't have a weapon," he explained, "and that was an issue that needed to be immediately rectified. I carved a little succulent on the handle, see."

I turned the knife over and saw the crude drawing of a cactus on the polished wood handle. It was the most violent present I'd ever been given, but my heart went soft regardless. It had taken time and care to carve the cactus, and even though I didn't appreciate the reminder of the world's most embarrassing name, it was sweet. Really fucking sweet.

"Thank you," I breathed, running my thumb over the carving. "I love it."

His brown eyes lit up and he leaned over me, careless of the knife, to kiss me. "Keep it on you at all times."

"I will," I agreed, relieved to have something to defend myself with if Nightmare threatened me again. I sighed, pushing the thought away.

"What's wrong?"

"Nightmare. She's going to find me. If you're right that cursing us is part of her plan for power, she's going to hunt me again. She would have caught me if you hadn't found me yesterday."

Tor's upper lip peeled back, a low, threatening noise revving his chest. "She won't get anywhere near you. You are *mine*, not hers. I'll beat her head into a shattered pulp if she even *looks* at you."

"That's… a vivid picture," I murmured. But having two death gods on my side—the jury was still out on Miz—gave me a level of comfort and reassurance I didn't have yesterday. "Thank you. I appreciate you protecting me."

"Always," he swore, gently taking the knife from me to set it on the bedside table.

My eyes widened when he laid me back against the cushions and glided down my body.

"What?" he asked, demur and wicked all at once. Those light brown eyes were glittering with mischief again. "Did you think I was finished with a single orgasm?" He scoffed. "My wife deserves more than one."

CHAPTER TWENTY-ONE

CAT

*A*fter the way I'd woken—and the way Tor kept me occupied for a whole *hour*—I needed a run, needed to clear my head in the way that only early morning exercise could. Not only did I have the curse and Nightmare to stress about, but my new marriage to three death gods, and the fact that one had woken me with oral[1] and the other had dropped by to leave breakfast, a lime green tulip, and *my phone.* That gesture made my heart full.

I'd eaten the bread, delighted to find it filled with chocolate cream as I cleaned up as much as I could. I changed into activewear leggings, a loose vest, and a hoodie with my knife in the pocket, and then jogged down the stairs of Lawrence Hall, taking a direction at random when I was outside.

It wasn't raining yet, though I could have used a cold shower to cool the heat in my blood when I thought about Tor. I swore I could still feel his tongue on me, the sensation so much more intense than it had ever been before. Probably because Tor actually knew what he was doing. Honey's derision for Clay, my one and only boyfriend, made me smile as I jogged around the side of Milton Hall, curious about what lay behind the main building. I'd glimpsed graves from the windows while I took classes yesterday, so I was prepared for the graveyard with its weathered headstones. But I blinked at the massive circle of mausoleums, towering high above my head, each decorative and ornate.

"Wow," I breathed, unable to resist the urge to stop and inspect them. My family travelled three times a year, so I'd seen a lot of curious things, but I'd never seen a circle of mausoleums. I supposed the travelling would stop now I was at school. It hadn't been the same without Virgil anyway. Maybe we could all go to Sydney to snoop around his university.

I fished my phone from my pocket and snapped photos to send to Mum, Dad, and my brothers, stepping back to show the circle of mausoleums as a whole, then getting closer for the details—roses carved around the doorway of one, Ford's sea serpent motif recurring in most of the small, stone buildings, names etched above doorways, each one a Ford except for one: Caishen Malevollus.

"That," I said, "is one hell of a name."

Caishen Malevollus sounded like a Disney villain. I traced my fingers over the black dahlias etched into the stone around the doorway, leaning onto my tiptoes to see through the thick glass panels. Unlike the other tombs, this one was plain inside, lacking the luxury and details of the others—no gilding, no stars on the ceiling, no sea of serpents below. It was bare stone, almost austere. Lonely.

"I'd hate to be left to rot in one of these things," I said, as if the ghost of Caishen would hear me, and walked to the next mausoleum, peering inside. This belonged to Rosalind Ford, presumably the same woman the woods was named after—Rosalind Woods. She must have been well loved to get a wood named after her. The inside of her mausoleum was ornate and full of faded colour—enamel and frescoes that someone had taken care to paint.

As far as distractions from my problems went, this was a pretty good one. I must have spent an hour in the graveyard, going from mausoleum to mausoleum. There were thirteen in total, an eerie number that called to mind bad luck and Friday the thirteenth. I was just about to move on and continue my run, the path taking me around the side of Milton Hall towards the lake, but footsteps crunched a twig behind me, and I spun with a gasp.

I only realised I was expecting one of the death gods when I saw Alastor Carmichael storming towards me, his golden hair bright in the new sunlight and his long coat open, flaring as he rushed across the graveyard.

"Alastor?" I asked, a ripple of unease in my belly. "Is something wrong?"

He laughed, a sharp, stunted sound, and it was too late to back up when he came at me.

Rough hands met my shoulders. My back slammed into Rosalind Ford's mausoleum door, and I gasped at the shock of pain, the unexpected attack.

"What the fuck…?" I breathed, my unease turning to full panic when I saw the look in his eyes—sharp and bright with rage. Hatred. He *hated* me. But he barely knew me.

"I know it's you," he hissed, spittle hitting my face and making my stomach turn. I cringed away, trying to push off his rough hands and failing. "I know you summoned Nightmare. Summon her back, you psycho bitch, and get her to undo whatever the fuck she did to me."

Shock made me hesitate a moment too long and he wrenched me forward, slamming me back into the stone so forcefully that I cried out. My eyes burned with tears.

"I'm cursed too," I snapped, breathless, terrified. We were alone in the graveyard. There was no one else around, the campus deadly quiet. I suddenly felt so stupid for running alone, for lingering so long exploring the mausoleums. "She cursed *all* of us. I didn't summon her. I swear."

Alastor laughed, his handsome face hideous with anger. "You're lying. I *know* it was you, I can feel the evil in you."

I flinched, a lump pressing against my throat. "I didn't summon her. I didn't ask for this."

But Alastor could feel the wrongness in me. Could he sense that she'd ripped me apart and put me back together wrong? That what happened at the party had changed me in ways I hadn't even begun to understand yet.

His nostrils flared, fingers pressing bruises into my shoulders. "I know you did it. I know what you are."

"I don't even know what I am," I cried, my hands shaking fiercely where I pushed against him, straining so hard that my hoodie slapped my thigh, heavier than it should have been. My knife! "I didn't summon her, and I didn't ask for this, I swear to you. I want to *undo* this curse. I didn't call her here. I swear it. Get off me."

Alastor's laugh made me cold all over. "You're a good liar, but you *are* a liar."

His hands tightened until I cried out. I fumbled at my hoodie pocket, a raspy sob escaping when my fingers closed around the cool wooden handle. I whipped it out and pointed it at Alastor's throat.

"*Back off. T*hat psychopath killed four people; why would I bring her here? And why would I be cursed too, if I was one of her followers?"

Peel the skin from his bones, make him scream, make him afraid the way you're afraid. Teach him that no one will ever make you run, make you cry, make you beg. Not ever again.

The voice slid through my mind, seductive and compelling.

My breath quickened.

Alastor smirked and released me, but there was cruelty in that smile, and a mean glint in his eye that made my stomach knot. He didn't back up, only released me. I was still trapped between him and the mausoleum. I was going to throw up.

Both our heads snapped up when voices neared, along with footsteps pounding the path. Alastor took several quick steps back and smiled, his whole face transforming. He was a monster. With the easy way he flipped from threatening to friendly, he could be called nothing else.

"Darya!" I cried, spotting the friend Honey and I made at the costume shop. I shoved my knife back in my pocket, careful not to stab myself, and ran towards her. "Hey, I've been meaning to talk to you. How are you doing?"

She brightened at the sight of me. "I've been better, but I've been worse. You're another early morning jogger, I see. Meet the crew, Phyllis and Wilfrith—" She gestured to the tall, athletic brunette girl on her left, her clothes bright Barbie pink to match the ring pierced through her eyebrow, and the rugged blonde guy currently frowning at me behind aviator sunglasses, the only one not in athletic gear. Instead he wore a navy blue Ford hoodie thrown over sweatpants and a shirt that said I DON'T THINK YOU'RE READY FOR THIS JELLY, BABY with a cartoon of a Jelly Baby on it. I smiled at it even as he frowned at me.

"Oh!" he said suddenly. "We met at the party. I remember your..."

"Costume," I supplied hopefully.

"Heaving bosom," he finished with a wicked smirk that made me like him more than I had at the party. I thought he was a leering fuckboy then, but there was more humour to him now, and besides, that was a great T-shirt.

"It was heaving," I admitted, "despite my best attempts. Mind if I join you guys?" The back of my neck burned; Alastor was watching us, probably with his Golden Boy smile still in place.

"Sure," the brunette said easily, giving me a genuine smile as we all set off jogging again, Wilfrith with a husky groan of complaint. "And I'm Phil, by the way. Please do not, under pain of death, call me Phyllis."

I gave her a dry look, wrapping myself in humour to ward off the chill of Alastor's ambush. "You think that's bad? Try being called Cactus."

All three winced.

"Yeah," I agreed, forcing a laugh.

Wilfrith slung an arm over my shoulder, and I wondered if he was using me to hold himself upright—he wasn't, shall we say, a natural runner. "Welcome to the secret gang of awful names."

"Hey," Darya protested.

"Your middle name is Eunice, honey," Wilfrith quipped.

He gave me a kind smile. "You're gonna fit right in with us."

A weight fell off my shoulders—I had backup, I was safe —but when I glanced back, Alastor hovered, not taking his eyes off us until we rounded the corner of the building.

CHAPTER TWENTY-TWO

CAT

*T*he last thing I wanted to do after this morning was leave Lawrence Hall, where I could lock myself inside my room and convince myself I was safe despite Alastor living somewhere in the building. But I had classes, and unless I wanted to fail in my first week, I had to show up to them.

So I showered, got dressed, ate some of the grapes Death left for me[1] and went in search of my friends. Honey's room was empty—worry stabbed through my chest—so I knocked on Byron's door, my eyes stinging with tears when he swung it open, looking rumpled and tired.

He flung his arms around me and hauled me into a fierce hug before I could speak, and didn't let go for long minutes. "I'm so fucking sorry for snapping at you. And for being a raging dick since. You deserve better than me pushing you away when I'm stressed. I've already come up with a ten-step plan for how to be better at handling stress in the future."

"I love you," I blurted, because it was true and I'd missed my best friend. "Please don't shut me out again."

"I won't. That's step number one."

I laughed, a little weakly. A tear slid down the bridge of my nose. "I've been stressed too, so I get it. And I don't have a baby sister expecting *her own* baby."

Byron groaned and released me, giving me a beleaguered look. "She calls me twice a day to panic-vent. Mummy and Daddy still don't know."

"She'll have to tell them eventually," I pointed out, hauling him into another hug, this one quick and squeezing. "I missed you like hell, By."

I didn't know how to tell him about Nightmare, the curse, and the death gods that were apparently my husbands. But I couldn't keep all of it inside so I blurted, "I met someone. Someones."

"Someones?" Byron demanded, releasing me to stare at me. "A threesome? Cat Wallison, who *are* you?" He grinned. "Good for you. Tell me one of them isn't Duncan Ford."

I made a face. "He's hot but no."

Entitled, arrogant asshole wasn't my type. I wasn't sure what *was* my type. Apparently ageless, terrifying death gods who brought gifts and said sweet things.

"You haven't met them. They're... third years," I said in a stroke of genius.

Byron grinned, his face transformed, the life returning to his eyes. "Damn, Cat. University really brought out the wildcat in you."

I glanced down, my face on fire. "It might not last. It probably won't." I shrugged. "When in Rome, or whatever the med school equivalent is."

"When in Rome, try all the dick available to you?" By

suggested, ducking inside to grab his coat and satchel. "Speaking of dick…" he said shyly enough that I shot him a look.

"Byron," I breathed, my eyes popping out of my head.

"I know, I know, I hate people and humanity makes me want to scream, but I met a guy at the party." He shrugged, shooting me a surly look as he locked his door. "I don't hate him."

Coming from By, that was a declaration of love. "Fuck me."

"I'd rather not. Shall we grab Honey? We'll be late. Again."

Ah, shit. I thought living on campus would mean we were always on time, but Ford was so big and there was a whole park to run across, that we always seemed to be late or *just* on time. It resulted in people staring at us as we filed into lecture theatres and I hated it, Byron hated it, and yet we never learned.

"Honey must already be there; her room's empty."

"We could probably learn something from Miss Punctual," he pointed out, making me laugh. "Anyway, it's very early days, and he's not great with people he doesn't know so don't say anything okay? Shit," he said as we jogged down the stairs, "there he is."

Curiosity and excitement made it very hard to keep a smile off my face when I saw the guy Byron had pointed out, just locking the door to his room on the first floor. He had sandy-brown hair in an artful flop, deeply tanned skin, and an elegance about the way he moved, the way he was dressed—in a white shirt tucked into black trousers ringed by a gold belt of laurel leaves and *I was staring at Byron's boyfriend belt, send help, oh my god.*

"Hey, Gustin," Byron said, colour entering his cheeks.

Gustin—the elegant, sandy-haired boyfriend—turned

to see who'd spoken and smiled. "Byron. Hi. You're in Infection and Defence with me later, right?"

"Yeah." Byron nodded, turning a colour of scarlet.

"I'll see you there."

Byron nodded and hurried me down the stairs, all the while I grinned. I'd seen Byron nervous and anxious and stressed to breaking point but *shy?* I nudged him with my elbow when we burst out onto the campus, the weather miraculously holding. "You're so cute."

"Shut up," he muttered, scowling.

I laughed, and for a moment I forgot about Alastor accusing me of summoning Nightmare, and the fact he— and Nightmare, and all her followers—could find me again at any time.

CHAPTER TWENTY-THREE

CAT

*M*y head swam, stuffed full of so much information I feared it would erupt. There was only so much I could learn about scientific principles before I hit my limit, and my laptop had obviously agreed because it froze halfway through the lecture and refused to start up again. I was tempted to blame Nightmare for that too, but I knew that was reaching.

Then again, she had fucked with my car...

"Stop it," Byron hissed, slapping Honey's arm. We were sitting halfway up the lecture theatre, the whole thing arranged like an indoor coliseum, with a big mullioned window beside us. Honey had insisted on sitting the closest to it, and now I knew why: so she could bird watch. I didn't begrudge her the twitching hobby, but it would have been great if she didn't make a demonic guttural chattering every time a bird landed on the trees outside the window. "Don't make me muzzle you, Honey."

She shot him such a sour look, I was surprised he didn't wilt on the spot.

"Pay attention," I warned them both, my eyes straight forward so Professor Radclyffe didn't single us out. His stoic, clipped introduction had warned us that any childishness or misbehaviour would have us kicked out not only for the lecture but his entire semester. I was right to be glad he hadn't caught me returning to campus late at night.

Honey chattered again, but at least she turned away from the window with a sulky hiss. Byron laughed under his breath, typing a few notes on his laptop.

"Did you find anything in the library?" I whispered as Professor Radclyffe launched into a new tirade.

"Nothing Nightmare related, but I've only just started looking." She squeezed my hand. "We'll find something."

I expected Byron to shoot us a strange look if he overhead, but he was too busy studying his laptop. Relief sagged my shoulders a fraction. I wanted Byron to stay out of this for as long as possible.

I opened my mouth to suggest going to the library with Honey after my next lecture—they were both abandoning me for their own classes this afternoon—but there was a loud commotion when Professor Radclyffe tapped the riding crop he was using in lieu of a cane[1] against the desk of the red-faced guy who hit on me at the party. The guy grabbed the end of the cane—and Radclyffe jerked as if he'd been electrocuted.

Voices rose, filling the lecture theatre. Around the ruddy blonde guy, people jumped back.

"Shit," Honey breathed, blue eyes as wide as saucers. "What just happened?"

"Oh, calm down," the guy laughed, a little high, a little crazy. "It's just a hand buzzer."

I shot Honey a look, but she didn't see the guy at Halloween; Byron had been with me instead. Unease spread through me, restricting my breathing when the guy laughed again, eerie and high, and I remembered what he'd worn that night: a clown costume.

Maybe he was a jerk anyway. Maybe this was normal behaviour for him. But clowns were famous for shocking people with hand buzzers. Radclyffe threw his crop onto his desk and rubbed his hand, his skin probably scarlet red.

"Get out," he seethed, throwing a hand towards the door. "And never return to my class."

Blonde Clown snorted, climbing out of his seat. "You can't take a joke, Radclyffe. You should lighten up."

"Out!"

I jumped at the shout, and beside me Byron swore under his breath.

"What a dickhead," he muttered, watching the clown leave. I wondered if, beneath his perfectly ordinary if a tad horsey face, the blonde guy still wore the face paint he'd caked on for the party.

"This… is not good," Honey whispered, sitting so stiffly I had no doubt her hackles would be raised if she was a literal cat.

The curse was showing itself, the secrets becoming harder to keep. And this was just a clown; what about the more obvious, more dangerous costumes worn that night?

"No," I agreed as Radclyffe yelled at the rest of us, ordering us out and snapping directions about chapters to read. "It's not good at all."

CHAPTER TWENTY-FOUR

CAT

I jumped when my pocket vibrated, Radclyffe's yelling voice echoing down the old stone staircase that led to his lecture theatre. For a second I thought the vibration was nefarious, irrationally scared it would kill me.

"Cat," Byron said, brushing my shoulder. "Your phone."

God. Fuck. "Right," I breathed, quickly taking it from my pocket and pressing answer. "It'll be the mechanic about my car."

I'd told Byron I broke down on the moor road last night but not why, and the less he knew the better.

"Hello?" I asked, the phone pressed to my ear, its screen cold against my hot face. I hated being shouted at, even by professors, and added to my unsettling morning, it was just the crap icing on a shitty cake.

I expected the gruff voice of the mechanic—I presumed all mechanics had gruff voices, apparently—but for a moment there was only silence. And then more silence, and—

Breathing.

A chill skated down my spine. Was it Nightmare? Or—a somehow worse thought—had Alastor Carmichael got hold of my number? It was in my school records, and someone had found out my name was Cactus; Mason Lindgren had known it. My number would be easy to find, too.

Lindgren... When I blinked, I saw his body behind my eyelids, splayed out on the floor of Ford House, his mouth open on a silent scream, eyes empty. I shuddered.

"Hello?" I demanded, angry with fear.

There was only silence, and breathing. *Fuck you, asshole.*

I wrenched the phone from my ear and ended the call, swallowing hard when I realised Honey's and By's eyes were on me. "Silent call. Probably one of those scam callers," I said, convincing myself. It was a good explanation. I got those all the time.

Byron slung his arm across my shoulders, sensing my unease. "Did I tell you about the back-to-back calls I got the other day?"

I frowned. "No."

"I'm sensing shenanigans," Honey said, stifling a yawn. She paused on the staircase in a square of bright sunlight, lifting her face into the warmth; I caught her arm and tugged her down the stairs after us.

"Morbid shenanigans," Byron confirmed. "I got a call from a very lovely man with a thick accent eager to sell me ten—I repeat, ten—packets of Viagra."

A snort left me, so sudden it surprised even me, and loud enough that it echoed around the stairwell.

"I politely declined him, obviously," Byron said as we passed the first floor landing and kept descending, his sapphire eyes glimmering. "And then ten minutes later I got *another* call—"

"Why do you answer them?" Honey asked, her eyes narrowed in judgement.

"One part fun, one part malice. This one was a woman very insistent on selling me a funeral plan despite me being nineteen, who was so ruthless I had to put the phone down. But maybe she knew something I *didn't*. And if you put the two together..."

I chuckled. "You're going down in a blaze of Viagra."

"Death by erections," Byron agreed with a crooked grin. "What a way to go."

Better than whatever Nightmare intended for Honey and I. Maybe I should order a shipment of lady Viagra...

"I bet I could climb that," Honey said suddenly, eyeing the three-storey wall ahead of us. The old stones were uneven, some jutting out further than others, but they were hardly safe handholds, and the way was interrupted by several austere paintings of what must have been the Ford family.

"No," Byron warned, and grabbed her wrist. If he thought Honey was acting strange, he never voiced it. "No suicidal climbing trips today, thank you very—"

He stopped abruptly when we reached the bottom of the staircase and a dark shadow stepped into our path—all I saw at first was a black leather jacket that seemed to swallow all light, then jeans that followed the sleek lines of his thighs, biker boots Dad would have called skull crushers, and a deep olive face both soft and sharp, illuminated by blazing eyes the exact colour of latte.

Tor was here. In Ford. In Milton Hall. *In front of Honey and Byron.*

I was malfunctioning.

"Can we help you?" Honey asked rudely, eyeing him

down her nose in a way that was nothing like her friendly self and everything like cats meeting a new person for the first time.

"Nope," Tor replied, quite mildly. He lifted an iced coffee cup and held it out to me and I swore my heart melted into a pile of sap. "Here's the coffee you wanted last night. I noticed you left it in your car when it broke down."

I blinked, a smile forming. "How did you even find me?" Ford was huge... Had he used death god magic to locate me?

"Oh, I memorised your schedule," he said casually. "Have fun in your Circulation and Breathing lecture this afternoon."

He ducked closer while I was disarmed and pressed a kiss to my forehead, then glanced at Honey and Byron who'd been struck both still and silent. Miracle of miracles.

"Goodbye, Cat's friends. Goodbye, my cute little succulent."

"Goodbye, Tor," I laughed, completely stunned, utterly flushed, and probably beet-red. "Thank you for the coffee."

I glanced down at the clear cup, my heart stuttering when I saw the message he'd written there: *you are so beautiful it's like a knife to the heart.* When I lifted my head, he'd slipped away again.

"Marry him," Honey said suddenly and seriously, grasping my arm. "He's hot, he's sweet, he's got a unique term of endearment for you. What else do you need?"

"A massive cock that knows what it's doing?" Byron suggested, making me laugh. By was the grumpiest and quietest of us, and by far the dirtiest. I bet he'd know all those kinks I listed to Honey.

Honey pointed at him like he had a point, then pinned me with a bright blue stare. "As soon as you see his cock, just propose on the spot, Cat."

I shook my head, amused and—happy. "I'll take it under advisement."

"You do that." She hugged me suddenly, brushing her cheek against my shoulder. "I'm in the Ingrid Morris Building next, but I'll see you later?"

"Meet in the library?" I suggested.

She headbutted my neck in response, which could have meant anything, grabbed Byron into a fierce hug, and then slinked out the door with a grace she hadn't possessed last week.

"The crazy lady's right," Byron said with a laugh, shaking his dark head. "Based on the coffee and the nickname, that guy's a keeper. But be careful, alright? There are some psychos out there, and he did memorise your schedule. That's red flag number one."

"I know," I assured him, squeezing his arm but not quite able to push off the warmth of Tor bringing me coffee. I'd worry about the stalking later. "I'll be careful. And you be careful with—" I clicked my fingers. I'd already forgotten his name.

"Gustin," Byron supplied.

"Yeah, that guy. You be careful, too."

"I will." He backed away a step. "See you later?"

"Deserter," I teased. "Everyone's leaving me."

"You'll live," he teased right back, and tugged his collar up before he went outside, leaving me alone.

Right now, I hated being alone.

CHAPTER TWENTY-FIVE

CAT

*T*he back of my neck burned. I squirmed in the uncomfortable plastic chair in the cold basement room, trying to pay attention. Ironically, I was struggling to breathe while Professor Lancashire, a stout, bespectacled man with greying hair, explained the airways of the body in acute detail. Anxiety was a bitch.

At least I was getting my car back; the mechanic called while I was on my way down, and it turned out there was nothing wrong with my car at all. He still expected five hundred pounds, and I knew he was overcharging because Ford students were privileged, but I was just happy to be getting my car back.

My neck burned more intensely, and I reached back to itch it, convinced someone had their eyes on me. I took a subtle peek, pretending to reach into the satchel hanging on the back of my chair and—yep. There was a guy staring at me so intensely I'd think he hated me if I'd ever met him before. But he was a stranger.

I didn't even recognise him from the ill fated Halloween party, or from the people who'd got caught in the crimson light outside. I'd never seen this man before— his face was all sharp angles, cut cheekbones, and stern beauty under a mop of black hair, with eyes the colour of ice behind wire-frame glasses. They pinned on me like he was picturing skinning me alive.

I quickly turned back around, my heart quickening. Was he in the cult of Nightmare? Cold dripped down my spine, a sharp contrast to the scalding burn of his glare, and I slid my phone out of my pocket to text Byron but... I bit my lip. He was stressed enough as it was. I texted Honey instead, my fingers flying over the screen while I tried to look attentive to the lecture.

> There's a guy staring at me. Not in a she's hot kinda way, in a planning to drug me, throw me in the boot of his car, and bury me in a hole in his garden kind of way.

I waited for her reply—and waited. My stomach sank the more minutes ticked by. I took notes on the lecture, misspelt diaphragm twice before giving up altogether, and waited. By the time it reached ten minutes, I gave up on a reply, and the back of my neck still burned.

I curled my hands into fists and pretended everything was normal, that everything had been fine since I got to Ford's End, and nothing was out of the ordinary. I listened to Professor Lancashire explain the process of respiration in a straightforward manner I appreciated. My head was in too messy a state for any complexities right now.

"—and these nerve impulses are what stimulate ventilation and make it possible for us to breathe. Does anyone know how often the impulses occur?"

"Every three seconds," Phil called from several rows in front of me, her glossy brunette hair pulled into a high pony, all her notes in an A4 notebook.

"Three to five," Lancashire agreed with an approving nod. "Someone else this time—what is caused by…"

She trailed off when a deep male voice began loudly intoning Latin. I jumped to my feet, my heart hammering a rapid beat, and I wasn't the only one. Phil leapt out of her seat, and so did Duncan Ford, the blonde clown, Justin Merchant, and three others I vaguely recognised from the party.

"Fuck this," Duncan spat and rushed down the steps to the door, a MacBook slung under his arm.

"What's this about?" the professor asked briskly, striding toward the guy chanting as I threw all my stuff into my bag and got, shaking, to my feet.

He chanted louder, his voice carrying enough for me to pick out words—espiritu santo. I didn't know what it meant, had vaguely heard it in religious ceremonies, but I wasn't about to stick around and find out what Nightmare planned this time.

The burning on the back of my neck intensified, but I had worse things to worry about than some creep staring at me. I rushed down the steps, Phil right ahead of me, but I glanced in the direction of the chanting and frowned when I realised the man who was chanting wore dense black robes and was holding up a wooden rosary.

Nightmare had holy men working for her now…?

I didn't stick around to question it.

"Hang on now," the professor said at our mass exodus. "There's no need to leave."

But seven of us were already out of the door, heading

up the cold stairs and not looking for a repeat performance of the Halloween party. If I'd had any doubts about Duncan, they were disproven by his jumpy reaction. He was as scared as I was and—

Wait. The guy in the dungeon classroom wasn't a priest; he was a student, no older than I was.

I stopped in an alcove off the stone steps and scrubbed a hand over my face. *Fuck.* He wasn't one of Nightmare's henchmen, he was one of us. Cursed. I bet he'd dressed as a priest for Halloween.

"Fuck," I breathed, staying in the alcove long after the footsteps faded to the higher floors. Shit. I was too fucking paranoid for this, for classes and day to day life and students cursed to be priests.

I dropped my hands to text Honey incessantly until she deigned to reply, but when I blinked away the spots over my eyes, I flinched back with a cry.

The staring creep was right in front of me, his ice-blue eyes narrowed with intense hatred that ripped all the breath from my lungs. I backed up, my spine pressing to cold brick, my blood dropping to the same icy temperature. I fumbled for my phone's keypad and hit my third speed dial after Mum and Virgil, praying Honey picked up quickly.

"Who are you, and what do you want?" I breathed, not understanding the hatred tightening the guy's sharp-planed face.

That face came threateningly close to mine, until I could see my own face in the reflection of his glasses.

"What makes you so fucking special?" he demanded, snarling and furious.

I jumped violently, holding up my hand, palm out, my phone clutched fiercely in my other. *Come on, Honey, pick up.* "I'm not special, I swear. Leave me alone."

Gut him. Carve his stomach open from side to side until his organs spill out.

My breath caught. I shook harder, my fingers twitching, wanting to grab my knife and answer that dark voice. But I couldn't. Not again. Not here, where someone would see.

"I don't see it," he hissed, leaning so close that my stomach swooped.

"Back off," I warned breathlessly, panic dumping into my system. Twice in one day I'd been thrown around and threatened, and my fight or flight reactions were intense.

Rip his tongue out so he can never snarl at you again.

His eyes flashed, ice blue and intense, a bright warning. I shoved my hands into his shoulders, pushing him away, but he rocked back a step and came right back at me.

"I'm warning you," I began, my voice low, the way it had been low that night three years ago.

The dark-haired psycho just laughed and—kissed me.

A high sound of panic and surprise and hysteria escaped as his mouth crushed mine, a rough hand finding my hip, pressing cruelly. I shoved at him, my breathing faster, that dark voice far louder, but he was undeterred, his lips moving over mine, tongue flicking out to trace my bottom lip. I wished I knew how to summon a death god, because I'd call Death right now to rip the soul out of this bastard.

I drove my knee up into his balls, braced to shove him aside and run, but he just moaned and leaned into me like I'd stroked him.

"I like it when you play rough," he told me, icy eyes hooded. "And the way you taste…" He licked my bottom lip again. Darkness surged and the next thing I knew, the tang of copper filled my mouth, and he staggered back, his hand to his chin.

Blood dripped.

When he grinned, tongue flicking out, I realised I'd bitten him. Good. He deserved it. But my heart beat panic-fast. I hadn't meant to bite him. The blackness took me. It only stole seconds this time, but it was bad enough that chills covered my arms.

I darted out of the alcove, but he caught my shoulders and crowded me back into the stone nook, his eyes bright, glowing with something that made me shake harder, something that made the dark voice roar.

"You drew my blood," he said, rough, quiet.

"Let me go, or I'll do worse," I threatened, shaking uncontrollably.

For a moment he just stared at me, then his lips surged against mine, tongue forcing its way inside. "You drew my blood, so take what you claimed."

When his knee pressed between my legs, adding sudden and visceral pressure to my clit, I jolted at the shot of pleasure to my fear. My clit was already swollen. Oh god, I was wet. Shame heated my face.

"You drew it, so it's yours," he panted and tore himself away from me. "Vile, intoxicating creature. Stay away from me, Prick."

"You stalked *me*," I snapped, rage and arousal mingled with fear. "You picked the wrong girl to fuck with, psychopath. I have very dangerous friends."

"So do I, Prick," he replied, licking blood off his bottom lip as he backed up a step, then another. This time I realised it wasn't an insult, but a name. Prick. A cactus reference, no doubt.

He took another step back, his body vibrating with tension, and I bolted through the space he put between us, my hand clammy where I gripped my phone. I didn't look back as I fled.

CHAPTER TWENTY-SIX

CAT

I didn't meet Honey in the library, didn't do anything except run all the way to my room in Lawrence Hall, lock the door, and prop a chair against it so it couldn't be rammed open. First Alastor and now this black-haired, blue-eyed psycho. Two students who lived in the same building as me, who both wanted to hurt me. And then there was Nightmare's cult and whoever the disciple who summoned her was.

I shook so hard my bones rattled. The blue-eyed guy had to be one of them. Nightmare's followers. Miz was right; she would drive me into a breakdown. I was already halfway there.

"Fuck," I exhaled in a shuddery breath, my hands shaking as I dragged them over my face.

All I wanted to do was crawl into bed, but I still had that asshole's blood on my face and I had chapters to read before tomorrow.

"You can do this," I psyched myself up. "Shower, bribe By and Honey into bringing dinner up, speed-read two chapters, then sleep for ten hours. Easy."

It didn't sound easy. It sounded impossible. But I threw clean clothes, underwear, and my toiletries into a Ford School of Medicine bag, the dark green of the serpent emblem watching me with red eyes. Reluctantly, I pulled the chair away from the door.

Ten minutes and I'd be back. Fifteen tops. I could do this.

I opened the door and locked it behind me before I could doubt myself, rushing down the hall to the shower room. My hands shook as I fumbled open one of the stalls and hung the bag on the back of the locked door where it wouldn't get wet.

You can do this, I told myself over and over, spinning my crown ring for courage as I undressed and turned the taps of the bronze overhead shower, probably the newest thing in the whole building. The water was ice cold when it sprayed out, but I was already shivering so I barely noticed.

I stepped fully under the spray and kept going until my forehead rested against the cool white tile, tears burning the backs of my eyes. I couldn't do this. My encouraging motto was bullshit; I really couldn't do this. I didn't mean the shower—I meant Ford, Nightmare, threatening assholes in my classes, and curses turning people into clowns and priests and fuck knows what else. I'd been on edge all day, and my mind was all too happy to replay the reasons I got that way—Alastor cornering me against the mausoleum, the silent phone call, Honey chattering at the bird, Byron glancing at us like he knew something was different, the chanting during the lecture, and then whatever the fuck that was in the alcove.

I only realised tears streaked my face when my breath

hitched, stuck, and broke apart. A sob crashed from my chest, loud enough to be heard over the drumming of water on white tile. I wanted to spool the cries back into my chest, keep them there where no one might overhear them, but I couldn't stop them now. They had their own force, like a storm that wouldn't be slowed, let alone stopped.

I screwed my eyes shut, my face against the wall, and gave up trying to fight the sobs. They came in ruthless waves, crushing my chest until it hurt, tears streaking my face until my skin was puffy and tight. The water slamming into my shoulders was too hot now but it didn't matter. None of this mattered.

I wanted to go home, to drop out of Ford, but I was *cursed.* I didn't think going back to Harrogate would really be escaping from Nightmare. I'd only drag her to my family, get them cursed too, and I couldn't bear that. Thoughts of what she'd do to Mum and Dad burned vividly in my mind and I flinched. What if she didn't curse them; what if she killed them, like she killed Lindgren?

My breathing turned jagged, desperate.

I flinched when I was turned from the wall, the hands on my body gentle but alien. Tears and water veiled my vision but I snapped my head up, staring—

"Death?" I asked in a small voice.

"I'm here," he said, drawing me into the safety of his arms and holding me so tight that I couldn't speak, could only sob brokenly. "It's okay, little one, it's okay."

Hot tears burned their way out of my eyes. I brought my arms up and clung to him, not caring that I'd only known him for days, or that a curse was the only thing that linked us. He was familiar and comforting and safe. It was a relief to be held while I cried, a relief to have someone hold together the jagged pieces I'd become.

Warm lips pressed to my forehead and he lifted a hand from my back only to turn the water to a more comfortable temperature, replacing it in the same spot, splayed against my hip while he hugged me as close as possible.

"You're okay now," he murmured against my temple. "You're okay, Daddy's here now."

I screwed my eyes shut, a desperate sound in the back of my throat. I didn't know how he knew what I needed; maybe the death gods were all psychic, maybe Death had taken one look at me and known I was both submissive and little. I didn't care. I was grateful for whatever brought him here, promising I was safe over and over, his body like a shield between me and the world.

I knew it couldn't last forever, but I clung to him, my head on his chest, listening to the steady rhythm of his heartbeat and marvelling at the fact his heart beat at all.

Kisses rained gently down my face and across my head, each one accompanied by a murmur of reassurance.

I'm here.

I won't let anyone hurt you.

You're my little bride.

You're safe now.

I'll take care of you, Cat.

Whoever made you cry will die screaming.

His words wrapped around my soul until I pulled my breathing back under my control, until my frantic sobs softened to hitching breaths, until I wasn't sure if the water on my face was tears or from the shower.

"How did you know?" I asked hoarsely when I was sure I could speak.

"How did I know you needed me?" Death clarified in a low, comforting rumble. "Tor mentioned your car was at the garage. I came to tell you I'd returned it to the garage on Ford's grounds." He kissed my temple. "I didn't know I'd find you like this."

"Sorry," I mumbled.

Death squeezed me to him, his body clad in a tight black shirt and jeans that were now soaked through. "No apology needed, pussy cat."

I groaned, which seemed to be his intention; I felt his smile against my forehead.

"I'll always be here when you need me." Another kiss to my temple. Then my neck. My shoulder. He froze there and his body—muscular but languid, fluid—hardened to steel. His spine stiffened in an instant. "Who did this to you?" he asked very, very quietly, barely audible over the shower.

"What?" I drew back with a frown, a tremor of nerves in my belly at the complete shift in his body language and tone. Danger throbbed from him in waves, quickening my heart.

Death splayed a hand at the base of my spine, keeping me against him, and trailed the fingertips of his other hand over my shoulder, pressing them carefully, gently.

"Oh," I breathed when his fingers wrapped around my shoulder, aligning with what must have been bruises from this morning. "It's nothing. It won't happen again."

I wouldn't go anywhere alone; I wasn't stupid enough to go running in the graveyard. If I needed to run tomorrow morning, I'd drag Honey with me or just run in the public areas where other people were. Alastor had proved he wouldn't hurt me in front of an audience.

"Nothing," Death repeated, and I became very aware of the fact he was clothed and I was entirely naked, on full display before him. But the way he was looking at me, his eyes black from edge to edge in a way that made my breath catch, was far from the way Tor had looked at me this morning. "There are fingerprints on your shoulders, Cat, that is *not* nothing. I want a name."

I swallowed. "I can't."

He inhaled slowly, nostrils flaring. "Whoever did this deserves to die a horrific death, my bride. There are consequences for hurting my wife."

Even as unease wound through me, my belly fluttered. I shouldn't have liked hearing that as much as I did. *My wife.*

"If I tell you who did it, you'll kill him."

"So it's a man," he breathed.

"And I'll be as bad as Nightmare." I shook my head, trying to move away from him and failing completely. "I won't kill someone."

His fingers slid along my cheek and into my hair, cradling the back of my head as he brought his face down, peering intently into my eyes. For a moment I thought he'd force me to tell him with magic, compel me into speaking, but he only read the fear in my eyes.

"Alright, little bride, you don't have to tell me. I'll find his name another way." Death pulled me back into his arms like that wasn't an alarming statement, and I meant to argue, but... why? If he killed Alastor, he wouldn't be able to threaten me anymore. He couldn't hurt Honey, either.

Instead of speaking, I squeezed his waist and rested my forehead on the swell of his pec, stepping closer—and jolting when his erection pressed against my hip through his wet jeans. Oh. I thought he'd been completely unaffected by the sight of him naked but nope. Definitely nope. And he was *huge.* The girth on what I felt was insane.

"Ignore that, my bride," he said, kissing the crown of my head. "I didn't get into the shower for sex. I'm here because you need me to hold you."

But now I'd felt it—and was *still* feeling it—I couldn't think about anything else. All my awareness had gone to that point of contact, where his thick cock pressed against my belly. This morning with Tor made me bold, and instead of stammering and blushing I looked up at Death and asked, "What if I need more than you holding me?"

His hand at my back travelled slowly up my spine, waking up my whole body. "Do you?"

I nodded, not taking my eyes off him. Now I wasn't crying, I could see him clearly and *fuck*, he was attractive. His hair flowed over his shoulders in thick black braids, his shirt clinging to the curves of his chest, and his smoke-grey eyes were sharp with a hunger he'd done such a good job of masking, I hadn't seen it before. His wide mouth curved into a slow smile at whatever he read on my face.

"I should tell you," he murmured, pulling my hands from his back and resting them on the button of his jeans, "I came to see you yesterday and I overheard a conversation you had with your friend."

I wracked my brain for anything we'd said and came up blank.

He tucked the fingers of one of my hands into his waistband, the command obvious, and when I dared to unfasten his jeans, his warm hand cupped my cheek and lifted my face.

"You were telling her a list of your interests."

A list of my— "Oh god," I gasped.

His small smile curved deeper into his cheeks, his voice rich and sweet like caramel when he said, "I should tell you, a great many of them overlap with my own interests."

Mortification quickly burned to surprise—and thrill. "They do?"

"Mm." His voice deepened, gruffer when I tugged down the zip of his jeans for me. "Dirty talk is a favourite of mine. So is giving praise. And you already know you're my little one."

I flushed, but I was smiling, my stomach fluttering madly.

"Dominance and submission, too," he went on, flicking his tongue over his bottom lip when I had his pants unfastened. Water cascaded down his rugged face and muscular chest, enticing me. "Tor's the one you want for primal play and chasing."

A shudder went down my whole body. Tor would chase me, catch me, and fuck me? Holy fuck. Holy, holy fuck.

"You love that," Death observed, smiling with a wickedness that was new to me. "Do you want Torment to hunt you like prey, then fuck you like a good little slut?"

My entire body electrified. A gasp caught in my throat.

"Yes, you do," he breathed, pressing closer. He groaned when I slid my hand into his pants and squeezed his cock, needier with every word out of his mouth. "I bet that pretty pussy is soaked at just the thought."

"It's wet because of you," I said, and didn't know where I found the courage. My heart hammered against my chest, but the warmth and presence of him here against me freed me from the usual cage of my anxieties. I didn't hesitate to slide my fingers under his underwear and wrap my hand around the silken warmth of his cock.

His hips jerked, a sexy little groan in his throat. "Cat," he breathed, "my bride, my wife." He surged forward in a desperate rush, kissing me hard, and the hint of roughness clashed with the kindness and care I knew of him. The perfect combination. My ultimate weakness.

The taste of him burned out everything else, spicy and sweet like aniseed, and I kissed him like I was possessed by need. The kiss was instantly hot and greedy, my tongue in his mouth, his devouring mine with deep groans of satisfaction, teeth sinking in my bottom lip, my fingers twisting in his hair, grabbing fistfuls of braids even as I squeezed his cock.

"Does my perfect little wife need my cock?" Death asked, sending lightning to my clit. He was breathing hard, his chest rising and falling, the shirt clinging to every rise and fall of muscle.

"Yes," I breathed, *pleaded.* I released his hair to push his jeans over his hips, my heart beating faster when he flicked his wrist and all his clothes vanished in a rush of dark smoke.

CHAPTER TWENTY-SEVEN

CAT

"*L*ean back against the wall for me. That's it," he praised when I instantly obeyed. For a moment he just stared at me, grey eyes devouring the sight of my face, my body on display for him. "You are so beautiful you ruin me."

I sucked in a surprised breath when he sank to his knees in the shower stall, warm hands on my knees, encouraging my legs wider. Oh, he was going to... What was with these death gods and their obsession with eating my pussy?[1]

"Devastating," Death breathed, and glided his hands over my thighs and around their pale curves to hold my ass as his tongue dove into my pussy. He licked a long, slow stroke, his tongue vibrating with a groan like I tasted amazing.

"Fuck," he breathed, hands tightening on me as he dove

back into my pussy with a passion that edged into wild, frantic need. Like he'd die without another taste.

I covered my mouth with my hand but a moan escaped. Tor had been all cleverness and skill, finding exactly what made me gasp. Death ate me with a wild ferocity, mouth dragging over me, moaning against my pussy, tongue moving in insane strokes and flicks. He wasn't careful, wasn't precise; he wanted to taste everything at once. He buried his whole face in my pussy, and growled when my legs began to shake, my breathing quickening.

"Oh shit," I gasped when he flicked his tongue over my clit. A whining moan clawed from my throat at how fucking good it felt. I pulsed, ached, tightened.

"Don't you dare come," he growled, dragging his mouth back to my entrance, possessive hands squeezing my ass as his tongue dove inside, curling, undulating.

"Death," I breathed, my hand shooting down, grabbing a fistful of his braids.

"I can feel you holding yourself still, little one," he chided. "You want to ride my face, then ride my face."

"God," I choked out, my body shuddering, legs weak. I leaned back against the wall and rolled my hips against his tongue.

"Too polite." He dragged his mouth up my pussy in a deep, sucking stroke; the suction made my eyes cross. "Ride my fucking face, Cat. For every second you hesitate, I'll hold back one climax from you."

I gasped, my eyes flashing wide.

"That's one second," he said, watching me from where he knelt on the floor. "Two. Three."

Oh god, I wouldn't survive. He would kill me. I tightened my fist in his hair and pushed his face into my pussy, jerking my hips up and struggling to breathe when he groaned his approval. He ate me with a rapid ferocity that made my eyes cross. *Oh god, yes.* "Fuck, fuck."

I bit my bottom lip, warmth wrapping around me, pleasure building so swiftly in my lower belly, my clit sharp and throbbing—

"No," I gasped when he tore his mouth away, overpowering me so easily that my control over him had been an illusion. "Please."

"You hesitated, little one," he said with disapproval that made my heart hurt. Sitting back on his heels he watched my pussy throb, desperate, *pleading.*

"This is cruel," I complained, my inner muscles tight, so close, so painfully close. They clenched when Death's warm hands skimmed up my legs, gliding over my wet skin.

"You need to learn proper behaviour, my bride. I can feel you holding back, and with me you *never* need to hold back any part of you. You don't need shields. When you're with me, you leave all your anxiety behind."

"I don't know how to do that," I laughed, a little sharply.

His hands skimmed up and down my legs. "Take a deep breath for me. There you go, that's perfect. Keep breathing deeply, and relax your muscles, starting with your feet, your legs, your arms and chest, and all the way up to your neck. Beautiful," he praised when I did, haltingly and a little nervously. I didn't relax like this with anyone. Sometimes not even with myself. But Death's gentle tone and the warmth of the water made it easier.

A deeper breath expelled from my lungs, and I felt a weight lift.

"That's it," Death murmured, kissing the inside of my thigh, his breath hot on my skin. "That's my girl. Stay like that for me, and when you want me harder or faster or deeper, you just roll your hips up against me, grab my hair, whatever you naturally want to do—don't fight it. Take everything you want."

"Except an orgasm?" I asked sourly, making him laugh.

"Don't worry, my wife, I'll give you plenty."

I scowled, the expression coming freer now I'd relaxed. "Liar."

"I never lie," he said, and dove his tongue back into my pussy, eating me with the ferocity that made my breath catch. This time I didn't hold myself against the wall; I rolled my hips into the wild thrusts of his tongue, and grabbed his head to keep that euphoric sensation against my clit until a deep sigh punched from me.

"Fuck, that feels good," I groaned, my eyes fluttering shut. The contrast between his soft tongue and the vicious hunger guiding his motions sent me crashing towards the edge so fast. My hips jolted against his face, my breathing lighter, sharper. "Please, Death. Please."

He tore away when I was right on the edge, and my back arched off the wall, my hips bucking, jerking, begging.

"Please," I whined, my whole body gripped by the sharp intensity of near-orgasm. *"Please."*

He rose from his knees in a rush, crowding me back against the wall. He kissed me so hard I couldn't keep up, wilting from how fucking close I was, how much I ached, *hurting,* to come. I reached between our bodies, but my fingers barely glanced over my clit before a strong hand wrapped around my wrist and pulled it away.

"No. You're going to be my perfect, obedient wife and come on my cock. Aren't you?"

"Yes," I gasped jaggedly, my hips stuttering, my skin so sensitive that I burned where we touched.

"One more edge, little one, and then you can come as many times as you need." Death's lips pressed to my forehead, and then he was catching me up in his arms, my legs around his waist, my back to the wall and—

My eyes crossed. I came instantly, a half-thrust all it took to throw me violently over the edge. Death swore softly, reverently as I gasped and shook, my pussy clamping down around his cock in powerful waves as pleasure wrung everything from me.

"You tried so beautifully," he murmured when I stopped shuddering. "I'm not mad or disappointed, little one. It's my fault you were so sensitive, you couldn't help but come."

I cried out loudly when he withdrew and sank in deeper, my pussy so fucking sensitive. "It's too much—too much."

"If it's really too much, you can tell me to stop. Just say my name." His lips brushed my ear as he held me to the wall, thrusting even deeper, stretching me around his thickness until I couldn't breathe. "Just say *Jermaine,* and I'll stop. But you won't say it, will you, little one?"

"No," I whimpered, clinging to his warm shoulders, my eyes slamming shut when he fucked me faster, still hitting so deep, stretching me so much, that I couldn't take it. "I won't—but it's—ah, please, Death, please—"

His lips dragged down my sensitive throat, placing a kiss on my pulse. "Call me what you really want to, and I'll give you what this pussy is begging me for."

I spasmed around him, my hips shaking, and buried my face in his shoulder. "Please, daddy."

"Good girl," he praised, and tightened his hands on my ass, driving harder, so much faster.

Oh, god.

Oh, I couldn't—

He drew back to watch me, his eyes roving across my features. "I love those faces you make. Such pretty faces."

I whined, squirming. Unable to do anything but take what he gave me.

He fucked me over the edge and into a second orgasm so fast, I couldn't bear it. Liquid lightning charged my bloodstream until I shook violently. My eyes rolled all the way back into my head. I whimpered and cried and moaned, clinging to him.

The door to the shower room creaked open. My hips jerked. I tightened around his cock, my orgasm drawn out mercilessly.

The thought of getting caught was terrifying, mortifying, but it made me come harder.

Death's hand covered my mouth, his smoky eyes intense when I blinked up at him, mine heavy lidded.

"Be *very* quiet, little one," he warned, his lips finding my forehead, his cock not slowing for one second. The slap of wet skin against wet skin would give us away in an instant, but the warning and his hand over my mouth heightened everything until I came apart in a rush, my third climax hitting with so much force that my back arched and I froze, locked in place.

"That's my girl, that's my girl," Death chanted in a whisper, driving all the way into me and hauling my body against his until I splayed against his chest. "That's my fucking girl," he breathed, gasping, holding me fiercely as his cock went wild inside me.

We stayed like that for long minutes, and I was glad for Ford's expensive showers never going cold as water washed over us. In the stall beside us, someone was clearly showering, hopefully unaware of what Death and I had done beside them.

My husband cleaned me with whispered praises, always returning to my lips for kisses. We waited until whoever was in the stall beside us left to shut off our water and get dry and dressed, Death clothing himself with a gesture and a rush of power.

He walked me back to my room where he indulged me in another kiss or five, and stroked his hands down my wet hair.

"I'll be back tonight. Go spend time with your friends. Eat. Sleep." His next kiss landed between my eyes and lingered. "You were perfect, Cat. So fucking perfect for me."

I swallowed, a lump rising in my throat. "You were perfect, too."

His smile was contagious and unbearably handsome. I leaned up for another kiss, greedy for more.

"My insatiable wife," he said against my mouth, then groaned when I sucked his tongue into my mouth. "I suppose one more orgasm won't hurt."

He fused his mouth to mine, vanished our clothes with a single thought, and took me on the desk until all my things crashed to the floor and the shape of his body was imprinted on mine.

I hated Nightmare for cursing me, but I loved this, loved having two husbands who were sweet and sexy and insane in bed.

I just didn't know if I'd get to keep them if the curse broke.

CHAPTER TWENTY-EIGHT

MISERY

I could smell her on Death. My teeth ground together as I threw myself into the chair by the fireplace, across from him. My mouth set in a hard line, my whole body bristling. I hadn't slept a single fucking minute last night, and it was all her fault for stealing him from me.

"I told you to join us," Death said gently, watching me and seeing far too much.

I bared my teeth. Dragged in a breath and smelled peaches and cream instead of the logs in the fire. I couldn't even smell the burned sugar or the amber and sandalwood of Death and Tor's scents. She'd invaded my life, and now here she was, clinging to my home. I hated her more than I'd ever hated anyone.

No. Not more than Nightmare, but almost.

"Why would I join you?" I demanded eventually, casting Tor a dirty look when he sank onto the chair arm beside me and slung an arm over my shoulders. It had the usual calming effect, but I didn't *want* to be calm. I was tired and furious and jealous. I met Death's worried eyes and said, "I don't know why you're drawn to her. I don't feel it at all."

"Nothing?" Tor asked, frowning as he wrapped a strand of my pale hair around his finger.

"Nothing," I confirmed, my skin crawling even as my heart beat faster.

I felt nothing. Yesterday was an experiment. Clinical. Necessary. And now it was over, and would never happen again.

Tor shrugged, leaning closer to me. "Maybe it'll take a while for your bond to develop. She's amazing, Miz, you're gonna love her."

"She's pathetic," I sneered. "Mortal and dull and placid."

"Misery," Death said in the note of warning that told me I'd gone too far. Well, so had he. He stayed with *her* for two nights in a row when he should have been here with us.

He'd never been away overnight before. I loathed to discover I couldn't sleep without him. Just another misery to add to a long list of them.

"She's not dull," Tor argued, although without fire or sharpness. He tugged the strand of my hair. "She's sweet and perceptive and so fucking sexy when she comes." He groaned, as if remembering, and I sucked on a tooth so I didn't snap at him. So they'd *both* been with her. No wonder our home smelled of peaches and cream. Too sweet. Sickly. Taunting.

"Miz," Death said, watching me. "Cat might change things, but she doesn't change how much we want you. You know that, don't you?"

I laughed, a little strangled, and shoved out of the too-hot chair by the fire. I was burning, incinerating. I wanted to tear her hands off my men, wanted to make her pay, wanted to watch fear fill her pretty grey eyes again. I wanted to scare her so badly she ran away and never went near Death and Tor again.

"Don't be an idiot," Tor huffed. "You're ours, like we're yours. That shit won't ever change."

"Fuck you," I snarled, stalking away and getting a sick satisfaction from crusting mud from my boots into the rug. "Fuck both of you. Go back to your fucking girlfriend."

"Misery," Death said, his voice too close for him to still be sitting by the fire. "Don't walk away from us."

His voice cut under my skin and raked claws through my heart. How long would it be until he decided he didn't need me? Who would need misery incarnate when you had someone *sweet* and *perceptive* and *sexy?*

I made a rough sound in my throat, storming through the foyer to the front door, the domain of death feeling colder than usual, forcing goosebumps on my arms.

I didn't make it to the door. Death snapped warm arms around me from behind and held me captive, his chin resting on my shoulder, beloved lips pressing a kiss to the side of my throat. My eyes burned. I clenched my jaw.

"You said she's our wife," I muttered, "but you're the only one she's bound to. Nightmare's magic links *you,* and if you don't think the real curse is to take you away from me, you haven't been paying attention all these years."

"Impossible," Death replied, so soft, so loving. "No force in any domain can take me from you, Misery."

I flexed my hands in and out of fists. "I've already lost Tor to her. Nightmare has won."

"Like fuck you have," Tor snapped, and I jumped at the proximity of his voice. "And like fuck she has. Her plan is obviously to use Cat against Death, but Cat would never do anything to hurt him. Or us. She isn't like that."

"Nightmare won't give her a choice," I laughed, my

chest tightening when Tor walked around me and stopped with inches between us.

"We're already winning, because she's our girl, and she's on our side. She's scared of Nightmare but not of us. That bitch isn't going to win this time, Miz."

She would. She always did. I stiffened, harsh words on the tip of my tongue, but they eddied into nothing, my mind emptying when Tor grabbed my cock through my loose black pants.

"And you are *not* fucking losing me," Tor said with enough gravel in his voice that my stomach twisted.

I swallowed. "I'm sorry."

Death expelled a hard breath against my neck, then brushed another kiss to my pulse. "Our bond is unbreakable. Fuck whatever Nightmare has planned."

But I could still smell her—peaches and cream and smug satisfaction at stealing the men I loved.

Tor squeezed my cock, reading the thoughts on my face, and my stomach hollowed. "Do you need a reminder, Misery, of just who you belong to—and who belongs to you?"

A roaring silence started in my head, my walls obliterated. My fears tripped off my tongue before I could stop them. "Are you angry at me? Do you hate me now, because I don't want her?"

"Fuck no," Tor replied, slipping his hand under the waistband of my trousers to close his hot hand around my cock. I hissed a sharp breath at the grip. "We're worried as shit about you, but we're not mad at you."

A knot unwound in my chest. I swallowed. "Okay. Please—" But I didn't know what I needed or how to even ask for it. "Tor," I whispered, a broken gasp.

"I know this is new, and we've never all been interested in the same woman before," he said, stroking his hand up and down my cock. My mouth fell open on a groan. "But," he continued, "she's not about to come between us. Well, unless she literally *comes* between us."

He winked. I couldn't help but laugh even as hatred for her filled my chest. I was so angry, so tired, so... bitter.

Tor slammed his mouth into mine, his eyes especially dark as he forced my lips apart and claimed my tongue with rough strokes and violent sucks. My heart quickened when he ripped open the button of his jeans and pulled his own cock free, the veins wrapping his length fucking beautiful, the curve to it destructive when it was inside me.

Tor grasped my cock and thrust his own along my length, and all thoughts of the sweet, enticing scent wrapped around my men melted away. When he dragged his mouth from mine to haul down air, Death caught my chin and turned my face for a deep, plundering kiss that made me whine and buck, frantic for more of his aniseed taste, driving my cock faster against Tor's.

"Fuck, Miz," Tor grunted, stroking our cocks harder, his fat tip grazing a sensitive area that made me gasp into Death's mouth. He swallowed the sound with a deep, approving noise.

"Such a pretty fucking cock throbbing for me, dripping all over me." Tor groaned. "You're wound so tightly today, my Misery. Think you'll come so hard your knees give out?"

I nodded frantically, my hips bucking when Death kissed harder, trying to own every part of me as if I didn't already belong to him.

Please don't stop, I wanted to beg, but even when I was forced to haul down air, parting from Death, I couldn't string the words together. My body buzzed with pleasure, heat roiling through my cock, making my balls tighten.

"Tor," I managed to gasp, my head thrown back on

Death's shoulder as Tor dragged his cock along mine, gripping us tighter so the pressure made me strain against him, frantic, needy.

Death's warm hands slid around my hips, one pausing there to grip me fiercely while another continued lower. A rough breath punched from my chest when he gripped my balls, squeezing, massaging.

"You belong to us, Misery," Tor said suddenly, gruffly. "You can never escape. No matter how far you run, we will hunt you down and drag you back. You're etched on my fucking soul, and I'd rather kill you than lose you."

My eyes slammed shut, breaths coming as fast pants. I was his. He'd rather kill me than lose me. He'd never let me go.

"Try to run," Death dared, the hand at my hip caressing a path up my body. I jerked when his hand closed around my throat. Hard. "Try to leave, Misery. See what happens. See how we react to losing what is *ours.*"

I shuddered between them, struggling to catch a breath, my balls swelling, my cock full of impatient fire. They both claimed me. Owned me. It was all I needed to cry out and find release, my cock frantic in Tor's hand, throbbing against his hard length, covering us both in cum.

Death's hand tightened around my throat. A strangled, breathy whine crawled up my airway and broke free, another wave of pleasure hitting so hard my legs buckled.

Tor laughed as they both followed me to the floor in the foyer, but he didn't stop thrusting his cock along mine for a damn second.

"Tor," I begged, my eyes crossing, stomach hollowing as I sucked in a wild breath.

"No," he replied, husky and rough. "You doubted us, Miz, so you'll pay the price. You get to stop coming when I come." He leaned closer to kiss my cheek and breathed, "And I think I'll last a long, long time this morning."

"I can't." My voice strangled as a sharp sensation cut through my nerves. Oh god. I was too sensitive. I couldn't come again.

"You can, and you will," Death replied, steely as he kissed the side of my face. "Because you're ours."

I struggled for air. Oh god, I was gonna come again and it was already too much.

"Say it," Tor ordered, grabbing a fistful of my hair to wrench my face closer, lips moving over mine. "Fucking *say it.*"

"I'm yours," I breathed.

"And don't ever forget it," he hissed and made me come again.

CHAPTER TWENTY-NINE

CAT

"*I*'m so so so," Honey said, clinging to my arm as we sat at breakfast the next morning, "so so so *so* sorry for not answering my phone."

"It's fine," I said dully, not pushing her off but not encouraging her either. I picked up my toast and bit into it, the sweetness of Nutella bursting across my tongue. Death brought me breakfast as he did every morning, food miraculously waiting for me when I woke up. It was always fresh and with a lime green tulip sitting beside it, but I needed comfort food. Hence Nutella toast, Pop-Tarts, and pancakes drizzled in honey and cream.

"It's not fine," she said fiercely, a furrow between her blonde brows. "You're my best friend and you needed me. In the Best Friend Code, section thirteen verse two, it explicitly states besties must always answer the phone when their bestie is in need."

"You just made that up," I said, humour entering my

voice. I met her eyes, my heart crushed at the misery and apology there, and forgave her on the spot. "And you can't help not answering, Honey."

She made a throaty sound, scowling into her cereal. "I fell asleep and slept through five texts and *three calls.* Who does that?"

"People cursed to be a cat that needs eighteen hours of sleep a day," I pointed out quietly, glancing up when a shadow fell over the table. My entire body buzzed, and I tensed all over, ready to fight or run. But it was just a pale-haired, white-faced girl floating past us. *Literally floating.*

I stared, my heart quickening.

Honey made a soft sound.

"Yeah, I'm a ghost," the girl lamented and floated on, out the door. She had nothing in her hands, no bowl of granola or plate of avocado toast. I had to wonder if she could even eat, or if she'd come here to mourn her loss of food.

"First a sexy nurse and now a ghost," Honey murmured, propping her chin on her hand and stifling a yawn despite *just* waking up. "This is so fucked up."

I was trying very hard not to look across the room to where a black girl with a *very* low-cut shirt was leaning over the table, tending to the world's most pathetic paper-cut. She kept cooing over the 'injured' guy and promising to make it all better, while he blatantly stared down her shirt. He was one of the fuckboys who ogled my heaving bosom at the party, dressed as a werewolf.

"Any progress with the library search?" I asked Honey. She was supposed to check out a stack of books for us to read—she'd found a promising one about the violent history of Ford.

"Shit," she hissed, rubbing her eyes. "I was supposed to check them out yesterday but I fell asleep and forgot."

"It's fine," I said even though it wasn't, and it felt like

I'd lost my best friend. It wasn't Honey's fault she was acting differently, and it wasn't her fault she was cursed to be a cat forever. Unless we could break the curse. "I'll come with you later. I was the one who bailed on you anyway."

Because the dark-haired, blue-eyed psycho accosted me, and I ran home to cry and lock myself away.

Honey must have been thinking along the same lines because she lowered her voice and hissed—actually *hissed*— "If I find out who hurt you, I'll gouge his eyes out and claw his throat."

I blinked. "I think the feline Honey is a little violent."

She shrugged, unapologetic. "I'm protective of my friends. Speaking of friends, plural, where the fuck is Byron?"

"Probably with his new boyfriend," I said, a real smile crossing my face for the first time since Death left me with a kiss and a promise to return later.

"He needs to introduce us," Honey said, a little sulky. "The people want to know what this new boyfriend is like."

The people being Honey.

"Extremely shy," I murmured, finishing my toast and reaching for my Pop-Tart, barely holding back a groan at the warm strawberry filling.[1] "My guess is he's socially anxious and terrified of new people."

"Well, so are you, and you do okay!" Honey complained.

"Thanks," I said, my brow knotting, "I think."

"Oh!" she said suddenly, digging through her cardigan pocket. "I got you this as an apology gift."

She held out a yellow pen balanced on both her hands like she was bestowing me with a sword, and I gave her a strange look but accepted the apology gift—and grinned when I saw it was covered in mallards.

"Okay, you're forgiven," I said, and laughed when she

groaned and splayed across the table, barely avoiding knocking over her cereal bowl.

"Thank *fuck* for that. I knew the duck pen would work."

"Ducks will always earn my forgiveness," I agreed, tucking it into my pocket and startling when my alarm went off on my phone. "Fuck, ten minutes until my first lecture. I better go get my bag. Thank you for the pen." I dragged her into a hug when she stood too, and said, "We're good, Honey, don't worry. I still love you."

She sagged. "I still love you, too, Cat. Even if you haven't told me anything about your three hot husbands today."

"Later," I promised. And god, did I have a lot to tell her.

I ran upstairs, searching every person I passed for Alastor Carmichael, boneless with relief when I didn't run across him. That was one thing I hadn't worked out how to tell Honey yet. She was enamoured with him, and I needed to warn her what kind of person he was, but how did you tell your bestie her crush had thrown you up against a mausoleum and threatened you?

Coat thrown on and bag hanging over my shoulder, I locked my door and ran back downstairs, giving a wide berth to a girl with voluminous straw-coloured hair and freckles who cast a spell in the hallway. She was currently making a plant pot float, and I wasn't keen to get levitated next.

Getting out of Lawrence Hall unscathed was like a slalom course, moving around cursed student after cursed student, but I made it out—and skidded back before I could step on the paw of the tiny grey tabby kitten limping across the path.

"Oh," I breathed, kneeling, my heart skipping when I realised what I'd thought were stripes were actually streaks of blood. "Oh no, baby," I cooed, very carefully scooping up the kitten and cradling it to my chest. I meant to take it to the laboratory building where I knew Professor Palmerston—part time teacher, part time surgeon—would be, but the second I held the kitten to my chest, a deep *clang* went through my soul.

It throbbed like a sick heartbeat, like the pulse of magic I felt when Nightmare killed, and I jolted forward a step before I could process the intention. I glanced down and cried out when I saw my hands were empty.

There was never a kitten. Nightmare had set a trap, and I'd walked directly into it.

CHAPTER THIRTY

CAT

*L*ight struggled to reach the ground here, the dense tree canopy encouraging the darkness that ebbed and flowed around me. It was the same thriving dark I'd seen from Death, Miz, and Tor, but where that had never felt malevolent, this darkness wanted to hurt me and would revel in it.

I'd tried to speak, tried to choke out Death's name and pray names had power like in old fairy tales, but I couldn't open my mouth or choke out even a gasp.

I felt so stupid for walking directly into a trap, for playing into her hands. Terror caught me in its icy grip that Nightmare had learned enough about me to know I'd instantly pick up the kitten and try to help it. She'd used that against me—the part of me that wanted to care for vulnerable animals, that wanted to nurse them back to health. She'd taken the one good part of me that anxiety had never touched, and made me resent it.

"There you are," Nightmare's sultry voice called through the trees, and there she was, standing in a clearing. Her golden skin and long red hair were dappled with sunlight, darkness gathered around the skirt and train of her black lace dress. I couldn't bear to look at her unnatural beauty, but with her curse in my veins and whatever she'd done with the kitten, I couldn't tear my eyes away.

Tears gathered, burned, and streaked down my cheeks. I didn't even have enough agency to flinch when she neared, the train of her dress gliding over the ground. She brushed the tears off my cheeks with sharp-nailed thumbs.

"No need to cry, my terror," she soothed, holding my face in her hands. Inside, I screamed, fought, and threw up, but outwardly I did nothing. Stood there like a sacrificial lamb. "I won't hurt you."

She smoothed ragged strands of white hair from my face and said, "I only need one little thing from you. An act of loyalty, a tiny test of how amenable you are to my commands."

No, I hissed, screamed, pleaded. *No. Please. I don't want to do anything.*

She smiled, her face so unnaturally beautiful and blood-chilling at the same time, the iris of her white eye leaking blood steadily down her face. "I just need you to get Darya Henderson alone and bring her to me. Use any means necessary to get her here. You can do that, can't you, Cat?"

I couldn't. I wouldn't. I wasn't going to hurt Darya; she was my friend.

I tried to wrench away from Nightmare, tried to spit in her face, to snarl, scream, and curse her a thousand times, but all I did was stand in place, my face unchanging, lips utterly silent.

And when Nightmare stepped back, her nails dragging

along my cheek, so sharp they left tiny cuts, I found myself turning. My feet lifted one by one until I left the forest, crossed the campus, and stopped finally under a tree outside Milton Hall.

I waited, as still as a statue, until lectures ended and students arrived, and then the expressionless mask of my face changed, twisting into distress. Tears overflowed my eyes again. I didn't choose to cry, didn't choose to race out of the tree's shadow and grasp Darya's arm. I felt the texture of wool against my fingertips, but I was distant, any control I had overruled by Nightmare's command.

"Cat?" Darya asked instantly, grasping my shoulders with warm hands. "What's wrong?"

"Come with me," I blurted. "Please. I found something."

I didn't choose the words. Had Nightmare chosen them, or was this the curse's own command at work? My voice was just panicked enough to be convincing, but I sounded unnatural to my own ears.

"Of course," Darya agreed, her eyes wide in her face.

And like I'd been led to the slaughter by the kitten, I led Darya to it. She followed me as I rushed through the trees. I fended off every question she had with tearful, breathless exclamations of *there's so much blood, I didn't know what else to do, I'm so scared.*

And then we were in the clearing, and Nightmare stepped out of the darkness with a slow-blooming smile as Darya ground to a halt, her breath hitching.

"Well done, Cat," the goddess praised, her voice low and sensual, sliding along my nerves like a caress. "You've proven very effective."

Darya had frozen; I saw her from the corner of my eye. But *I* could still move because my body shook. I gasped down air while I still could.

"Now," Nightmare said, brushing the backs of her golden fingers over my cheek, "kill her."

I reared back. *What?*

"No."

Nightmare sighed, her eyes narrowing, one beautiful, one bloody. "I suppose you feel safe under his protection. But shields can fall, and he won't be around forever."

My heart jolted. Death. The *he* was obvious. What did she mean he wouldn't be around forever?

"I have a little plan for that too, my terror. But first—" Her voice changed, growing deeper, harder, hypnotic. *"Kill Darya."*

When Nightmare held out a knife, my hand lifted.

When she gestured for me to turn, I faced Darya.

I looked my friend in the eye, saw panic bleach the colour from her brown skin, but I had no power. Nightmare's will controlled every atom of my body.

I screamed and ripped at the cage of her control, but I was powerless. Useless.

I took one step, then another, and drove the silver dagger so deep into Darya's stomach, my hand angled up, that I knew I pierced her heart.

She dropped instantly, her eyes flat and empty, lifeless.

And I died right there with her.

CHAPTER THIRTY-ONE

CAT

*T*he second Nightmare released me from the iron grip of her command, my legs went from under me. I landed beside Darya, blood soaking into the knees of my jeans, the red damning and bright. All I could do was stare at the knife buried in my friend's stomach. The knife I'd put there.

Oh god.

Oh god, I killed her.

Nightmare brushed her fingers over my head as she walked past, her fingernails ripping out strands of hair. I barely felt the sting; I couldn't take my eyes off Darya, off the knife driven into her middle, the blood pouring from the hole I'd made. I'd stabbed her in the heart.

I choked on air, my wheezing the only sound in the clearing except for the slow drip of blood hitting the grass.

Darya was dead. I killed her.

I really—oh god—

I twisted aside as vomit sprayed up my throat and hit the ground, acid burning as I retched miserably. My stomach cramped, and my eyes stung, but the rest of me was starting to ice over.

Fingers caught my chin, but other than pressure I couldn't tell if they were warm or cold, smooth or calloused. They tipped my head up, and then I was staring into piercing gold eyes that watched me so sharply I felt the look scour my very soul.

"I'll get the others," Miz said, a frown tugging at his beautiful mouth as his fingertips traced the shape of three lines on my cheek. The scratches Nightmare made.

I just stared, my chest hollowed out, my body covered in what must be a rime of ice, as he stood and vanished in a cloud of shadow. Darya's blood was on my hands. It soaked into my jeans. Stained my skin beneath the denim.

Another rush of acid and bile poured up my throat and I heaved, doubled over, but then there were hands pulling my hair back and others stroking up and down my back, and Miz was crouching in front of me, carelessly stepping in Darya's blood.

"This is Nightmare's doing," he said, looking beyond me. "I can feel her here."

Her name triggered another spasm of retching, and I curled over myself as my stomach cramped painfully.

"Get rid of the body," Tor said, his gravelly voice easily recognisable. I felt better for hearing him, and for hearing Death's murmured reply. The hand stroking my back vanished, and darkness wrapped around Darya's body. When I blinked, she was gone, only a pool of blood and the knife Nightmare had put in my hand remaining. Miz picked it up to inspect it and dropped it instantly, flexing his hands.

"She made this knife," he said, eyeing me with an expression I couldn't decipher. Nor did I care to. "It has your signature on it," he said. "And you have blood on your hands. She forced you to kill, didn't she?"

I dry-heaved again, tears squeezing out of my eyes. I didn't speak, didn't want to say it out loud.

"Such misery," he breathed, fingers returning to my cheek where Nightmare had slashed me. "So much suffering."

"Don't be an asshole, Miz," Tor muttered.

I swallowed hard, my mouth dry as I rasped, "Take it away."

Miz took my anxiety away when we first met. He could do it again.

Misery stared at me for a long moment, his golden eyes flickering with thoughts I couldn't guess at, but after a moment he leaned closer, soft lips brushing over my forehead. The crushing grip bruising my chest lifted, and I could breathe. The tightness in my stomach eased. The headache that had begun to pound at my temples faded. But I was still sickened by what I'd done, still ashamed, still crying.

"I can only remove the physical misery," he said, leaning back and watching me uncomfortably closely. "If I took it all away, there'd be repercussions."

I frowned.

"With an event this big," he explained, gazing at the pool of blood with a frown, "it becomes a formative event. To take away your misery would be to change who you are, or who you'll become. It could make you someone who kills without feeling remorse."

I shied away from the possibility, leaning back into Tor who released my hair to wrap his arms around me. "I don't want to kill anyone. Ever."

Miz's mouth flattened, something like sympathy in his bright eyes. "Your wants rarely come into it," he said and pushed to his feet, glancing over my head when Death returned, his boots trampling grass as he came to my side.

"What happened, little one?" he asked gently, crouching in front of where I'd collapsed in the clearing. His smoke-grey eyes were unbearably soft; I glanced away, convinced I didn't deserve his softness. Not when I'd just killed my friend.

Oh god, what if Nightmare ordered me to hurt Byron or Honey? I couldn't live with it. I couldn't bear it.

"Cat," Death prompted, still in that soft tone. It made my entire chest hurt.

I opened my mouth to tell him, to tell all of them, but I choked on my tongue. Pain wrapped like a chain of thorns around my throat, and my bloody hands flew for my neck.

Panic erupted like a star through me. I opened my mouth to gasp out a plea, to confess how terrified I was, but that chain dug deeper into my skin.

Nightmare lured me here. She compelled me to bring Darya to the woods and then kill her.

The words were on the tip of my tongue, burning in intensity, but when I reached for them, only air gurgled up my throat. And after it came the bitter copper of blood.

"Stop!" Miz said urgently, rushing across the distance he'd put between us, pale hands reaching for me, his beautiful eyes wide with panic. "*Stop,* Cat, you need to stop speaking."

I swallowed blood, hot tears falling down my face.

"She gagged her," Miz told the others, each word bit out, harsh and short. "Nightmare fucking gagged her."

"Shit," Tor said softly, holding me tighter. "We'll figure this out, Cat. We've beaten her once before, remember."

Death's mouth pressed thin, his nostrils flaring. It was

the same rage he wore when he saw the bruises on my shoulder. "We need to get you home. You're staying in our domain tonight, Cat."

"But—my friends—" I complained, and realised I could speak again. I wilted in relief, more tears scalding my cheeks.

"I'll get a message to them," Death offered. "Let them know you're safe but spending the night with us."

Honey would be supportive of that; she'd told me to go after my three husbands after all. Byron might be a little more suspicious, but I could come up with an explanation by tomorrow. Right now, I just wanted to curl into a ball and cry somewhere I knew I was safe.

My hands shook as I brushed tears off my cheeks and nodded, wincing at the sting from the cuts. I remembered the veil of darkness Death had spread across the gates of his home, and how Nightmare had shouted in rage that she couldn't get through. The castle was the safest place for me right now. And the safest place for everyone else, where I couldn't hurt them.

"Thank you," I rasped, and tasted blood.

"Don't try to talk about what happened," Miz said seriously, his brow knotted as he watched me climb weakly to my feet. "Or even mention Nightmare's name. Don't write it down either, or your fingernails will fall off."

"How do you know this?" I asked, my throat closing up.

He just stared at me for a beat longer than was comfortable. Had she... done those things to him? Did she make him kill, too?

I covered my mouth in horror, my breathing quickening. Miz glared at my reaction, hatred changing his face so drastically that I only now realised it had been absent since he found me here.

"Let's go home," Tor said gently, turning me so he could

pull me into his arms, my face to his chest. I dragged his woody amber scent into my lungs, my breath hitching. "This won't ever happen again, Cat. We won't let it."

I let that promise wash through me like safety and relief even if I didn't quite believe it.

CHAPTER THIRTY-TWO

CAT

I ended up in a massive four-poster bed, bundled into red silk covers, with pillows propped around me and a cup of chamomile tea brewed from plants grown in Death's own garden. Misery had been unceremoniously pushed into bed beside me, Death giving him a stern look that clearly echoed a warning given when I wasn't present. He left us sitting in silence while he joined Tor, cleaning up the murder scene and trying to follow Nightmare's signature to her hideout.

"I haven't seen Death that angry in years," Misery muttered, his arms crossed over his loose white shirt, the cuffs stained in Darya's blood. Tor had painstakingly cleaned me with a warm cloth and careful hands, murmuring reassurances the whole time, but there it was on Miz's sleeve: proof of what I'd done.

"He should be angry," I said quietly, staring at the tiny flowers that flocked the silk covers. "I killed someone."

Miz scoffed. "He's not angry at *you*. He's angry at her."

He hadn't said her name since it made me throw up, I'd noticed. Probably because he didn't want me to soil the covers with vomit.

"She doesn't give you a choice," he added, hands flexing in and out of fists. "Don't blame yourself."

But I did blame myself. I killed Darya, my friend, and I didn't know to live with that knowledge. When I closed my eyes, I saw her empty face staring at me, her dead eyes accusing. My stomach cramped, and I swallowed a mouthful of tea like I could drown the sickness in botanicals.

I jumped when Miz reached across the scant distance between us to lay his hand on my stomach, and the nausea eased by half.

"Thanks," I said, scratchy, and then: "Why are you helping me? You hate me."

Misery sighed, and from the corner of my eye I watched him frown. "It's hard to hate you when you're so pitiful, Prick."

Wow, what a glowing compliment. I slid a glare at him.

"Do you deny being pitiful?"

"No," I muttered, "but you didn't have to point it out."

He laughed quietly, the sound every bit as silken and soft as his speech. I finished my tea and set the empty cup on the bedside table. All the furniture in this room matched the gothic castle—dark wood, elegantly turned arches, carved details, and foreboding tapestries. The drapes around the bed were heavy red velvet the same colour as the curtains at the window and the sheets Death had pulled up around my waist.

When would Tor and Death be back? I had the strange sense Misery wouldn't hurt me but it wasn't the safety I felt when the others were here. I needed comfort and reassurance and Miz wasn't offering it, so I slid my phone out of my pocket and pulled open my favourites folder on Youtube.

"What in damnation?" Misery hissed, leaning over my shoulder to stare at the screen.

I shot him a look and laughed at the bewilderment tugging his pale brows together, pinching his eyes. "You've never seen a duck before?"

"What is it doing?" he asked in a confused murmur.

"Drinking Dunkin' Donuts' strawberry water," I informed him. At his blank look, I explained," Dunkin is a fast food chain. A shop that sells food," I elaborated when his eyes went dull.

"I see," he murmured. "And you can watch Dunkin on your phone?"

"Yeah, there are millions of duck videos on here. And even more cute videos of other animals."

He went very still for a reason I couldn't pinpoint, and then looking at me with wide golden eyes, he asked, "Are there prairie dogs on your phone?"

"On Youtube? Yeah, I bet there are loads." I closed the video and searched for prairie dogs, darting glances at Misery who was very, very close all of a sudden. His face lit up when I opened a short and scrolled through a few others when it finished, and I swear I saw actual stars in his eyes.

"I'm getting Peach," he said, pulling back abruptly. "She'd love this."

"Um—" He jumped out of bed and raced from the room before I could say another word, and I blinked at the open door. "Who the hell's Peach?"

The video drew my attention again and I smiled, watching the groundhog steal a man's snacks. I glanced back up when movement came through the door, and then I shot upright in bed, my mouth falling open.

"Holy shit!" I exclaimed, and then because that wasn't enough, "Holy adorable fucking shit."

"Language," Miz chided, carrying a *real life prairie dog* across the room. "You'll corrupt her."

I couldn't resist a smile. "I bet she's learned plenty of swearwords from Tor already."

Miz groaned. "Despite my best efforts." He settled in bed beside me, Peach cradled in his arms, adorably fuzzy, her eyes big and dark and luminous. Wow. I'd never been so close to one before, had only been this close to a cat or dog, actually.

"Can I...touch her?" I asked, my heart jumping when she turned at the sound of my voice. "Oh, hi. I'm Cat. It's very nice to meet you, Peach."

Miz groaned and whispered, "Torment was right."

"About what?"

"Nothing," he said quickly. "You can touch her; stroke her head, she likes that."

My stomach swooped as I reached out, very lightly stroking Peach's head, surprised at the texture of her fur. The smile on my face widened until my eyes curved. "She's so fucking cute. Oops, sorry for swearing."

The look on Miz's face was... different. Almost tender. He clearly loved Peach a lot.

"Let's show her some videos," I said, grabbing my phone again and scrolling until I found a good one.

Peach showed no interest at all until we got to a video of a prairie dog yipping, the high pitched sound drawing her attention.

"No biting," Miz warned her in a stern fatherly tone as she leaned closer. "Watch your fingers, Cat; she likes to nip them." With a wicked smirk, he added, "Tor's been bitten more times than I can count."

My heart faltered at that smirk, the familiarity of it— the mixture of malice and joy in it.

And as if it had stuck in my consciousness, waiting for me to finally notice it lingering there, something he said minutes ago came back to me.

It's hard to hate you when you're so pitiful, Prick.

Fury rose so swiftly that I saw red. Relief was there too, that the blue-eyed psycho who kissed me wasn't one of Nightmare's followers. But rage was the dominant emotion that took over me.

"Put Peach at the bottom of the bed," I told him, and I must have sounded serious because he immediately did as I said, setting Peach up on a cushion. The second Miz sat back against the pillows, I leapt onto him and wrapped my hands around his throat.

"You," I hissed, the sound coming from deep in my throat. "You were the psycho who shoved me into that alcove and forced your tongue in my mouth."

"You drew my blood," he replied like that made it any better.

I squeezed viciously hard, and hoped his throat collapsed under my hands.

He'll regret ever crossing you. He'll learn never to fuck with you again, or he'll suffer for eternity and—

"Why do your eyes glaze over like that?" he asked, raspy and raw.

I squeezed his throat tighter, watching his pretty face turn pink. "None of your fucking business," I snapped, getting close, my teeth bared as an animal instinct drove me. Another animal instinct reared its ugly head when I felt his cock harden under me, pressing enticingly against my clit.

"Are you picturing all the things you'll do to me?" he asked, his voice weak but amusement and something dark, something thrilled, in his golden eyes. No fear. Fine. I needed to try harder.

"You'll die for this," I promised, breathing hard. My heart beat fast, exhilarated.

Miz flicked his wrist and I braced for pain, for magic to attack me, but it never touched me. It rushed past me, wrapped around Peach like a blanket, and whisked her away.

I should never have taken my eyes off Misery. The second I was distracted, he hooked his leg around mine, caged me in his arms, and flipped me onto my back on the bed.

"Bastard," I seethed, struggling, blinded by fury. I tore at his skin with my fingernails and tried to sink my teeth into his arm.

"If you're going to bite me anywhere," he said, looming over me, his hips trapping mine against the bed, "you should bite here, where everyone will see." He tilted his head, baring his neck, and my breathing came faster. I needed to rip his throat out, to make him bleed more, to drain his entire body until he was dead and staring up at me with the same unseeing eyes as Darya.

Darya. That name drained all the strength from my murderous haze and I flinched, my breath catching.

"Don't go all tame on me now, Prick," Misery taunted, a mean smile curling his mouth. "Where did all that darkness go?"

"Fuck you."

"Mm." His face came at me too quick to escape, and my skin crawled as he licked my face. "That is a very good idea."

"What?" I breathed, panic quickening my heart.

"Don't worry, Cat. I won't hurt you too badly."

Oh, god.

"But I don't mind if you hurt *me*," he went on, pressing his chest into mine, teeth raking down my jaw. "In fact, I insist on it. Put your pretty hands around my throat again."

I—what?

"Now," he commanded, his voice nothing but cold steel. It sent a shiver through me, awakening parts of me that really should have stayed asleep.[1]

I was still furious that Miz was the asshole who backed me against the wall and forced his tongue into my mouth, so wrapping my hands around his throat was no chore. But I jumped when darkness rippled in the air, thin streams of it winding around my torso, my own throat, others catching my ankles and—oh god—spreading my legs for Miz to settle between them.

"I was so determined to hate you," he told me with a sneer, spreading his hand across my stomach, where a single flex of his fingers made my shirt vanish. "You took Death from me, and stole all his nights so I couldn't sleep. I *do* hate you. But then you had to call Peach cute, and be kind to her, and make me like you."

His face came close to mine, anger in his golden eyes but mostly drowned out by a furore of lust. "And you had to choke me, getting my cock all hard like a bad girl."

A flash of heat and warning went down my body, concentrated where his hand now rested on the curve of my bare stomach. I tried to let go of his throat to push him away but more tendrils of power snapped around my wrists, pressing my hands back to his neck, encouraging me to squeeze tighter.

"You just *had* to make me like you," he spat, like I'd done something evil, "and now I have no choice but to fuck that grief and guilt out of your eyes."

"You don't even want me," I said, a weak protest. The scent of him was dizzying, his closeness a new brand of torture. "This is insane, Miz."

In answer, his hand splayed lower, stroking from hip bone to hip bone and my jeans dissolved to nothing. I began to protest again because this was complete and utter madness, but he pulled my underwear to the side and drove his cock all the way inside me in a single thrust.

My eyes blew wide. I cried out loudly at the pressure, the stretch, the sudden and harsh fullness.

Oh god, when did he even lose his clothes? How was his cock hitting so deep, making me arch off the bed, frantic to escape him, frantic for him to move, to fuck me.

Pure insanity. I clenched around him in a wild flutter.

"Pick a safe word because I'm not holding back."

"I hate you," I seethed, squeezing his throat harder as I struggled to adjust to him inside me.

"Works for me," he said with a shrug and drove the last inch into me, cool hands coming to settle on my thighs to push me wider for him. "Look at you," he laughed, his pretty face twisted with wickedness, "taking my cock all the way like a little slut. This cunt was made for me, wasn't it?"

"No," I moaned, unable to trap the sound of pleasure. Oh shit, oh god. I wanted to say it was all discomfort and *too deep* and *god, stop* but that would be a lie. I dug my fingernails into his throat, panting as he inflicted a brutal pace on my pussy. My eyes slammed shut. They might have crossed at the sudden onslaught of sensation.

"No?" Miz asked, the shadow encircling my throat tightening a fraction. "Then why is your pussy squeezing me like it can't get enough? Why have you soaked my cock and my balls? Why does every word out of my mouth make you twitch and gasp? Hm? Why *is* that?"

"You're a piece of shit," I snarled, straining against him, my whole body hot and sensitive. I wanted his hands everywhere. Wanted to mutilate him until he begged me to spare him.

"I know," he cooed, a tendril of darkness stroking my cheek with faux gentleness. He made me cry out when he slammed his hips into mine, ruthless and rough—once, twice, three times. "But you're gonna come anyway, aren't you, Prick?"

"No," I scoffed.

He stilled on the next thrust and rotated his hips, over and over. I felt like my skeleton would fly out of my body. I tensed, gasping. The shadow tightened around my throat until I whimpered, the world hazy and spinning. I'd never tried this before, had never anticipated that it would blur out everything except the warm body on top of me, the cock grinding against all my weak spots until it was unbearable.

"There you go," Miz said when I shattered, my eyes crossing at the intense pleasure. "Good little whore. I knew this cunt would come for me, because you *love* this, don't you? You love getting your pussy railed by a man you can't stand. You love getting the life fucked out of you by a man you *hate*."

His lips brushed my cheek as I squirmed, the aftershocks cruel. "Don't worry, Cat, I love the way you hate me. Makes it even hotter when you can't help but come." His thumb stroked my clit, and I gasped. "Over and fucking over."

"No," I protested, my eyes flashing open in panic.

Misery's lips covered mine. The magic wrapped around my wrists pulled them from his throat, and then my hands were pinned to the bed above me. Every atom in my body came alive, shivering and gasping for more.

"I know you're a dirty slut, Cat. I know you love being choked, and tied down, and fucked so roughly you can't take it anymore. Death thinks you're a good girl, but you're not, are you? You're my needy slut, my pretty whore, my fucking bad girl."

I thrashed, aching and close to a second orgasm, my whole body alive with an awful kind of buzz. I refused to beg, refused to gasp his name, but it clung to the tip of my tongue and burned there.

"So you're going to come over and over, until you've soaked the bed and I'm happy there's not a single thought left in that wicked brain of yours, not a single speck of grief or guilt." The darkness tightened around my wrists, until I was sure it would leave marks.

"Oh god," I breathed when his hand left my thigh and plunged into a shadow, pulling out a magic wand vibrator. "No, no, no."

I was too sensitive. I couldn't take that. I knew the vibrations would be unbearable, un—

I screamed when he set it on the highest setting and pressed it to my swollen clit. My eyes rolled all the way back. I came so hard I blacked out for a few seconds and when I came back, Miz was fucking me again, a cruel grin on his face. His cock hit so fucking deep, it was unreal.

"Bastard," I panted, my body on fire, legs trembling with the ripples of vibrations that *had not stopped.*

His grin turned lopsided. So fucking pretty. A beautiful poison. "I thought you wanted to be dominated, Cat? You should be thanking me."

"Ah!" I squirmed, trying to escape the deep stab of stimulation through my clit.

He pressed it harder, finding an angle that made me scream.[2] "Say it. Say *thank you.*"

I whined, my breathing wrecked, traitorous pleas escaping with each breath.

He thrust his cock into me roughly, deeply, a grunt in his throat with each thrust. "Say it. *Fucking say it.*"

"Thank you!" I cried, so loudly my voice echoed off the high ceiling.

"Beautiful," he laughed, almost delirious. "What a good slut, thanking her god."

Not mine. Oh, god, not mine. My eyes slammed shut when he adjusted the wand's angle, and then I was coming again, warmth flooding me in a rush, making my mouth hang open. I lost control of what sounds escaped, what words I spoke. His grunts rose in volume, hips frantic and wild, his cock filling me so deep that it dragged my orgasm into another.

I was so wrecked, I barely noticed the ropes of dark magic leaving my body, only truly conscious that the wand left when my legs stopped shaking. Thank fuck. Oh, thank fuck it was over.

But on the flipside, I felt so. Fucking. Good.

Miz had ripped every bit of tension out of me until I was as limp as a ragdoll. I didn't even bother to open my eyes when he rolled onto his back and arranged me splayed over him, his chest rising and falling fast. I really, truly hated him. I did. But *fuck.* He'd just brought five different fantasies to life, and I didn't know how he could have possibly known unless—

Death told him. I stifled a groan. When he overheard me talking to Honey, he must have told Miz and Tor everything I said. Bastard. I was angry, but that emotion felt very far away, my mind floaty and my body extremely satisfied. The warmth of Misery under me satisfied my soul's need for companionship, too. I had everything I needed right here, with a man I hated.

He expelled a long breath, his face moving against the side of my head. Nuzzling me, I realised after a minute. As if Misery could ever be gentle.

"Well," a sweet, rich voice said, startling me but not enough that I bothered to open my eyes. Death was back. "This is unexpected."

"Peach likes her," Miz said softly.

"Hm."

I made a soft noise of complaint when hands moved me on top of Miz, spreading my legs again, presumably Misery's hands but I wasn't sure. I was comfy and warm and held close, so I didn't much care.

"I filled her up for you, see."

Death groaned.

I tried to open my eyes to see them both but I was so tired, my eyelids so heavy.

"Just don't make her come again," Miz murmured, his hand flexing on my bare back. "I don't think she can take another."

Alarm should have pulsed through me but I was too floaty for that. A cool tongue swiped over my pussy and I made a quiet sound of surprise, but it felt nice. Soft, gentle, swirling over me slowly enough to not arouse me again. The moan Death let out threatened to wake up my body again, but the warm hands caressing the backs of my thighs lulled me to calm again.

"Fuck, the taste of you both together..." Death groaned, curling his tongue inside me. Oh. He was—eating Miz's cum from my pussy. Well, that was... well.

When he was done, Death kissed my aching pussy, then my clit, and then rose up the bed and slung his arm across my back, holding us both.

"Sleep, Cat," he murmured, as if I wasn't already halfway there. "We'll all stay with you."

CHAPTER THIRTY-THREE

CAT

*H*aving breakfast with the living (ish) embodiments of Death and Torment was weird but even weirder that it felt easy and natural. There were no awkward silences, only teasing, laughter, and warmth that felt dangerously close to affection.

I sat on Death's lap in the kitchen, at his insistence, and wasn't even allowed to get my own food; he hand-fed me bites of pastries and fruit, and seemed to love every second of it. A pleasant happiness moved through my chest, making me lighter. I liked being cared for more than I'd realised, like I'd enjoyed being choked more than I ever realised.

Oh god, I'd never come as hard as I did on Miz's cock with his filthy words brushing my skin, his wand on my clit.

"Where's the bastard anyway?" I asked, sucking the juice of a strawberry from Death's fingers and enjoying the soft groan he bit back. It felt like I was living in a dream, and dream Cat liked to tease her husbands.

"Brooding probably," Tor replied with an eye roll where he sat across the solid wood table big enough to seat twelve. "He vanished a couple hours ago and hasn't come back."

Alarm went through my chest. "Shouldn't we be worried, with Nightmare around?"

"No." Death kissed my shoulder, and tugged down my borrowed shirt—one of Miz's, a loose white cotton lavish with embroidery—so he could kiss bare skin. "He's prone to disappearances when he's got a lot on his mind. This is normal for him. If he's not back in a few hours, then I'll go find him."

"A lot on his mind meaning me," I murmured, reaching for my cup of coffee and laughing when Death rushed to get it first, bringing it to my lips.

"Don't worry about him," Tor said, propping his chin on his hand and gazing at me in a way that made my stomach squirm. "He's always dramatic about everything, and he wasn't planning to like you, let alone sleep with you. He'll get over it and come begging for more."

I snorted. "I can't imagine him begging."

"He begs so beautifully," Death told me, lavishing more kisses across my skin. "I'll fuck him into submission some time so you can see it in person."

I nearly choked on my coffee, heat spreading further through me.

"I think our cute little succulent is done with breakfast," Tor observed, a slow smile spreading across his face, soft brown eyes dancing. He crooked a finger. "Come over here, pussy cat."

I groaned at the name. First Death used it and now it was catching. But I turned on Death's lap, ignored my squirming nerves, and kissed him chastely before hopping off his lap to obey Tor. You'd think with all the things they'd done to my body, I'd be bolder around them, but Rome wasn't built in a day. I couldn't help moments of self-consciousness. Dream Cat was a work in progress.

Death's arm hooked my waist and pulled me back, his lips catching mine for a deep, plundering kiss that made me groan. He set down my coffee and a soft pulse shot through my clit at the rough, beastly sound in his throat as we kissed, the throb stronger with every sinuous sweep of his tongue.

When he released me, I was throbbing and wet.

"Go to Tor, little one," he said, and spilled darkness and magic across the table as I walked around it, clearing some of the plates and bowls of food.

"You better have one of those kisses for me," Torment said, rising from his chair to meet me, surrounding me with the heady scent of sandalwood and amber.

I groaned when his lips met mine, rougher, more demanding than Death's. His hands moulded to my ass, wrenching my hips flush to his, and another moan shuddered from my tongue to his as his cock pushed insistently at my stomach.

"Mine," he breathed against my lips. "Fucking mine."

His possessiveness caressed my soul like his hands caressed my body, now wandering up my ass to my hips. I yelped in surprise when he spun me suddenly, pushing me flat to the table Death had cleared. A shudder went all the way through me, cold chasing down my arms and up the backs of my thighs. *Oh god, yes.*

Crazy how I'd gone years without good sex, and now I'd had a taste of it, I couldn't get enough. It was a craving. An addiction that dream Cat wasn't going to fight.

"So fucking beautiful spread out for your husband," Tor

groaned, his hands slipping under Miz's shirt and flipping it up so my ass was bared, my pussy bare and already dripping. "My pretty, needy, perfect wife."

His praise filled me with warmth, made me squirmy with butterflies. I glanced across the table, searching for Death, and my breath caught when I found him sitting regally in the dark chair, his hand wrapped around his thick cock, the head weeping like my pussy wept with aching need.

"*Our* pretty, needy, perfect wife," he corrected with a smile, his caramel voice a little huskier than before. His smoky eyes held mine, the prolonged contact making my butterflies swarm faster, like they were frantic to get out, to get closer to him. I didn't blame them. "Are you gonna be a good girl and take Tor's cock, little one?"

I felt the words across my skin, felt them deep inside me as I clenched, arousal dripping from me. "Yes," I breathed, and because it wasn't enough, because I needed more and more and so much more, I blurted, "I'll be so good for you, I promise."

Tor's hands stroked up my back under my stolen shirt, and maybe he sensed how frantic and desperate I was—desperate to please but also to keep them, to never let them go—because he murmured, "Shh, I've got you. I've got what you need, wife."

Tor's hand returning to my hip was the only warning he gave before he traced his cock around my dripping entrance and glided inside. The curve to his shaft raked his tip over my inner muscles, making him seem even bigger, and when he reached a sensitive spot, my hips jerked. The motion buried him all the way, and I moaned so loudly I didn't realise he'd made an answering sound, his body bowing over mine on the table.

"Oh fuck, that's it," he moaned, hands splaying on my

ass, pulling my cheeks apart so he—oh, fuck, so he could see where he stroked in and out of me, first in shallow thrusts and then deeper, longer, harder. I tried to keep my head up, tried to keep my eyes on Death, but Tor breathed, "You're too fucking good, Cat, I can't take how insane you feel wrapped around me," and my head dropped to the table as sensations overwhelmed me.

"Tor," I breathed, my voice edging towards a whine at those slow, rough thrusts, each one dragging a moan from him, the noises growing loud enough to echo off the kitchen's vaulted ceilings. "Oh, god."

"That's it, Beautiful," he panted, teeth scraping over my throat, his whole body covering me, "praise your god."

My hips jolted, obscene wet sounds coming from my pussy as his cock slammed into me, not hard enough to hurt but rough enough to make my whole body shivery.

"So," he murmured, dragging kisses down my back now, tearing Miz's shirt off my body. "Fucking." His lips mapped the curve of my spine, body sliding down mine. "Mine."

He lifted off me and grasped my hips so fast that I was moving before I realised what was happening. His cock slipped out of me for a second, but then I was on my back on the table, cups rattling at the other end, and he was driving back into me with a feral look on his sharply beautiful face, and that curve to his shaft—

My back arched, but that only made everything sharper, even more sensitive. He hit my weak spot over and over, quickening his pace now, his warm coffee eyes flashing each time he sank inside me.

"My Cat," he rasped, his stare fixed obsessively on my face. "My wife. My cunt. Every inch of you is fucking mine."

My whole body locked in its arch and then I was

coming, my inner walls locking around his cock, frantic to hold him inside even as Tor kept fucking me, dragging out my climax until I couldn't bear it anymore. He kissed me to muffle my pleas and fucked me until my eyes crossed, until I couldn't breathe, couldn't control my hands as they scratched at him, frantic for more, for less, for everything.

"Do you want my cum, wife? Gonna fill up this beautiful fucking pussy with every drop in me." His voice strangled, thrusts erratic now. "Gonna mark you with my scent, fill you with my cum so everyone knows you belong to *me.*"

"Fuck," I whimpered, his frantic thrusts and the dirty talk throwing me over the edge into an orgasm that made my toes curl.

Tor let out the sexiest growling whine I'd ever heard, and buried his cock inside me as he came, each powerful throb inside me matched by a tight, breathy cry from the man above me. He was undone, sweaty and glazed-eyed, and that filled me with power. With satisfaction.

His lips found mine, each press and lick coloured with desperation as he shuddered through the last few throbs, clinging to me like he couldn't bear it.

"Stay right where you are," Death ordered softly, his footsteps the only sound other than Tor's and my strained breaths. I couldn't have moved if I tried—my legs were jelly, my whole body made of the same substance. My eyelashes fluttered to half-mast but it was enough to see Tor sweaty and gorgeous as he slowly pulled out of me and dropped into a chair just as Death fell to his knees before me.

A groan tore up my throat and echoed off the ceiling when his mouth covered my pussy in quick, greedy sucks. "Death," I breathed and wasn't sure what I was asking for, wasn't sure I was asking for anything at all.

His warm hands came to my thighs, cradling them as he

ate Tor's cum from my pussy like he had with Misery's. A low rumbling sound filled the back of his throat like he loved it. His eyes flicked up to mine when he trailed his tongue from my entrance to my clit, circling it as his mouth stretched into a smile.

"You gonna give me an orgasm, little one? It doesn't seem fair that Tor got two from you and I got none."

"Just one," I warned, remembering the intensity of coming over and over and over for Miz. I loved it, and wanted to recreate it, but god, not the morning after. I was still recovering from the way it beat up my clit and my soul simultaneously.

"One is perfect," Death breathed, that gentle, praising tone making my cheeks flush with heat. "You're so good for us, Cat," he said, licking up the arousal that dripped from me. "You took Tor's cock so perfectly."

"Made for us," Tor input breathlessly.

"Definitely," Death agreed, and licked a broad stroke up my pussy, making every place he touched tingle. "You were made for our cocks, weren't you, little one? Not because of any fucking curse; because of *you*."

The words hit my insecurity and blasted it to pieces until I was smiling, melting into the table again and not particularly caring that its hard edge dug into my thighs.

"Yours," I agreed on a breath.

"Our wife," Death rumbled and made my hips jump when he closed his teeth around my clit. His hand splayed over my stomach and pushed me back down, and it was so hot I came there and then. "Our good girl, coming so prettily for all of us."

Hazy and pleasured, I thought he meant that I'd come for them all separately until Death added, "Clean off Tor's cock, Miz."

I prised my eyelids open to watch Misery round the

table, his body rife with tension. Insecurity came roaring back, but Death's gentle kisses along my inner thigh kept it from sinking its claws all the way. I didn't look away as Miz dropped to his knees before Tor's chair and cleaned his cock of both his cum and mine. It was the tender way Tor's fingers sank into Miz's pale hair that held my attention, and the way all that tension bled from Misery at the single touch.

He slid his mouth down the thick vein in Tor's cock and held eye contact with me the entire time. When he was done, he drew back and said, "Get dressed. I'll take you back to Ford."

I was a little stunned by the eye contact but mostly amenable because of the orgasms, so I hopped off the table and went to find my clothes.

CHAPTER THIRTY-FOUR

CAT

*M*iz was lucky I didn't break his nose; my hand curled into a fist, itchy with encouragement, and the dark voice in my mind whispered he deserved to bleed. I cast a sideways glance at him as we walked across the park in the heart of Ford's campus, and wanted to rearrange his entire bone structure. The least I could do was shatter his glasses and make his vivid blue eyes bleed. He'd adopted the form of the psycho he wore when he shoved me into the alcove, and I seethed with anger.

Last night hadn't warmed me to him at all, no matter how sweet he was with Peach or that he'd claimed to make to come to stop my grief over killing Darya. I didn't buy it. Miz was all about control and dominance; I bet he never did anything for others without something to gain first.

"Problem?" he asked, glancing at me with nerves instead of the hostility he'd shown before. Sweat shone at his brow and neck, too, but that could have been because he was wearing a heavy wool coat straight off Paris Fashion Week and it was a rare scorching day in Ford's End.

"Other than wanting to break your nose, no problem," I replied sweetly, surprising myself with the cold bite of acid in my words. There was just something about Miz that riled me.

He laughed softly, but didn't snap back at me, and didn't taunt. I cast him a weird look, but I didn't want to bring up the awkwardness between us. Clearly he had regrets about sleeping with me. And fine, let him regret it. He was the one who initiated it anyway.

"You can leave me here," I told him for the second time as we neared Lawrence Hall.

To which he shot me the same scowl as before and said, "I'll walk you to your door. Unless you want to give Nightmare a perfect opportunity to lure you away again?"

I glanced away, memories hitting me like daggers. Darya rushing after me, concern widening her innocent eyes. Nightmare ordering me to kill her. My hand burying a knife in my friend's gut. The emptiness in her eyes.

I jumped when a cold, clammy hand wrapped around mine, and Miz squeezed hard. "The clarity of the memories fades over time," he murmured. "It will always haunt you, but it won't always hurt this much."

I swallowed the lump in my throat and didn't know why he was trying to comfort me. "Thanks," I said anyway, because his words gave me hope. I could barely breathe or speak around the knives inside my chest, and maybe I didn't deserve it but I wanted to believe it wouldn't always be this way.

"There, isn't that your annoyingly upbeat friend?"

I glanced up, looking across the park where a few

students mingled near the benches, more sitting on picnic blankets on the grass to take advantage of the good weather.

"Honey!" I called, and immediately wished I hadn't when she turned, smiling wide enough to light up her whole face, and a tall, broad-shouldered man turned with her.

Alastor.

My body locked up, but Miz's hand was still wrapped around mine, and even if I wanted to break his face, I'd choose him over Alastor a thousand times. I might not feel safe with Misery, but I didn't feel *un*safe, and that was a powerful distinction.

"I'd call you a dirty stop-out," Honey teased, jogging across the park to us, eyeing up Miz's blue-eyed asshole disguise, "but I'm guilty of the same crime. Alastor, you remember Cat from the party, right? Or were you too trollied to remember anything?"

Trollied? I almost laughed.

"The latter," he replied, his golden face friendly and harmless. My heart stuttered in my chest. "But I've seen Cat around campus. I don't know you, though," he added, glancing at Misery with that same bright, open expression on his face. It was a fucking lie.

"I don't do parties," Miz said coldly, tugging me closer, and I didn't know if it was male possessiveness or if he was reading my body language, but I was glad for the back up.

Cat shot me a wide-eyed look at the *don't fuck with me* attitude Miz gave off, but I didn't mirror it. Even if I didn't have the nerve to show my real feelings about Alastor, I was glad someone did. He was evil at his core. I needed to get Honey away from him, but I knew what she got like when she had a crush—she was all in, and completely blind

213

to red flags. If I tried to get her to see the real him, she'd cling to him harder.

"I don't blame you," Alastor replied to Miz, completely ignoring his tone of warning. "That night was a shitshow. You didn't miss much."

"Where are you going now?" Honey asked, a smile tugging at her lips again like she couldn't resist it. I hated seeing her so happy when I knew I'd have to pop the bubble eventually. I hated knowing her crush was a monster and not knowing how to convince her of that.

"Lawrence Hall," I replied, and tried to keep all my true emotion out of my voice.

Something came flying at us and I flinched hard, seeing only a fast-moving shape. *Nightmare*, my instincts screamed, and I twisted away, my breathing wrecked. Miz squeezed my hand so tightly it hurt and put his lips to my ears.

"I would take every threat to you apart piece by piece, bone by bone, but you're safe, Cat. It's a frisbee."

I exhaled a hard breath, unable to say why the violent comfort worked so well, and I noticed both Honey and Alastor watching me with matching worried expressions. Like he'd studied hers and mirrored it. I wondered if he stole pieces from everyone, flawlessly mimicking human emotion.

"I'm fine," I told Honey, a chill rushing down my spine at the way her crush—boyfriend?—watched me. It was so believable, I'd never guess he was so dangerous. "Just shaken because of... you know..."

The Halloween party. Nightmare cursing us.

"Come on," she said kindly, her expression so soft it killed me. "We're heading that way so we'll walk with you." She gave Miz a stern look. "You better protect my girl."

"With my life," he swore, and sounded so believable I

thought he must be mimicking the emotion like Alastor did.

"And if I find out *you* hurt her," Honey said, going into scary sunshine mode as we crossed the park, "I will end you, and I'll make sure the pain lasts a long time."

"Good," Misery said softly, quietly. "I'd deserve nothing less."

I squeezed his hand, not quite believing this was fake anymore. That was real, and I didn't like the sound of it—small and loathing and fragile.

Honey nodded though, satisfied. "Alastor, tell Cat about the gala." She shot me an excited stare that softened to pleasure when Alastor held open the door to Lawrence Hall for all of us. A perfect gentleman.

"You have to come," Alastor said, smiling at both me and Miz, his mask impeccable. "I need all the numbers I can get. I'm organising a charity gala for the week before Christmas."

"It's for this group of injured kittens someone dumped in the village," Honey said, her lip pushing out in a sad pout. "It's *awful,* Cat. The poor things, left out in a cardboard box in the cold."

"I'm taking it as a chance to raise awareness about animal cruelty," Alastor went on as we headed upstairs, a riot of noise coming from the dining hall. Right, it must be lunch time by now. I was glad it was Saturday; I couldn't bear classes right now. "There are so many animals abused, so many pets discarded, but we have the money and privilege to do something about it."

One look at Honey and I knew she was a goner. The sun might as well have shone out of Alastor Carmichael's ass, and I really did not know how to tell her this was all a clever alibi while underneath he was poison and malice. I held onto Miz's hand for dear life.

"We might be busy that day," Misery said when I forgot to reply. "Cat will have to check her calendar." He said it with a tight smile that told him my calendar would be fully booked. But Honey shot me a pleading look and I knew I'd cave, that I'd end up going to the gala organised by a man who threatened me.

"I can't remember the date," Alastor said when we reached the second floor, glancing at Honey. "You wrote it down, didn't you, dear? Can you go check in your diary?"

Honey leaned up to kiss his cheek and darted to her room. When she was gone, Alastor kept up his good natured routine, but he said, "The gala's for injured cats actually," and looked right at me.

My stomach squirmed. That was a threat. I knew it was. He was threatening to hurt me, right here in the corridor in front of Miz. I cringed away, and expected Miz to jump in and threaten him back, maybe even eviscerate him, break his bones apart like he'd promised, but he was frowning down the hallway, distracted.

"Your door's open," he pointed out, his voice strange. He shook his head hard, like he was trying to dislodge something.

He was right. Shit. My door was open. And when I rushed down the hallway, releasing my death grip on Miz's hand, I saw the gouge the lock had left in the frame. It had been forced open.

A chill went down my spine and made my hands shake.

"If you did this—" I turned to hiss at Alastor, who was smirking, his real face exposed.

"Why would I give a shit what was in your room?"

I didn't believe him, didn't believe a single word out of his sneering mouth.

"Keep looking at her like that," Misery hissed, stepping between us. "I fucking dare you."

I fought a shudder as I pushed my door open, a soft sound catching the back of my throat when I found one of my curtains hanging off its pole, my mattress and duvet dragged off the bed frame, a crack going through the desk where Death had fucked me. Everything that could be broken *was* broken. I turned to look at Miz, my heart breaking, and swallowed hard at the look on his face. He looked sick.

"You can't stay here," he whispered, running a graceful hand down his face. "You'll have to move into a new room, Cat."

I stared at the wreckage, the back of my neck prickling with warning. Nightmare had done this, or one of her followers had on her command. What would they have done if I'd spent the night here? Killed me?

I padded carefully into the room, my hands shaking as I salvaged some of my things from the mess. My eyes welled with tears when I saw the ceramic duck Virgil got me for my last birthday shattered on the ground.

My knees gave out without warning and I knelt there, clutching the shards.

"Cat," Miz breathed, tentatively coming towards me. "You can't stay."

Because whoever did this would come back.

"Oh god," Honey's soft voice came from the door, horror bleaching her face when I glanced back at her. "They got into your room, too."

"Too?" I wiped the tears off my cheeks, dropped the broken duck, and stood. "Your room was broken into?"

She nodded, something new in her eyes—horror and grief. It was like looking in a mirror. "They didn't trash my room, but they left this," she whispered, holding out a red rose.

"A rose," I murmured, grabbing clothes from the

wardrobe that now slumped into the wall, a massive gash down its side. "Why would someone leave that?"

She shook her head, silent, and a tear dripped down her face. "Oh, Cat, I'm so sorry this happened."

When she rushed across the room and hugged me, not caring that I had my hands full, I rested my head on her shoulder. "This is Nightmare's followers targeting us," I said. "She wants us to be scared, but fuck her. Fuck her scare tactics."

Mind games—that was what she did, what she loved. She made me kill Darya because she knew it would haunt me. She trashed my room, but only left Honey a rose, so it would fracture us. I was supposed to wonder why Honey's room was spared, why she was left a gift, to all intents and purposes. But I refused to play Nightmare's games.

"I'll get you a new room," Miz said as Honey and I separated, both of us teary, traumatised. Exactly as Nightmare wanted. "And I'll make sure it's protected," he added, catching my eye so I understood he'd use magic to make sure no one could get in. I nodded.

"You're right," Honey breathed, wiping tears on her sleeve, her face red. "She wants us to be scared, but why should she get what she wants? Alastor—" she began, raising her voice, but he was gone.

Probably off to report to Nightmare. I didn't care that he couldn't be one of her robed followers because I saw him in that room on Halloween, unrobed. He did this. I knew he did.

"The person who did this will pay," I promised. "And— maybe until then, stay away from Alastor? We hardly know him, Honey."

Honey's eyes narrowed, as I knew they would. Fuck! "And you know your husbands so much better? You never approve of my choice in men, Cat."

"Sorry," I rushed out. "Sorry, I'm just upset and stressed." I gestured at my trashed room and hoped sympathy would win her back to my side, my bones melting in relief when her face softened. I cried harder.

I didn't know if I hugged her first or if she hugged me, but we both clung hard and only pulled apart when a sharp male cry came from the hallway outside. Distressed. Pained. Familiar.

"Byron," I gasped, and sprinted for the door. If Alastor had hurt him, I swear to all my death gods...

But it wasn't Alastor. When Honey and I burst into the hallway, it was a five-foot-nine guy whose name I didn't know throwing Byron up against the wall, his face parted on a guttural animalistic hiss and his skin greyish and peeling.

"Oh god, a zombie," Honey whispered.

"Miz?" I turned to him but he was already moving, grabbing the zombie in a grip so tight that he screamed, staggering back, clutching his chest as dark tendrils of smoke inflicted misery. "Don't kill him," I rushed out, Honey and I darting forward to catch Byron. "It's not his fault he's cursed."

Misery made a throaty sound and released the zombie, letting him collapse to the floor. "I'll shield all your rooms," he said, turning to meet my eyes. "I believe there's a conversation you need to have."

Ah. Byron was staring at the zombie, then at me, then at Honey, his eyes widening when we didn't run away screaming at the sight of a zombie.

"Yeah, By, there's something you should know."

CHAPTER THIRTY-FIVE

TORMENT

I startled awake some time around three a.m. when my bed dipped and a shivering body crawled under the covers, arms and legs wrapping around me.

"Miz?" I murmured, rolling over and pulling him into my arms. "What's wrong? You're shaking."

"I'm fine," he breathed, but he clearly wasn't. I came fully awake, alarm lancing through me. Miz came to me for sex and friendship, and humour on his bad days, but it was Death he sought when he needed comfort and reassurance.

And if he was lying about being okay, he must have been in a state.

"The castle's safe," I reminded him gently, tucking his head under my chin and marvelling at being able to. Standing, he towered over me, but curled up here in bed he seemed small, and my protective instincts kicked in hard. "Nightmare can't get in."

He flinched at the name. I tightened my grip, tangling my legs with his and making sure the duvet covered him completely. "You're safe here with me," I promised, an ache starting in my chest. "You know I'll rip her apart if she even tries to touch you. I've done it before."

"I know," he murmured, a nod moving his nose against my throat. "I know that, fuck, but—she lives in my fucking head. I can't get the memories out, can't ever forget—"

"Shh," I soothed him, squeezing him to me, fingers knotting in his long hair. "It's over. That time is *over*. She lost, Miz, and she'll lose again."

"She got to Cat," he said quietly, rapid breaths moving over my throat. "She forced her to kill that girl."

"That will never happen to you again," I swore, a growl entering my voice.

He shuddered, a hitch in his breath. "I want—I want to get her a duck. Cat."

"Not a live one," I said gently, carding my fingers through his hair.

"Fine."

"Get her a plushie. Littles love plushies."

He made a throaty sound, soft and doubtful. I feathered kisses across his head.

"Tell me what happened."

"No."

"Miz, please."

"No."

I bit back a sigh and just held him, and I was clearly a bastard because even as worried as I was, I fucking *loved* getting the chance to hold him like this, to be his protector for once.

He gradually stopped shaking, his arms squeezing me tight to his body, and eventually those arms slackened and his breathing turned deep and even.

I wouldn't let Nightmare hurt either of them. Hell, *any* of them. This whole fucked up crusade was for revenge, and she'd unleash that revenge on Death, too.

Over my dead fucking body.

It took me a while to calm down, to soften the anger that filled me like lava, but I brushed a final kiss to Miz's head and slipped into sleep just as the sun began to rise.

God help anyone who fucked with the people I loved.

CHAPTER THIRTY-SIX

CAT

*D*eath was gone when I woke up three mornings later, only a lime green tulip left behind, but I'd been prepared for that. It was nice to be in a relationship with someone who communicated openly, and told me he had a stubborn soul to bring to his domain the next day instead of letting me wake alone, wondering if I'd done something wrong.

And we *were* in a relationship—we'd had that conversation yesterday and he'd told me, in explicit terms, that he was serious about being my husband, and I was his for life. Life seemed a little unrealistic, but it put a smile on my face anyway. At least until he wiped it away by sinking his cock inside my pussy and making my mouth drop open.

Remembering that, a split second smile curved my lips until everything that happened in the woods returned with force. Darya's immobile body, the helpless terror in her eyes, Nightmare's voice hooking through my mind like a scythe. *Well done, Cat, you've proven very effective. Now kill her.*

Like it did every time I remembered, my whole body locked up, a weight crushing my chest until I could only half breathe, and my heart beat strained.

You're scaring me, Cat, what's going on? The last words Darya ever spoke to me. To anyone.

I rolled over and threw my torso over the side of the bed, aiming for the bucket I'd kept there for days. A cramp in my stomach sent bile splashing the bottom of the bucket. Ugh. This happened too many times a day; I was so wretched I hadn't made it to classes yesterday and I had no interest in going today either.

I didn't know this room yet. It was surprising how quickly I'd adjusted to my old room, and now I was thrown in a whole new space, I hated it. The desk and wardrobe were on a whole other side, the window bigger, throwing shadow and light across the floor in a new pattern. This room had a heater and extra blankets, though, and Miz had shielded it. Whatever that meant.

I flopped back onto the bed with a groan—and frowned at the yellow blur of colour in the corner of my eye.

"Huh?" I squinted, still bleary-eyed and miserable, but no, I was really seeing what I thought I was seeing: a 20cm tall duck plushie.

My bottom lip wobbled, and I wanted Death to come back so I could hug him fiercely—but when my eyes focused, they drifted from the plush duck to two iced drinks from Dunkin Donuts and a white paper bag with their logo. I couldn't take it. I buried my face in the pillow and cried, and didn't stop until I was hollow and my chest hurt.

It took me an hour to feel human again, and by then the sun was high in the sky, blazing through the crack in my curtains. I pulled myself up until I was propped against the pillows and reached for the iced coffee, sliding my phone out from under my pillow.

I dialled Virgil first, frowning when he didn't pick up after a solid minute of ringing. Then I tried again, to the same end. I left him a voicemail and tried Tannie.

"Darling sister," he greeted, "why have you abandoned me?"

I grunted in reply.

"Ten days without a call, and yes I counted." He tsked. "Do you not love me anymore? Are we over?"

"You're my brother, I can't break up with you."

He gasped, affronted. "So if I wasn't your brother, you *would* break up with me. Harsh, Cat."

I found it in me to laugh, but it was weak. "Are you okay?"

"Fine. Bored. I'm waiting for a placement so I'm just sitting here twiddling my thumbs."

"There must be something you can do. You're telling me you have no work due?"

Zoltan groaned dramatically. "Don't be a bore, Cat. You know I'm allergic to theses."

"Since when are you writing a thesis?"

"Ugh, don't. I have too much personality for this drabness. Why are you calling, anyway? What do you want?"

"Charming," I muttered.

"Ten days of silence, Cat. I'm suspicious."

"I've just been busy." Being tormented by a madwoman and her followers. "Sorry, I won't leave it as long again. I actually called to see if you've heard from Virgil."

"Not in a few days."

"I just tried calling him, and it went to voicemail."

"And you're panicking," Tannie said, not entirely a question. "You know Virgil, he's a swot. He'll be doing all that boring stuff you just told me to do. Last I heard, he had a practical coming up."

I chewed my bottom lip. Tannie was probably right. Virgil was a perfectionist when it came to work and grades. He considered it a disaster if he got a ninety nine score when a hundred was available.

"Don't panic," Tannie said, his voice softening. "He'll be fine, Cat. He's in Australia, not an active warzone."

"I know," I mumbled. But with everything going on here, it had me paranoid. "You're right."

He gasped. Obnoxiously. "Wait, wait, let me open my recording app and say that again."

I rolled my eyes, a smile tugging at my cheeks. "I want you to know, I'm giving you my middle finger right now."

"I'd expect nothing less from my grumpy baby sister. How's things on the creepy gothic island anyway?"

"Creepy and gothic," I muttered. "It's fine. The professors are okay, classes are good so far, and we've even made a friend or two."

"Wonders will never cease," he drawled. "Even Byron?"

"Even Byron," I confirmed.

"Fuck me."

"You've got to stop saying that, Tannie. Someone will take you up on it."

"Chance would be a fine thing," he huffed. "Everyone's straight or closeted here. Hence, I am *bored.*"

"You'll live." The smile was still on my face. I pointedly did not mention my three husbands. I could have told my brother I'd hooked up with three men and he'd praise my sexual liberation and encourage me to shake off the trappings of an outdated society's beliefs about sex and bodies, but explaining *husbands?* And gods? And a curse? I kept my mouth shut.

"Oh, this looks promising," Tannie said before he could

tease me. "Yep, I'm being given my placement. Gotta go, darling sister. Take care, and don't wait ten days to call me, or I'll share that video of you walking the runway as Kitty Corner in our hallway."

I gasped, clearly able to see the footage of me in drag, massive wig and sequins and all. "You wouldn't dare."

"Totally would, love you, bye."

I scowled when he ended the call, and stuffed my phone back under my pillowcase, staring at the ceiling. For a few minutes, I felt normal again. I felt *myself* again. I spun my crown ring around and around my finger and drank the rest of my coffee.[1]

"What am I gonna do?" I asked the duck plushie, hugging her to my chest. I decided to name her Yena, and I loved her at first sight. "Clearly I don't have the nerve to tell my family what's happening here."

But Honey knew, and now Byron did. He hadn't taken the news calmly—he'd paced from one end of his room to the other, fingers tugging at his hair, and when we finished catching him up, he just murmured, "Fuck. She's gonna kill us all. Fuck."

I hated it but Byron was right. And maybe that was why I didn't have the guts to tell Tannie what was happening. He'd steal a helicopter and fly his way here, and then he'd be right in the middle of it. And I didn't want him to be doomed, too.

Panic settled like an anvil on my chest, but I ripped the covers off myself and swung my legs over the side of the bed.

"Get up, come on, *get up*," I breathed, and tensed all my muscles, physically propelling myself out of bed.

I dressed robotically, chanting at myself to *keep going, keep moving.* If I stopped, Nightmare won. She wanted me broken, wanted me completely paralysed by fear and guilt and the memories of what I'd done. Death had murmured as much to me every time we were together. So had Tor, and even Miz when he dropped by very briefly to check his shields were holding up, his stare lingering on me when I just sat in bed, my knees to my chest.

I wondered if any of them knew I hadn't eaten, that throwing up multiple times a day made it difficult but I had no appetite to begin with. I didn't even check what was in the white paper bag.

Dressed and shaking and crushed with anxiety, I grabbed my satchel and threw it over my shoulder, more as a talisman than anything else. *This is normal, you are normal, everything is normal.*

I squeezed Yena to my chest for a last boost of courage, settled her among the cushions on my new bed, and rushed to the door before I could talk myself out of it. It opened with a creak that drew the attention of my old neighbour—the studious black guy I'd seen once, when he got the party invitation. I didn't know if he was cursed or if he escaped before that happened. He stood by the landing, speaking to one of Duncan Ford's friends, the tall, blond guy looking like he'd walked out of a fashion magazine.

"Hey, you know Darya, right?" my once-neighbour asked, something drawn and disturbed about his expression.

"I..." I wasn't expecting to hear her name. I couldn't bear it. *You are normal, everything is normal.* "Yeah, we've spoken a few times. Why?"

"She's gone missing," Fashion Magazine jumped in, his eyes bright with either fear or excitement. "So have Professor Lancashire and Jillian Pendleton."

I didn't know the last name, but... "They've gone *missing?*" My breath came faint, my head starting to pound again.

"All three of them," my neighbour agreed, pushing his glasses up his nose in an obviously stressed move.

"Three at once," I breathed, panic closing off my chest.

"And you know why," Fashion Magazine said emphatically. "This is Duncan Ford's cult bullshit."

I blinked. "Aren't you friends with Duncan?" I asked, trying to ignore the hammering inside my skull, the anvil crushing my chest. The room was starting to go dark around the edges.

Three were missing. Darya was dead. People were asking after her. But she was never coming back, because I *killed* her.

"I *was*," Fashion Magazine said, his mouth twisted and arms crossing over his fashionable jacket. "Until Halloween."

So he thought Duncan was behind Nightmare's resurgence to power. Duncan was one of the few I knew wasn't —I saw the look on his face that night, and it was honest and terrified—but I could understand how everyone would jump to conclusions.

"You got an invitation," my neighbour said, watching me with tense understanding. "Did you go that night?"

I nodded tightly.

"Me, too," he offered. Neither of us was talking about simply attending a party. What costume did he wear that night? What was he now cursed as?

"They're picking us off one by one," Fashion Magazine spat, the whites of his eyes showing. He angrily stuffed his hands in the pockets of his khaki slacks.

"They?" I asked. My blood pounded too loudly in my ears.

"Those robed fuckers. The cult."

Was he right? Had her cult killed the other two? Oh god, was I one of them now? Was I her follower, controlled by her whim, powerless against each command? I shuddered hard, cold all over.

"I can't do this," I gasped, and fled back into my room, locking it firmly behind me. I stumbled over the rug to my bed and collapsed face down onto the covers, shaking all over. Cold all the way down to my bones.

People knew Darya was missing. How long before they realised she was dead?

CHAPTER THIRTY-SEVEN

CAT

a week passed, but I only got out of bed to use the bathroom attached to my room. I wasn't sure this room was supposed to be ensuite but my gods had made it so. Magic, I presumed. They tried to coax me into eating, but beyond a few sips of soup every day, I couldn't keep anything in my stomach.

One morning I woke up with Miz squashed into the single bed with me, his arms and legs wrapped around me like a clingy octopus and his whole body shaking. I didn't ask what had freaked him out, and he didn't ask why I couldn't leave my room. I knew the answer would be the same: Nightmare.

My phone buzzed on the fourth day, and I reached for it, thinking it was Virgil finally, but instead five words stared back at me from an unknown number.

> I know what you did

I threw it across the room so hard it shattered the mirror on the wardrobe—Tor picked up the shards hours later so I wouldn't stand on them, and stared at the text I'd received with his nostrils flaring like an angry bull.

I hadn't checked my phone in the days since. Sometimes Tor scanned my messages and passed on any from my family and friends.

Honey and Byron had hammered my door down, and only relented when I finally let them in to see I was miserably sick. They didn't know why, but I couldn't bring myself to explain what Nightmare made me do, what my own hands had done.

Darya hadn't been found yet. She was officially missing. But Professor Lancashire had been found in Rosalind Woods, his throat cut, and the other girl had been found hanging from a tall tree's heavy limbs. Dead, all three of them.

On the fifth day, Honey forced her way into my room and curled up with me in bed, holding me so tightly the impression of her arms must have been imprinted on my ribs.

"It's awful out there," she whispered. "Everyone's talking about the murders, and Darya being missing. I can't stand it much longer."

"I'm sorry," I'd whispered, my body hollowed out, soul decaying in my body.

"So I've come to catch your flu," she informed me, trying for humour and falling short. "Feel free to breathe all over me."

I could barely breathe at all, but I didn't tell her that. I was sure she already knew, sure she knew it wasn't flu that kept me in bed. She didn't know what I'd done, but she must have guessed Nightmare had done something, like I guessed Nightmare did something to have Honey clinging to me so tightly.

She only left when darkness fell and Death arrived. Beyond startling hard, she didn't ask how he'd melted through the walls in a cloud of darkness, and he didn't offer an explanation.

"Take care of her," she'd warned, sounding tired and empty like me.

"I will," Death had promised, laying a hand over his heart before he unveiled food and drinks and a new blanket made of the same feathers as the cloak he gave me before.

I had it wrapped around me now, on the eighth day since everyone had learned Darya was missing. I was surviving on coffee and what little scraps of food my stomach would allow. Every morning when I woke up, the bucket was empty and ready for a new day of vomit. I never asked who changed it, but it must have been one of my husbands.

Miz was here now, sitting on the floor with his back to the repaired wardrobe, his eyes far away as he turned Yena over in his hands. It was comical, seeing this beautiful, tortured man playing with a bright yellow duck plush.

"Say the word and I'll take you away from this place. I don't need a ferry, Prick."

He didn't sneer the name anymore; it was almost soft and tender on his tongue. It reminded me of Virgil calling me Prickly, and it was more comforting than I wanted to admit.

"She'll follow me," I said numbly, turning my head on the pillow to look at him.

"Come to the castle with me," he countered, his golden eyes pleading. "Fuck school."

"I can't fuck school. My mum and dad think my future's

set by coming here, that I'll have this illustrious career. If I drop out, I'll let them down."

"You could never let anyone down," Miz replied in a whisper that made my bruised heart hurt. "And this isn't a normal circumstance. Tell them people are getting murdered, and they'll understand."

"I can't. They'll stress about it." The words were hollow, like my chest. I rolled onto my back automatically when Miz pushed off the floor and came to the bed, setting Yena in my lap as he fit himself awkwardly onto my mattress.

"Be selfish for once, or this is going to kill you. I've seen it happen before, Cat, and I won't watch you die, too."

I couldn't look him in the eye. "Who?"

"A man I called my brother," he admitted. "Nightmare got to him, too. Being alive is more important than classes, Cat. You're missing them now, anyway."

"Thanks for reminding me," I muttered, rubbing the spot on my chest where it hurt fiercely.

"Here, unlock this thing and watch your ducks," he urged, pressing my phone into my hands. I did as instructed and opened Youtube, but we'd only watched a single short before an authoritative rapping came at my door.

I jumped, ice drenching my body.

"Stay here," Miz murmured and kissed my cheek, stunning me in place as he erupted into a seething plume of darkness. He vanished for a moment before returning. "It's the dean."

"I'm being kicked out," I gasped, my panic escalating.

Miz knelt beside the bed and took my face in his hands, drawing the worst of my thorny anguish from me. "Answer it. I'll be close by."

My body shook as I crawled out of bed and opened the

door, aware that I looked like shit with my hair greasy, face wan and sickly, and my pyjamas unchanged all week.[1]

"Dean Fairchild," I said, my voice croaky. Great, I sounded like shit as well as looked like it. "I'd invite you in, but I'm sick and I don't want you to catch it, too…"

"You do look peaky," the head of Ford School of Medicine agreed, his brown eyes shadowed with concern. I'd only met him once during orientation, but enough to know he was in his early forties, scholarly in a rugged way, and he gave off a stern but fair vibe. "I just came to see how you're doing. You were flagged on the system as missing a week of classes and, well, no prizes for guessing why."

I smiled weakly. "I'll be back as soon as I can. I hate missing lectures."

"Don't worry about it," he said with an understanding smile that surprised me. I'd always expected Ford's dean to be a hardass. "There's always a few who end up getting sick the first week. The popular theory is a change in food, but I'm more inclined to believe it's the shocking amount of alcohol imbibed in a single night that's doing more damage."

"I wish I was hungover," I murmured thoughtlessly, and horror shocked me like a lightning bolt to the heart but he just chuckled.

"I don't doubt it." Dean Fairchild gave me a sad smile. "If this is Halloween-related, don't worry. I'll make sure it never happens again." There was something in his tone that made my heart thud harder, sweat prickling my upper lip. I got the sense he wasn't just talking about cracking down on wild parties, but how would he know what happened that night? "Lawrence House is safe, and I'll make sure it stays that way, so take as long as you need to convalesce."

I could only stare at him for a moment, my ears ringing. He knew. I didn't know how, but he knew.

"I appreciate it," I said with numb lips.

His smile was nothing short of sympathetic, and genuine enough that I was confused. Was he cursed too? Was that why he cared so much about Halloween?

"Right well, I'll leave you to recover. If you're not up to classes for a while," he added, half turned away, "have a chat with Erika about taking online classes. We've got enough online material to keep you busy for a month or so."

Some of my anxiety lifted at that practical solution. I didn't have to leave my room, but I could still learn, could still do my coursework and avoid letting everyone down. "Thank you," I said and genuinely meant it. "I'll do that."

He gave me a nod and headed down the hall.

I closed my door feeling cold and scared but the tiniest bit hopeful. Maybe everything didn't have to be ruined. Maybe I could have this one good thing.

CHAPTER THIRTY-EIGHT

CAT

$\mathcal{M}$y phone buzzed on my bedside table, one text after another. I barely glanced at them, but they were all of the same ilk.

I know what you did

How long will your secret stay secret?

What happened to the body, Cat?

Poor Darya

I flipped it over so I couldn't see the screen and dragged my hands down my face. Someone knew what I did, and it didn't take a genius to figure out who. Nightmare's cult. Her followers. It was probably Alastor Carmichael texting me, pushing me to breaking point.

That was the one good thing about hiding in my room for a week—I hadn't seen his vicious face in days. I'd ventured out today to use the shower, but only because Tor was with me and my death god promised to kill anyone who so much as looked at me.

I was alone for a few hours now. Death would come soon, and spend the night with me. Maybe Misery would come too, and they'd use their magic to make the bed big enough for three. I wished someone were here to take my phone away, to hide the awful texts from me or—in the case of Tor—reply with threats so viciously detailed and bloody that he never got a message back.

I'd blocked every number the texts had come from, but they always returned. Every time my phone buzzed, I saw Darya's empty eyes, and a spiral of thorns cut deeper into my chest. But it wasn't just fear and grief now—I was *angry*. Not only had Nightmare forced me to murder my friend in cold blood, she'd made her followers harass me, as if the whole thing had been my choice.

I didn't deserve this. The pain, the anguish, the guilt? I deserved those. But I didn't deserve to be hounded by a cult for it.

I laid there for an hour, my mind racing fast but my breathing faster, this time with anger instead of panic. *She* did this. She killed Darya, and now she was torturing me over it.

"Fuck you," I whispered into my silent room, and then snapped louder, "Fuck you!"

Two days later, I was just as angry, and I found the anger gave me enough strength to get me dressed, clean, and out of my room. I stalked to the staircase and up to the third floor, rapping on Erika's door before I lost my nerve. All week, I'd gone over and over Dean Fairchild's words, holding them like a life raft while guilt and grief tried to drown me. He'd never realise just how much his kindness had saved me when I was at my lowest.

When there was no answer from within, I knocked again, and jumped when the door swung open, not fully closed.

"Erika?" I asked tentatively, peering into the room.

Her bedroom had a lot more personality than mine, probably because she'd been here for two years to my six weeks. Her books were on a neat shelf above her desk, a poster of a punk band beside it, and her room was decorated in shades of pink and grey. Erika sat in a swivel chair at her desk, her back to me.

"Hey, it's Cat. Do you remember me from orientation? Dean Fairchild told me to come speak to you about changing to online classes."

I took a step inside when she didn't reply, figuring she had earphones in. "I'm sorry to disturb you," I said, tapping her shoulder and startling when the chair spun.

"Oh god," I cried, jumping back when I saw the slack scream on her tanned face, and the gaping cut across her throat. Blood soaked into her baby pink shirt, a fatal amount.

She was dead.

Someone had killed Erika.

My hands shook as I lifted them to cover my mouth, my legs shaky when I stumbled back. Someone had killed Erika.

I was back in the corridor before I'd realised it, tripping down the stairs to my room—and stopping dead in the middle of the hallway when I realised a black-cloaked figure crouched in front of my door, feeding something under it.

I saw red.

"Hey!" I yelled, all my stress, my grief, my *rage* bubbling out as I launched down the corridor. My head filled with buzzing and violence, adrenaline burning off my shakiness until I was ready to fight.

The robed figure jumped to their feet, clearly not expecting to be interrupted, and after a frozen hesitation they lurched towards me. I was ready for a fight, ready to beat the shit out of these people who thought they could torment me even if I wasn't quite sure *how* to beat the shit out of someone. I widened my stance, lifted my fists.

But the robed figure shoved me aside instead of attacking me, and I lost my balance. I slammed into the wall hard as they fled down the stairs, a sharp ache exploding through my shoulder, shooting across my ribs, until I had to grit my teeth against a whimper. But I sucked in a pained breath and raced after the robed bastard.

CHAPTER THIRTY-NINE

MISERY

Stalking Cat had become an addiction. It made me feel in control of my own life when everything was falling apart, when even now Nightmare closed her hands around my soul. If I thought I had the strength to fight her after all these years, that hope was swiftly killed when I blacked out.

Just like last time.

So I stalked Cat as penance, watching over her so no one else could hurt her. Keeping her close for selfish reasons, too, the sight of her a balm the way Death and Torment were. My bride. I no longer cared that claiming her was exactly what Nightmare wanted; it was too late for that the second she wrapped her fingers around my throat. Cat was mine, and I'd just have to find a way to stop Nightmare winning.

Even if it felt like she'd already won.

"Where are you going, Cactus?" I murmured, cloaked in

the darkness behind her as she climbed the stairs of Lawrence House, looking better than she had in days. There was fire in her grey eyes again, and her back was straight instead of slouched, her clothes free of creases and food stains.[1]

I hung back, watching as she entered a room on the third floor of Lawrence House, my magic like acid in my veins as I readied to jump to her defence. Nightmare could be anywhere, her followers in any guise. When Cat stumbled back out of the room, her hands pressed to her mouth and face especially pale, I shot past her in a seething veil of darkness, ready to unleash myself on her enemies.

I would break their bones, pull their skin until it tore, carve cautionary tales about hurting my wife on their organs as a message to whoever found them—

There was only a corpse in the room, a recently dead body of a student with blonde hair streaked pink. The comparison to Cat made me uneasy. This could have been her, in her own room, with her own friends stumbling in to find her murdered.

I raced out of the room, frantic to be beside her again, to have her in my sight so I knew Nightmare hadn't got to her. Any suspicion I had that she'd killed the girl passed when I remembered the shock bleaching her face.

"Where are you?" I hissed, pushing myself to the limits of my speed, nothing but a shadow streaking down the stairs, finally locating my wife as she burst out the doors in the lobby.

"Don't run, you fucking coward!" she screamed, more animated than I'd heard her in weeks. I reached for her, my shadow stretching across pavement onto grass as she sprinted through the park after a human draped in a black robe, a hood concealing their face. As much as I loved seeing her fire return, I'd have preferred my bride didn't race after a cult madman without a single weapon in her hand. What happened to the knife Tor gave her? Clearly we needed to give her an armoury of weapons so our wife could always be armed.

Our wife. I liked that more than I had any right to.

She'd hate me when she knew who I truly was, what I'd done. She'd be *their* wife then, not mine.

"Stop fucking running!" she shouted, her voice both loud and guttural. It went right to my cock, but now was a bad time to be turned on. I followed her across the park, finally reaching her side in a pool of darkness, and I lashed out a thread of power to catch the figure she pursued.

An unexpected chill went through me. My darkness slid off the robed student without grasping, like oil on water. I gnashed my teeth. Anger flared for a second before I realised the tree cover had disappeared above us. I'd blindly followed Cat past Ford House and into the shadow of Rosalind Woods where the lake shone silver.

Ice cold filled my veins. I ground to a halt, staring at that still body of water reflecting the setting sun, serene and quiet. A lie, a fucking lie, the calm was all a lie.

My darkness ripped away and I stumbled forward at the same time Cat breathed, "What the fuck…?"

Because the robed figure had vanished.

"Never real," I choked out, struggling to breathe and unable to tear my stare from the lake. My eyes burned, beginning to water.

I remembered soft hands on my cheeks, remembered the sharp sting of fingernails leaving cuts exactly like the ones they left on Cat's cheeks. I remembered the hollow, pleading eyes of my sister, and then her screams as I walked mechanically into the water with my arms around her and carried her all the way to the bottom. I'd already been a death god then, foolishly trying to live a life outside death's domain. I'd lived and wished I hadn't.

I could still hear her screaming, hear her pleading for mercy in the moments before I dragged her under the water.

"Miz?" Cat breathed, jumping before she reached for me. I didn't feel her hands on my arms, didn't feel anything. "When did you get here? Were you following me? Did you see her follower? They just... disappeared."

We both flinched when a scream cut through the silence, distant but too close, too close, too close—

"Miz?" Cat murmured, her hand moulding to my face. She hissed in surprise. "Shit, you're ice cold. What's wrong?"

"That's her," I breathed, the ice spreading until I shook. "She's screaming but it won't change anything, it never changes anything."

Cat flung a panicked look around us and then threw her arms around me. I was so startled I forgot to breathe as she hugged me.

"Let's get out of here," she said gently. "You can talk about what's going on back at Lawrence Hall, okay?"

I couldn't. I wouldn't ever talk about it. I'd barely stammered through a conversation when Death and Tor found me sobbing at the side of the lake. Cat would hate me if she knew everything I'd done, and I found the idea of her hating me intolerable. It would kill me. A few scant weeks and I was already attached to her. Stupid. So fucking stupid, when Nightmare would exploit every weakness.

"This way," Cat murmured as if speaking to a wounded animal, guiding me as if I hadn't known this campus for hundreds of years. My eyes only left the lake when she physically turned me away from it, an impressive feat given she was five-seven and not particularly strong, and I was six-foot-tall and a death god.

"Say something," she pleaded, her arm around my waist. "She's watching us. I can feel her."

Cat stiffened, breath catching in her throat. Nightmare's laugh echoed around the woods now, delighting in our fear, her location impossible to pinpoint. But she didn't appear to us, didn't attack or issue commands. She only watched, and laughed, and no doubt planned her next move.

We'd be lucky if it didn't kill us.

CHAPTER FORTY

CAT

$\mathcal{I}$ had the unsettling feeling that everything was getting bigger, and by bigger I meant worse. It had been three weeks since I found Erika murdered, and five others had been found dead.

The island had their own police—two men in their late fifties with matching paunches and balding spots. They'd made a cursory investigation, but either they were in Nightmare's clutches or they were just useless. Fear of my prints being found on Erika's door and desk chair had kept me awake, but the officers didn't even dust for prints.

According to Byron who'd seen the officers in the room of a third year called Willie Herbert[1] all they did was walk around the room squinting at stuff, put electricals in bags for later examination, and ask around if anyone had witnessed anything suspicious.

Naturally, everyone said, *no, everything was completely*

normal. Eight people were dead and one was missing, but sure, everything was normal.

Hell, maybe this was normal for Ford. There was a reason the school was cloaked in so much secrecy, so much information held back until a week before term's start. Maybe the administration at Ford *knew* Nightmare would rise.

I wanted to know how my gods had killed her the first time. All they'd said was they'd tried the same method this time, and it had failed. Clearly, Nightmare had expected the attempt. I didn't like the thought of them confronting the terrifying madwoman, but they were *gods,* I reminded myself. I didn't fully know what they were capable of.

Miz had returned to my room after we followed the cult member, but had told me nothing—not why he was as pale as a ghost, or why he was shaking. I hadn't seen him since, but I got the sense he was always nearby.

"Please," Honey begged, perched on my desk while I caught up on online coursework I'd missed while spending time with my husbands this morning. "Please, *please,* Cat."

"No," I said, slanting a narrow scowl at her. "It sounds hellish, and no thank you. Go ask Byron."

"I can't *find* Byron," she muttered, batting a lock of slick, dark hair from her face and giving me a pleading lock I pretended not to see.

"He'll be with his boyfriend."

The pleading look continued. "You only have to come for two hours."

Honey, I have no interest in attending a charity gala organised by your boyfriend who threatens me every time he finds me alone and vulnerable, and who the very sight of makes me want to throw up with fear or break his fucking nose.

But I couldn't say that. And besides, she didn't know he'd threatened me. She was so stubbornly attached to him, I worried she'd fallen for his sneering golden face. I'd tried to bring up getting a weird vibe from him several times, to which she'd said I just needed to spend more time with him.[2] When I told her he'd said some things that made me uncomfortable, she'd promised to talk to him. The next time he caught me unawares in the dining hall, he pinned me to the wall with his arm to my throat, so that worked *so well*.

I wanted to scream the truth at her, but I was scared she'd take his side, and then she'd be alone with a man I knew wouldn't hesitate to hurt a woman. At least if I was still her friend, I'd know if something was wrong. So far, she was in the honeymoon period, but the first hint I got that it had changed, I'd ask one of my husbands to deal with him. I'd come so fucking close to telling them about all of Alastor's threats, but I couldn't bring myself to hurt Honey. What if this came between us and she never spoke to me again?

"One hour," I muttered, because her pleading expression was changing to one of hurt, and I couldn't stand hurting my friends.

"And hour and half," she haggled, hope brightening her blue eyes.

"Fine," I groaned.

I couldn't resist a smile when she moved my laptop aside so she could throw herself on me, hugging me tightly. I hugged her back harder than normal but neither of us commented on it.

The scream Miz and I heard in the woods that day hadn't led to another murder, but it had shaken both of us, and I couldn't get the sound out of my head. *Or* the sound of Miz's fast, frantic breaths and Nightmare's laughter. She was toying with us.

I didn't want to think about going to the gala, where

Honey would be vibrant with happiness and I'd have to pretend to be okay when every moment of every day I waited for one of Nightmare's followers to break into my room and murder me.

Almost everyone at Ford had seen the cloaked person I chased now—they were calling him the Assassin. Duncan Ford had been beaten up because everyone, especially his blond friend Fashion Magazine had managed to convince everyone he did it. Duncan walked stooped with a limp now, and I would have loved to believe it was him who hunted and murdered people, who pushed that envelope under my door, but it was too convenient and I wasn't convinced.

When Miz and I got back that night, there'd been no envelope, but I knew what I saw, like I knew it was Nightmare's twisted magic that had removed it.

"Thank you, thank you," Honey was gushing, squeezing my shoulders. "You won't regret it. And it'll give you a chance to wear that amazing red dress you brought."

"Yeah," I agreed, trying to summon some enthusiasm. "That makes it worth going."

"*And* we get to save some kittens, and you get to support your bestie."

I smiled, unable to resist her enthusiasm. "And there'll be food, right?"

"There will, a hundred percent," she agreed, laughing, "be f—"

Honey's laugh cut off. The world seemed to pause. To muffle, like a blanket was thrown over every noise.

"Cat, Honey," Nightmare's voice came floating on the air, a ghostly call that snapped us both to attention. "Come to me, my terrors. I have a job for you."

And like puppets we climbed off the bed and obeyed.

CHAPTER FORTY-ONE

CAT

oney didn't speak. I didn't speak. We walked in tense, forced calm out of my room, down the stairs, and across the park to the stretch of woods behind the laboratory building. Nightmare gave no further instructions, but we knew where to find her without being given a location. Could she find us, too, no matter how far away we were? The thought made me ice cold.

I wanted to grasp Honey's hand but I didn't dare move, didn't want to know if I *could* move or if I was a captive puppet who couldn't even blink without Nightmare's approval. I'd rather hold onto that tiny illusion of freedom and ignore the reality that I was a puppet.

"Don't dawdle," Nightmare chided when we reached her, like we were wayward children. The tree cover sheltered us from sight, but the closeness of campus made my skin itch. Would someone see us and come to our rescue? Or would Alastor see, and take it as evidence that I was

Nightmare's disciple? That Honey was too? I wasn't naïve enough to think things couldn't get worse. I knew they could, and would, and that made it impossible to breathe.

"I've got something I need you to clean up," Nightmare told us, looking unnaturally beautiful as always, her deep red hair a sleek waterfall and her face both stunning and horrific, especially when she smiled like she did now. "It shouldn't take you too long."

She swept a tanned, long-fingernailed hand at the ground, and it was only when I stared at the spot that I realised it wasn't a shadow made by the trees overhead but a long black holdall.

"What's inside?" Honey breathed, her voice so faint I barely recognised it. She gripped my hand so tightly it hurt, but I didn't let go of her.

"Just a block of hay, my terror," Nightmare replied, the fondness in her voice terrifying. Goosebumps formed on the back of my neck and flooded down my spine. "All I need you to do is move it through the woods, in secret, and put it where no one will ever find it."

"Where?" I whispered, both relieved that my mouth moved and petrified when Nightmare's mismatched eyes fell on me. I dropped my gaze, a horrible pain stabbing my frontal lobe.

"The lake," she said, her feet not touching the ground as she drifted towards us. One hand came up to cup my cheek, ignoring my flinch, and one stroked Honey's face. "That's all you need to do. Just take this bag of hay and put it in the lake. You can do that for me, can't you, my terrors?"

My mouth went dry, my knees knocking together. I imagined Death was here with me, his presence at my back supportive and furious at once. And Tor beside me, holding my hand fiercely while he told Nightmare exactly how he was going to torture her for scaring me. And Miz, who burned hotter and stronger than anyone else, who knew pain so intimately he could inflict it on others with expert care.

I wondered if he'd learned that pain from her. And I said, "No."

Nightmare laughed like I was hilarious, her head thrown back, her tinkling laugh grating my ears and heart alike. I flinched, but this time my body didn't move. I was frozen in place.

"Say that again," she dared, her laughter cutting off so abruptly it was like a switch flipped. "Tell me *no* again, Cat."

My eyes—the only part of me I still controlled—darted from her to the bag of hay, and I didn't know what mind games she was playing, why she was so insistent we do this, but I knew it was designed for maximum impact. Maximum trauma. Like everything she did.

I tried to curl my hands into fists, but pain exploded in my skull at the defiance, worse than the sudden flare from before. This stabbed far deeper and gouged a space inside my brain until I gasped.

I *gasped.*

Knowing it was going to hurt, I prised my lips apart, and said through a guttural snarl of pain, *"No."*

It hurt so badly my knees buckled and I wished my husbands were here. I wanted them to sweep me into their arms, to surround me with safety and affection and care. But there was only me, Honey, and Nightmare here. Something kept them busy elsewhere, and I didn't doubt that was by design. *Her* design.

"No?" Nightmare gave me that look again—like I was amusing and adorable, like a kitten trying and failing to climb a staircase. "I hope you don't think it was a request,

Cat. Pick up the bag, both of you, carry it to the lake without being seen, and throw it into the water." Her voice hardened, and my next gasp of pain sent me to my knees on the hard ground. *"Now."*

Her words rocked through my head like the aftermath of an explosion, and I bit back a whimper when Honey knelt beside me—not to check if I was okay but because she was bound as tightly by Nightmare's order as I was. Her hands went to the black holdall but her eyes found mine, watery and full of pain.

We'll be okay, I silently conveyed. *We'll be okay, I promise.*

We just had to do what Nightmare wanted and the command would release, and we'd be free. Just like the day in the clearing, where—where I killed Darya.

Tears burned my eyes and acid razed through my stomach, but I didn't have enough control over my body to vomit so it stayed in my stomach, my throat, my mouth. I was glad I hadn't eaten a meal in hours.

My hands found the rough canvas of the black bag, and I gritted my teeth. Fighting. Failing.

Sweat beaded on my head. A scream scratched at the inside of my skull, but my fingers wrapped around the handle and slowly, against my will, I stood.

"Good," Nightmare praised, almost sweet now, nothing menacing remaining in her voice. I couldn't even shudder. "Now, take it to the lake."

All we had to do was carry a bag of hay to the lake. That was all. It was only hay—we'd seen it. And the lake wasn't far. We'd be fine.

We had to be fine.

CHAPTER FORTY-TWO

DEATH

$\mathcal{N}$ othing felt right here. I knew it in my bones, felt the clang of alarm through my body, but I couldn't explain it with any kind of logic. This magic was old and had a will of its own, but it was failsafe in my hands. As Death, it would bend to my command even if it hated it.

"I have a really bad feeling about this," Tor said gruffly, standing outside the triangle cut into the grass behind my greenhouse. The castle loomed over us, its dark shadow hiding the symbol we'd carved into the ground and the darkness we'd all sent to fill it. Mud speckled his black leather jacket and stained his hands.

"It won't work," Misery said quietly, his eyes on the triangle of power, arms crossed over his slim chest. "It's not enough."

"We'll never know until we try," I countered, matching his soft tone. "We agreed it's worth a try."

"I know," Miz muttered, his expression difficult to read. He looked moody and angry but I *knew* Misery, and I could tell he was concealing something bigger, some deeper emotion. I squeezed his shoulder, and when that didn't relax even an inch of tension from him, I pulled him into my arms, brushing a kiss over his lips. "If this works, we kill them all. I don't care if they're compelled."

"Fine by me," Tor agreed with a shrug. He was frowning at the symbol cut into the grass.

I released Miz with another reassuring kiss, each of us standing at a different point of the triangle. From Tor's casual surveillance on Cat's phone we knew she and Honey had been searching the library at Ford for any hints of a curse and how to break it. We also knew there was nothing there to find; any books that had been at Ford were moved here six hundred years ago to *my* library. And in one of them, we'd found one of the original sigils used to summon Nightmare—or in theory any death god. We'd adjusted it with a single scrawled symbol to summon her *followers*.

In theory.

Whatever happened, at least Cat was safe with her friend. Nightmare only attacked when she was alone.

"All this bullshit over a husband who didn't even like her," Tor muttered, shaking his head. "You'd think she'd want to die to go be with him, but no."

"Love ruins people," Misery said with a frown. "It leads only to madness."

Tor's face cracked in a grin, and he would have nudged Miz if he were close enough. "I happen to like that brand of madness."

"It'll kill you eventually."

"I can't be killed."

"Enough," I interrupted softly, not wanting to think about why Nightmare had crusaded for revenge all these years—because her husband died and she blamed me, Death. Everyone that had suffered at her hands could be traced back to me and the force I embodied. "On three, speak the incantation. And you're right, Miz, we kill anyone who comes through."

Tor nodded brusquely. Miz uncrossed his arms and reached for a swath of shadow, pulling out a knife. He nodded too, and we stepped forward, onto each corner of the sigil, shadows flowing around our feet to power the symbol in lieu of fire and blood. As much as I wanted to strike Nightmare a blow, I wouldn't kill for it.

Followers of Nightmare, you are summoned. Appear here, or suffer for eternity.

Our voices blended, overlapping in a droning chant of power, and at first nothing happened.

But then movement flickered from the rivers of shadow cut into the ground—pale silvery light. I caught my breath. It was working.

Figures were torn through the triangle of power, so many trapped in its magic that I lost count. Relief nearly weakened my knees. Her followers were here. We could deal her a dangerous blow, weaken her, and get the upper hand we needed to keep Miz and Cat safe.

But I realised too late, the figures were too transparent to be living.

The fifty people who appeared were dead. Ghosts. And the symbol had only been drawn to contain the living.

They swarmed before I could throw up a veil to shield us, their hands as cold as bone.

CHAPTER FORTY-THREE

CAT

$\mathcal{W}$e dropped the black canvas bag into the shallow water at the edge of the lake, neither Honey or I speaking but our rough breaths broadcasting panic and terror. The second the bag's weight tore the handles from our hands, I felt the dead weight of Nightmare's command lift from me and I sank to my knees in the mud.

Honey knelt beside me, shaking so violently that her teeth chattered when she wrapped her arms around me. "How do we stop her?"

"I don't know," I choked out, trying to speak past the tightness in my chest. Nightmare's magic left a residue, like oil covering my hands, taunting my soul.

I gagged, wanting to scour every trace of her off me.

Now I could move and breathe and think for myself again, I began to tremble. Why had it been so hard to pull a bag of hay? I knew hay was heavier than I might realise,

257

but it wouldn't have been backbreaking for two people to drag a bag full of it.

"Cat?" Honey whispered when I pulled away from her and reached for the bag. In the shallow water, it had caught on a rock protruding from the lake and it had stuck only a few feet from the bank. I waded a step into the water, so icy and numb I didn't feel the cold water fill my shoes or soak my jeans. I had to know. I didn't want to, but I *had* to.

"Cat," Honey said, almost a warning, a plea. She didn't want to know, but I couldn't live with never knowing what we'd carried across the woods.

So I pulled down the zip—and staggered back onto the muddy bank, a shudder wracking me from head to toe.

It wasn't hay. It was a person—pale and cold and empty-eyed.

"Who is that?" Honey whispered, grabbing my arm so tightly it hurt.

I couldn't look away. My stomach cramped.

"It's Dean Fairchild."

CHAPTER FORTY-FOUR

TOR

*N*ote to self: when you're performing a ritual based on a dead language, get very fucking specific with your wording.

I trudged up the stairs of Lawrence House to my girl, weak as fuck after being drained by ghosts for hours, and my head pounded a warning that I was weak. Turned out we should have specified Nightmare's *living* followers. We'd paid the price for that little error. Miz passed out, looking pale and fragile, but that was his regular look these days. Death was watching over him, and I was here to watch over our girl. Our wife.

Usually that thought, that precious fucking title, filled me with energy and thrill, but I was too exhausted for that. I wanted to collapse into her bed and fall asleep with my wife in my arms. It would be the first time I'd spent the night alone with her. It would have been nice to not be out of breath when I reached her floor, to have the stamina to

259

give her at least half a dozen orgasms, but I'd be lucky to give her one.

"In the morning," I promised myself, even my voice weak.

Honestly, fuck ghosts.

I used my last scrap of energy to pass through the door in a cloud of darkness, and grunted on the other side, completely fucking drained. I hated feeling like this. Vulnerable if we were attacked.

Cat was curled up on top of her covers, her eyes open and staring at the opposite wall, and panic paralysed me. She looked dead. But then she startled at the sight of me, sitting up suddenly before she wilted with a sigh when she registered it was me.

"Tor," she breathed, her voice as husky as mine. Her face was pale and splotchy but streaked with tears, her eyes as empty as the ghosts we'd fought tonight.

"What happened, beautiful?" I asked gently, my own torment forgotten in the face of hers. I kicked off my boots and climbed onto the bed with her, letting the dip of the mattress roll her into my arms.

"We—I—" Her breath caught and then she was sobbing, burying her face in my chest and clinging to me with fierce arms.

In halting, broken gasps she told me what had happened, from Nightmare's lilting voice summoning her to opening the bag and seeing the dead eyes of her dean staring up at her.

"Not your fault, Cat," I promised, my lips pressed to her forehead, moving over her skin with each word. The peaches and cream taste of her wrapped around my tongue, but instead of waking me up, she lulled me into a calm that made my exhaustion more evident. "Nothing you did is your fault."

I wanted to tell her we were working on bringing Nightmare down, weakening her power, but the idea of giving her false hope damn near killed me. But I couldn't say nothing, not when she cried harder, her tears soaking through my shirt.

"We'll be with you at all times from now on, okay?" I murmured. "At least one of us will be with you, or watching. I promise." Death and Miz would take no convincing. "Everything's going to be okay, beautiful. She won't get to you again."

Cat sniffled and nodded. "Thank you," she squeaked out, making my heart squeeze tighter.

"We thought you were safe in your room with Honey. That mistake won't be made again," I swore, my heart beating irregularly. What if Nightmare had ordered Honey and Cat to kill each other? What if we'd been fighting ghosts, and our wife was dead the whole time?

I held her tighter, the thought making me cold down to my bones.

CHAPTER FORTY-FIVE

CAT

The guys stayed at my side every moment of the next week, and it should have been stifling but all I felt was gratitude and relief. When they were with me, Nightmare couldn't get to me. Even if she commanded me again, they wouldn't let me hurt anyone or dispose of another body. I was safe.

That safety was the only reason I was able to shower and change into my red and silver ombre tulle dress today. I bought it on a bad day a year ago, when I needed something good among all the bad I'd faced that year, but I'd never had the nerve—or occasion—to wear it. The bodice was made of a bold crisscross of red fabric, with cut-outs and straps offering glimpses of my ribs and my sides, before beautifully soft tulle swept to the ground, a high slit baring my left leg. I loved it. I just wished I was wearing it for something other than Alastor Carmichael's fundraiser.

Someone would be with me all night, though. I'd never be alone.

I jumped at the cold knuckles that skimmed my bare back, but all my tension melted at the kiss Misery brushed over my shoulder.

"You look to die for, Prick," he said tenderly, his knuckles trailing lower and sending a rush of shivers through me. When his hand moulded to my ass, I turned my face to kiss him, wondering when hatred had turned to tolerance and tolerance to affection. Probably all those days he spent with me at my worst, watching animal videos and making sure I ate, offering solidarity and comfort.

The first kiss was disconcerting, and I drew back with a frown at the roughness of his mouth instead of the silken warmth I was used to. It was the blue-eyed asshole who stared back at me, and even though I knew it was my Miz underneath the façade, I still couldn't help but feel a sense of loss.

"All your pretty hair," I murmured, turning to run my hands through his much shorter black hair. When he frowned, the expression familiar even if the face was not, I added, "This hair's pretty, too."

"It was, until you messed it all up," he agreed, scowling behind his wire-framed glasses.

"Oh," I said, a smile tugging at my lips. I dove both hands into his hair and made an even bigger mess. *"Oh, no."*

Miz's eyes darkened, not rich gold but piercing ice blue in this form. They still made my stomach leap and drop, though. I knew the punishment they promised, and I couldn't help but remember when he'd pinned me to the bed and made me come over and over with his wand.

"You look more debonair this way," I told him, flattening a few choice strands before I laid another kiss on his lips, lingering this time, his cock growing hard where it pressed against my hip.

"Debonair," he repeated, a glow of pleasure in his eyes. "Hm."

He liked the compliment, and we both knew it. I kissed his jaw and drew out of the circle of his arms, giving myself a last check in the mirror, twisting the crown ring around and around my finger.

"I'll never leave your side, Cat," he reminded me, missing nothing.

"I know," I agreed, and summoned a smile, grabbing my clutch and jumping when it vibrated. "Shit," I hissed and fished out my phone. "It's probably Honey with another disaster."

She'd been roped into organising the fancy shindig by her boyfriend—yes they were official—and had been putting out mini fires all day. Caterer fuck ups, missing flowers and evergreen boughs, a Christmas tree lacking ornaments. Every few hours there was a new tragedy, and while I hated hearing my friend stressed, I couldn't bring myself to feel sad about Alastor's event falling apart.

I answered the call and put the phone to my ear. My heart stuttered at the silence on the other end.

I ripped it away from my ear and ended the call without sticking around to listen to them breathing. This was the sixth call I'd had.

"Wrong number," I said to Misery, shoving off my unease and dragging a deep breath into my lungs.

Miz's eyes turned murderous, but I just faked calm and headed for the door.

I was disappointed when Miz and I walked out of Lawrence House, hand in hand, crossed the park with its many trees and double fountains[1] and found the gala set up in a giant gazebo behind Everard Tower wasn't in flames or falling apart.

Miz paused with me beside the tower—it was a three-storey building, and not even cylindrical, so calling it a tower seemed aspirational—to watch the staff, students, and esteemed guests who'd flown onto the island mill around in their white-tie finery.

"We can go home," Miz reminded me, squeezing my hand. He looked insanely good in a fitted tuxedo, his shirt as white as snow but offset with an ice-blue bow tie that matched his eyes. I wanted to see *my* Miz in the suit, though.

I shook my head. "It'll be fine. I only have to stay an hour and half, then we can bail."

"Bail?"

"Leave."

He scowled at the gazebo, at the sculpted topiaries that had been wrapped in golden fairy lights, the mammoth Christmas tree by the entrance to the gazebo where tables had been set out, laden with drinks and leather-bound catalogues. The whole area looked like a festive explosion, and even smelled of Christmas—fir and cranberries and cinnamon. I didn't know how they'd managed it, and I was annoyed to find myself admiring the area.

"Language is annoying," Miz said, and led me out of the shadow of Everard Tower towards the throng of people, his head swivelling as he scanned the area. We were pretty enclosed here, between the tower and the woods, but the lights made it seem brighter, bigger.

"Are you okay?" I asked as we approached the table. We were close enough to the lake to be able to glimpse it between the trees.

"I'm fine." He lifted my hand to his lips and brushed a kiss to my knuckles. "Are you?"

I swallowed. The last time I was on this side of the campus, Honey and I pushed Dean Fairchild's body into the lake. "I'm fine," I echoed his words. I wondered if we were both lying.

"Honey," he pointed out, lifting our joined hands to gesture at my friend dressed in a gold silk dress and heels, storming across the ground[2] to throw a single red rose into the woods.

"Honey?" I called, hurrying across the space past mingling guests, snatches of conversation reaching me—business deals being done on the downlow, a trio of judgemental women sneering at the latest equality bill passed in parliament, even a marriage being arranged between a businessman and a politician, with zero input from their children. "You're still being sent roses? Why didn't you tell me?"

Honey sighed, crossing the grass to meet me halfway. "I thought it had stopped, and honestly, you've been stressed enough after—"

Yeah. After.

"I didn't want to give you anything else to worry about," she said with a sad smile, giving Miz a questioning look. "Do you think you can let my bestie go so I can hug her?"

"No," he replied, point blank.

I snorted and pulled my fingers free after a reassuring squeeze. The second he let go, Honey flung herself at me.

"You look hot, Cat. Megawatt hot."

I laughed, hugging her back. That's what we used to say when we were tweens—there was a whole scale of hotness, and we had ranked boys on it. Harry Styles was megawatt hot, but we'd argued about Tom Hiddleston.[3]

"You look megawatt hot, too, Honey." I stepped back to look at her, the gold silk hugging her curves and trailing artfully behind her. I told myself she dressed killer for

266

herself and not her boyfriend, but I was pretty sure it was denial. "Seriously. Do you know how much money you'd make for homeless cats if we auctioned you?"

She rolled her eyes, her cheeks flushing pink. "Oh, shut it. It's items and experiences only, no humans auctioned."

I tilted my head. "What do you class as an experience...?"

She elbowed me, giving me an unimpressed—but thoroughly amused—look. "Who's your date, anyway? Don't tell me you have a fourth husband."

"If she had a fourth husband, I would slit his throat in his sleep," Miz informed her conversationally.

"This is Miz's med student face," I told her. And when her eyes widened with disbelief, her mouth popping open, I added, "I've found it's best not to think about the *how* of things, and just shrug it off as magic."

"Yeah." She still stared at him, looking for a seam of where the illusion met his real face. She wouldn't find one. "Magic. Got it. Hey, is that Byron's guy?" she asked, looking beyond me to where the path snaked between Everard Tower and the laboratory. I spotted who she meant instantly—a tall guy our age dressed in fitted trousers and a white shirt with a narrow tie, his sandy hair swept back from his deeply tanned face and an expression of anxiety tightening his features. Yeah, I knew that feeling.

"That's him!" I confirmed, grinning. Honey hadn't met Gustin, Byron's boyfriend yet, but now was the perfect chance. As little as I liked being social and talking to new people, Gustin was one of us by extension of Byron, so I had to make an effort.

Miz held out his hand—calloused and deep gold compared to his usual soft, pale hand—when I took a step, and I answered his plea, or command, and slid mine into it as we crossed the light-strung field.

"Hey, Gustin!" I called, and smiled when he turned, recognising the dread in his body language. "I don't know if you remember me, we met once. This is Honey, we're Byron's friends. Is he coming tonight?"

He'd been absent more and more, and increasingly hard to track down, but I couldn't blame him for spending all his time with Gustin. The man was elegant and pretty and seemed really sweet.

His soft green eyes narrowed with confusion when we reached him. "Byron...?"

"Yeah," Honey said with sly glee, "you know, your boyfriend."

Gustin blinked, and then blinked again, looking from me to Honey to Miz. "I know who you mean, but he's not my boyfriend. I barely know him. Maybe you've confused me with someone else?"

My world, previously turning on its axis, screeched to a halt. "Yeah, maybe," I heard myself saying. I nodded when he excused himself politely, clearly uncomfortable.

"Maybe it was a different guy," Honey suggested, her voice brittle. "There's an endless supply of pretty men at Ford."

"He pointed Gustin out to me, and addressed him by name," I replied, my voice strangely dull. "He said he's shy, and that's why he didn't want to spend time with us. Because he had anxiety."

Honey didn't say anything. There was nothing she could say.

"It's clever if you think about it," I said bitterly, holding onto Miz like a raft in a storm. "I'd empathise with anyone who had anxiety, so I'd give them space. And if he chose someone shy as his fake boyfriend, he'd always have an explanation why they weren't spending time with us."

"And the fake boyfriend would give him a cover when

he disappeared for long periods of time," Miz pointed out, his mouth pressed into a thin line.

Honey's shell shocked expression morphed into understanding and disbelief. "He lied to us."

It wasn't just me he'd lied to—he'd given Gustin as an excuse when he left Honey and I at breakfast, at dinner, during study sessions. My stomach knotted.

"But why would he lie?" she asked, her hands crumpling the fine silk of her dress.

My heart hurt. "There are so many reasons, but one really obvious one." Miz pulled me against his side, his arm around me. "He wasn't there that night we got cursed, or there'd be a mark—his hair colour different, his behaviour changing—but Nightmare got to him. She must have."

It was the only thing that made sense.

"What if...?" Honey began, chewing her bottom lip. "The Assassin..."

"No," I argued instantly. "No."

Byron wasn't the one who tormented me with texts and threats, who I chased across campus that night, who'd been seen by multiple people stalking the grounds of Ford with blood dripping from a knife. The same days people were killed.

That wasn't Byron.

CHAPTER FORTY-SIX

CAT

I don't know how we got through the introductions and into the auction. I blinked and I had a catalogue in my hand, and Alastor was standing proud and smug on the stage that'd been built at the far end of the marquee, guests murmuring as he announced the auction for a signed Lakers jersey. I hadn't bid on anything and I didn't plan to. I was counting down the minutes until I could run home to Lawrence Hall as soon as possible. Or I'd beg Miz to take me to the castle, where I could hide behind the shields and cry my heart out.

My best friend had lied to me. He didn't have a boyfriend. He'd been absent so often it was strange. And there was a cloaked madman stalking the grounds of Ford, threatening and killing people. I didn't want to connect the dots, but I couldn't help it. Honey's words burrowed deep into my brain.

She stood on the stage beside Alastor now, handing him

items to display with a smile fixed on her face, the curve of her cheeks visibly strained. They'd already raised a hundred thousand pounds with three lots, and satisfaction radiated from Alastor as he presented items like a king looking down on his lowly subjects. I hated him.

No matter what I thought about Byron, and even if I'd seen him slip something under my door—if he *was* the Assassin—I knew it was Alastor calling me, texting me threats, grating my nerves to shreds. The messages echoed his threats from the graveyard, when he threw me up against the mausoleum.

Miz snagged a flute of champagne from a roving waiter and handed it to me, tucking me tighter into his side. "Tor should be here soon."

I glanced up at him, taking a sip of champagne and wincing at its sweetness. "Sick of me already?"

Miz replied with a throaty sound. "I'd spend my life with you if you let me."

"Who says I won't?"

His eyes softened, icy blue but unfathomably warm. "Let's go. You've shown your support of Honey."

"I don't feel good about leaving her with Alastor" I admitted, glancing at the stage.

"Why?" Miz's tone changed, like sharp steel. "Has he done something to you?"

"It's fine. It was only once, and he's stayed away from me ever since—"

A lethal sound rattled his throat and he jerked forward, like he'd rip Alastor limb from limb right here, with an audience. I caught his sleeve and held it tight.

"Don't. Miz, *please.* I need you here with me."

His wrathful expression didn't change, but he stopped charging through the crowd. "Fine, but I want you as far away from him as possible. And he *will* meet the consequences of harming you." He brushed my cheek with the backs of his fingers, a strange mix of affection and murder in his eyes. "No one hurts my wife."

I swooned, even with my heart broken over Byron's lies —and the texts he'd ignored from both me and Honey tonight.

"Not going to beg me to spare him?" Miz asked, a black eyebrow raised.

"No," I replied, and watched his eyes flash.

His arm tightened around me, drawing me closer so his lips could brush my ear. "The only reason I'm not ripping that beguiling dress off you right here, in front of all these people, and fucking you until you scream my name for all to hear, is because I don't want *him* to see."

I sucked in a breath, tingles rushing down my neck and across my chest.

"Otherwise," he continued, not entirely keeping his voice down, "you'd be gasping as you struggled to take my cock all the way inside your hot little cunt right now. I wouldn't give you time to adjust, or make sure you're ready for me. I'd take you the way I want, because you—" He bit my ear lobe. "Are." Scraped his teeth down my throat. "Mine."

"Oh, god," I gasped.

I caught Honey's gaze when Miz drew back, looking far too pleased with how affected I was, and I gave her a silent signal that I was leaving. *Are you okay?* I asked with a look.

I'm fine, go be ravished by your hot husband, she replied with a roll of her eyes.

"Let's go," I said and caught Miz's hand, leading him through the crowd and into the sharp cold. The sun had mostly set now, and a low mist had crept in, weaving around the trunks of evergreens, obscuring the pegs holding up the marquee until it looked like a scene from a fairy tale. Around us, the fog in the air caught the glow of fairy lights and diffused it until the whole space was full of hazy, magical illumination. It was romantic, and the perfect place to stop and tug Miz close for a slow, heated kiss.

"I'm going to bury myself so deep inside you that you'll never get me out," he panted against my lips, his eyes like shadowed ice. "I'm going to fill every aching, desperate hole in your body until you're wrecked and messy and pleading with me to stop. I'll write my name on your pussy in my cum and you can write your name wherever you want in my blood—"

"I'm not making you bleed," I breathed, my head spinning, my pussy pounding with head and furious need.

"Spoilsport," he said with a pout. "You've drawn my blood once before."

"I hated you then."

His eyes softened, lights twinkling in their depths. "But not anymore?"

"No," I said, linking my hands behind his neck. "Not anymore."

He dipped his head for another kiss, but jerked back with a low, threatening sound. "There. The one you call the Assassin."

My breath caught, the sudden chill clearing out the heat of our kisses, and I saw what Miz had seen—a cloaked, hooded figure slinking down the side of the marquee and into the shadows.

I didn't stop to think; I chased after them, my heart pounding in my chest. *Please don't be Byron, please don't be—*

I skidded around the side of the marquee, Miz catching me before I tripped, and stared at the empty space. "He's playing with us."

"Nightmare is," Miz corrected, his hands tightening on

my waist. "We need to go. Something's happening tonight and I don't want you involved."

I stared at the empty stretch of grass, and as much as I wanted to search the woods, the lake, and every building on campus until I found the hooded figure, I didn't want to know. I wanted to cling to the last few scraps of doubt. *It could be someone else. It might not be Byron.*

"This way, Cat," Misery said, something flat in his voice now. I wrapped my arm around his back, pulling him close. My own voice did that sometimes when I was overwhelmed.

"Miz?"

"We need to go this way," he echoed, guiding me past the marquee and down the back of the laboratory building, the warm lights falling away here until the fog seemed less magical and more threatening. The twisted silhouettes of topiaries looked like watchful figures. I remembered the first time I met the guys, when fog had crept across the moors as Nightmare hunted me. I remembered her howl of frustration when Death stopped her with a veil of dark magic.

"Okay," I soothed Miz, stroking his back. I didn't know what had triggered his panic, but I could guess. The lake was too close here, and his memories must have been eating at him. "It's okay, we'll go this way."

"Do you trust me?" he asked, trembling.

"Yes," I answered without hesitation. I might not have trusted him two months ago, but I did now. He was an asshole sometimes, but he'd never physically hurt me. He'd never lied to me, unlike Byron. Did I still trust By...? I couldn't answer that question until I spoke to him and found out what was going on.

It could be something innocent. He might not be

working for Nightmare, stalking Ford students. I prayed for another explanation.

Miz led me across the manicured field where the garage sat, Rosalind Woods hugging the right edge of it. I kept my arm around him, kept him close for comfort, for warmth as the biting wind cut through my tulle dress. My fingers were so numb I could barely feel my silver clutch against my palm.

I scanned the field, and startled when I saw we weren't the only ones here—ahead of us, strolling towards the garage was a squat female figure in a butter-yellow gown, her bronze skin luminous in the moonlight and long brown hair like a ribbon of silk down her back. For a moment, my heart stuttered and I thought it was Darya, but Darya was dead. I killed her.

I hugged Miz tighter, shivering against the cold both inside and outside my body. I wished Tor and Death were here, too, wanted them all at my back, wanted the safety of knowing they were with me.

"Are you okay?" I asked Miz.

Ahead of us, the woman in the yellow dress turned at the sound. My breath strangled in my throat.

I shook my head, staring at the woman, time slowing until she faced forward and began to run.

It was impossible. I stabbed her. She *died*. Death had to dispose of her body. But there was no denying it. The woman in the yellow dress was Darya.

I didn't stop to think. I ran after her.

CHAPTER FORTY-SEVEN

CAT

*D*arya fled past the garage and over a low wall onto the moors. I tore the tulle skirt of my dress climbing after her, but I didn't stop to inspect the damage. I ran until I was out of breath, using the moonlight to see the rough grasses and heather underfoot. The Christmas scent of the gala had given way to wild grass and cold, biting air.

"Call Death and Tor," I called as I ran, breathless and strained.

"Already done," Miz replied, his stress at an all-time high because his voice was even flatter. I wanted to stop to hug him, but I couldn't let Darya get away. I needed answers.

I *killed* her. But there she was, running across the moors ahead of me, the skirts of her yellow dress flying behind her. There was no mistaking it was her, even in the silvered light. She was alive.

276

"Darya!" I shouted. "Stop!" And because she might think I'd come to kill her again, I breathlessly added, "I don't want to hurt you, I just want to talk. Please."

But she didn't slow, let alone stop. A stitch pulled across my side, until pain flashed like lightning through my body, my breathing strained and sharp.

"Stay close," I panted to Miz, lifting the skirts of my dress above my ankles so I could run faster, never taking my eyes off the yellow dress streaking across the moors ahead of me.

I didn't stop to wonder why Darya was running, didn't think she might be leading me on an intentional chase until a cloud passed over the moon, casting the island into temporary darkness.

When it cleared, light beaming down on the moors again, Darya was no longer running. She stood a few metres ahead of where I ground to a sudden stop, a tall, robed figure and a familiar, smiling woman beside her.

Nightmare.

Darya had led me into a trap.

CHAPTER FORTY-EIGHT

CAT

I spun, breathless enough that a sudden flare of dizziness made the island whirl. "Go," I panted to Miz. His gaze was so wild with panic that it hurt me. "Run, get out of here. Go get help, I'll be fine."

He flinched every time I said her name, and he'd been terrified for weeks, and I didn't want him anywhere near the goddess.

"*Go*," I pleaded, my heart breaking when he stayed by my side. He wouldn't leave me alone, even though he was terrified.

"He won't leave until I command him to," Nightmare said, her low, sultry voice carrying across the distance like a song in a smoky room. "Did you think Darya was the one leading you to me?" She laughed softly. "Darya was just the distraction."

A frown pinched my brow, tightened my mouth. Cold began to spread through me.

"You want to deny it," Nightmare said, tilting her head as she watched me through mismatched eyes, the white iris in her eye bleeding fresh blood down her golden cheek. "But all the little inconsistencies are starting to add up, aren't they, my terror?"

"Shut the fuck up," I snapped, too breathy, too afraid. But in snapping I showed her my hand. Stupid. I began to shake.

I wouldn't believe what she was insinuating. No fucking way. *He won't leave until I command him to.* That was bullshit. She couldn't command Miz. He was a death god.

But I couldn't look at him. I didn't dare to.

"Now," Nightmare said lightly, glancing from me to Miz, "I have a few minor things to address, a couple items to check off my to-do list. You know how it is, Cat, always busy busy."

My name in her mouth made my blood run cold. I twitched my fingers to test if I was frozen, but I could still move. She hadn't compelled me yet. Miz was so close I could feel the heat pouring off him, sense the fear and rage even if I didn't dare look at him. I linked my little finger with his, the only movement I allowed. He showed no reaction.

I wish I'd brought the knife Tor gave me. I felt so stupid for leaving it behind because it wouldn't fit in my clutch. I had no weapon, no magic, *nothing* to stop Nightmare doing whatever she planned to.

The only thing I could do was run, but Miz was frozen beside me and it didn't seem like fear paralysing him. *He won't leave until I command him to.* She had him under her thumb. I wouldn't leave Miz to her non-existent mercy, no matter—no matter what he'd done. It was painful to think, to even consider that he was under her control.

What had he done while she compelled him? I didn't want to know.

"First of all, Cat say hello to my followers." Nightmare waved an elegant hand from Darya to the robed figure I prayed was a total stranger. "Neither are the disciple who restored me to power, you understand. I wouldn't be so foolish as to reveal them so soon in our little game, but these are both my valued followers. I believe you call them cult members."

"Is that how she's alive?" I breathed, a chill spreading through my blood. I glanced at Darya and found her watching me with deep amusement that made my heart jolt. A second later, rage poured through me.

How dare she smirk at you that way? You don't need a knife to claw the smile off her smug face; fingernails will prove just as effective.

My breath caught, but I shut out the dark impulse. If I hadn't had the voice for years, I might think this was Nightmare fucking with me. I wished I could blame it on her, but this was all me.

"Don't be ridiculous," Nightmare laughed, her eyes creased at me like I was both stupid and adorable. "She's not alive; you killed her. Darya Henderson is as dead as a doornail, and I have you to thank for that." Her mouth widened into a smile and I stumbled back an instinctive step when she focused all her attention on me. My head pounded, pain thumping against my skull. I was forced to look away. "What made you think I needed my followers to be alive?"

What? Goosebumps rippled all down my arms. Darya was really dead. I really killed her. I didn't realise until that moment how much I was hoping she was alive so I could absolve myself of the guilt of murdering her.

"Oh, poor thing," Nightmare crooned, her eyes hooded

with sadness when I flicked a rapid glance at her. "So much suffering, so much misery. This must be exciting for you, Cai," she said, looking at Miz.

Cai. I couldn't help it; this time I looked at him, forcing myself to be brave and stop sneaking cowardly glances at him. His expression was smooth and even, as calm as he was in sleep, but his golden eyes roared with fury and dread. The same emotions tangled in my chest, twisted my gut until I felt sick. White hair danced in the wind, the tails of his translucent shirt fluttering around his stomach.

Earlier, I'd wanted nothing more than to see Miz's true face, but now it hurt to look at him.

"She's controlling you," I rasped, forcing the truth out.

"I am," Nightmare confirmed mildly. "He won't speak unless I give him permission, which I won't. It'll ruin all this delicious tension, don't you think."

I spun to face her, my eyebrows slamming down over my eyes. "Let him go."

Nightmare laughed, a tinkling sound of beauty that filled the night. It cut off as suddenly as it began, and she looked at me with bright, delighted eyes. "Not yet, my terror, not yet. Besides." Her smile deepened. "You haven't met my second follower yet. This one's alive," she whispered with a wink.

God, Darya was dead. A ghost. I really killed her.

Nightmare smiled indulgently at the robed, hooded figure to her left. "Of course, I wouldn't have this follower in my grasp without my darling Misery."

"He's not *your* anything," I hissed, my pulse hammering against my throat. I held onto Miz's pinky finger harder. He was his own person, and if he belonged to anyone, he was *mine*.

Nightmare gave me a pitying look and turned to the robed follower.

"Where are the other four?" I blurted, stalling, terrified. A tremor started in my legs, threatening my knees. "At the party, there were five robed people."

"Now, those *were* ghosts," Nightmare said with relish at my flinch. I'd been in the room with *ghosts*. I'd spoken to one, had felt its stare on me.[1]

"I must say, it's been entertaining to watch you all turn on each other, playing your violent guessing games about who's my disciple. I didn't even plan that part," she added with the air of someone confessing gossip. "The paranoia and bloodthirst of mortals never fails to impress me."

I hooked my finger tighter around Miz's, holding on for dear life. "You set us up to attack each other, and sat back and watched."

"I did, didn't I?" She looked immensely pleased, her eyes trailing over the hooded figure. "I'm sure you have your own theories about my dear follower. Or as I hear my terrors calling him, the Assassin."

Calling him. So it was a male. My stomach sank. *Byron, what have you done?*

"Of course, none of you could know that some of the hooded figures you saw since Halloween were my new followers—not dead, but living. Like this gentleman. I believe you're acquainted."

I shook my head hard. "No."

"Forgive my flair for the dramatic," Nightmare said, savouring my panic as I cringed away. *I don't want to know, I don't want to know—*

She ripped the hood off his head and there was Byron, his dark, shaggy hair falling over his forehead, tears clinging to his long lashes. His eyes begged me to understand, to forgive him, but I glanced away, staring at the dark, empty moors. Why was there never anyone around when I needed them? *Please, someone, anyone.*

Nightmare had two men I loved under her control, and I didn't know what to do. I didn't know how to save them.

"There, that's better," Nightmare murmured, stroking Byron's cheekbone. "Now everyone can see each other. But I see you're not falling to your knees in shock, Cat."

I swallowed, scraped my teeth over my bottom lip. "He lied about having a boyfriend."

"The boyfriend," Nightmare sighed, shaking her head. "I should have taken him, too."

Taken. I shivered at the word. "Are you going to take me, too?"

She laughed, a sharp burst of sound that rippled across the moor. "Heavens, no. That would hurt Death far less than what I have planned."

"Hurt Death," I echoed, barely above a whisper. I trembled harder as the wind picked up, fog whispering around my ankles. "Why would you care about hurting Death?"

I knew he'd vanquished her once before, but I realised now I knew very little about how or why he'd done it. And for some reason, that felt deliberate. They'd all kept me in the dark.

"This whole enterprise has been about making Death pay, you understand," Nightmare said, a laugh lingering in her voice. She gave me a half pitying, half judgemental look. "Why else would I care about making you his bride? Everything has been to weaken him so when I get the chance, when every domino has fallen and the right cards are in my hand, I can kill him."

"Why are you *telling* me this?" I demanded, pain spreading through my chest. My husbands had lied. Miz was under her control. Byron was one of her robed followers. And she'd led me here, to the moors where she could torture me with these truths, and had yet to reveal *why.*

"Because it amuses me," she replied, patting Byron's

cheek. "And it furthers my agenda. Did you know Byron failed his entrance exams?"

The question was so abrupt that I didn't understand at first, and then frowned. "No, he didn't." Now she was just bullshitting me, trying to turn me against my best friend, and it wasn't fucking happening. I needed to be as clever and cunning as her, needed to get him away from her, needed to take him and Miz and run to Death's domain.

He said, all those weeks ago when we first met, his domain would answer to me. Surely, I could call up the castle. He told me death was everywhere, that it could be accessed from any place. All I needed to do was find a way to summon the domain and then—

"He *bribed* his way in," Nightmare said with a grin, her eyes gleaming. "Isn't that delightful? He couldn't get to Ford on merit, so he used his parents' money to buy a place." She laughed, the sound grating my ears, scraping my soul.

"Byron would never." I shook my head hard. "You're lying."

"I never lie, my terror. Why do you think he ran out of the party before the ritual was enacted? I gave my first disciple explicit instructions to send him a message and then call, ordering Byron to leave unless he wanted the truth leaked to both the governing body of Ford and the press. Can you imagine the scandal?" She gasped. "Son of the CEO and CFO of Everett Corp *buying* his way into university. It would have ruined him. And ruined his family, by extension. Of course he ran out and followed my every command. Of his own free will," she added with emphasis.

I shook my head. This was bullshit. There was no fucking way—

"His sister isn't even pregnant," Nightmare laughed.

"Tell her, Byron. She thinks you're frozen and under compulsion but we both know the truth, don't we?"

I forced myself to look at Byron for longer than a second, a sharp pain cracking through my heart at the devastation in his sapphire eyes.

"It's okay," I whispered. "Whatever she made you do—"

"Made?" Nightmare smiled wider, really enjoying herself. "Oh no, my terror. He *chose* to do everything. Didn't you?"

Byron jerked, a sharp flinch that told me he could move, like I could move, like Miz clearly couldn't. What would Misery have done if Nightmare released her grip on him? Killed her? I believed he would. He wouldn't stop until she was dead, and maybe he knew that.

"I'm so sorry," Byron said suddenly, his eyes darting to me. Full of shame. I didn't want to believe it; I clung to the possibility he was compelled. "She would have ruined my family." A tear tracked down his cheek. "I didn't want to do what she told me, but I didn't have a choice."

"You did," Nightmare chided. "You chose yourself, and preserving your reputation, your family's wealth."

"I would have been kicked out of Ford, Cat," Byron said, his voice breaking, pleading. "I'd have had no future in medicine, no future at all. Do you know what my parents would do if they found out I bribed my way in?"

I sucked in a pained breath. Oh god, he really did bribe his way in. My ears began to ring. I remembered how my voice sounded when Nightmare commanded me, remembered speaking to Darya, my voice not quite right. But this was *Byron's* voice, the voice I'd known for years. My bottom lip wobbled. He wasn't compelled at all.

"My dad beat the shit out of me the night before we came here because I told him and Mum I'm gay." Byron was pleading, willing me to understand. I remembered him

285

holding his middle the first few days we got here, and my chest ached fiercely.

"Why didn't you tell me?" I asked, unable to hide the hurt in my voice. "Honey and I would have had your back, By. You know we would."

A shadow moved across his eyes. "I didn't want you to hate my parents, and I knew the second I told you Dad was a fucking homophobe, all you'd talk about was him being a piece of shit."

"Because he *is* a piece of shit!" I exploded, all my stress, anger, and betrayal blasting out. "We would have taken care of you, and we'd have figured out the bribery shit, too —you didn't have to... what have you done?" I asked, realising all they'd done was hint at it.

Byron dropped his gaze, pain tightening his features.

"What did you do, Byron?" I asked, my voice hardening. I held Miz's pinky tighter.

"Not volunteering the information?" Nightmare asked, visibly gleeful. "Alright, then I will. From the moment Misery called him the night of the party Byron was my willing follower." I snapped my head around to stare at Miz. *He* called Byron? Fuck. *Fuck.* "And from then on, he's done all manner of little jobs for me, haven't you, Byron?"

"Fuck you," Byron said weakly.

"All those text messages you received? Byron. The threatening notes left for you? Byron. The kitten you thought you found outside Lawrence House? A scrap of my magic left there by Byron."

Every word made my chest tighter. Made it impossible to breathe.

"I killed Darya because of that kitten."

Byron flinched.

"You did that?"

"I'm sorry," he said miserably.

I couldn't look at him. Couldn't stand the sight of him. I was a murderer because of him.

Nightmare gloated. "The events that led to Dean Fairchild's murder were placed, meticulously, by Byron. I couldn't have done it without your help, dear." He recoiled from her reaching hand, his face twisted into hatred. "That nuisance kept me out of Ford's grounds for as long as he could, but ultimately he fell. Thanks to your precious Byron."

Dean Fairchild... protected us? Kept Nightmare away?

"You killed him?" I whispered, staring at my friend.

"In spectacular fashion," Nightmare confirmed, making me sick. "Oh, and that sweet girl in the year above you, the one you found tragically murdered in her room?" Nightmare's smile widened. "Byron."

"I didn't want to," Byron choked out, tears falling freely down his cheeks.

Erika. He killed Erika. *Byron.* My Byron. My best friend. I couldn't process it.

"No," Nightmare agreed softly, her expression changing to one of sympathy, so convincing I almost fell for it. "You didn't want to. But the difference between you and Cat is you had a choice, and you *chose* to kill to protect yourself. Cat did not choose. That makes you the greater monster, don't you think?"

All the things I thought were Alastor Carmichael—the threats, the texts. It was Byron. I covered my mouth with a numb hand, cold and sweaty all over.

"Now, for the pièce de résistance," Nightmare said with a flourish, her eyes flashing with delight. "Darya, my dear, go retrieve that object from the grass over there."

I watched as Darya moved freely, not robotically. Not even floating like a ghost should. The smirk on her face and the knowing glint in her eyes made me sick. The

287

second I saw what she'd retrieved was a knife, I dropped my hand and lunged into a run towards her.

I'd heard enough. Now it was time to grab my husband, my traitorous best friend, and get the hell out of here.

I'd wonder how a ghost could hold a knife later. Now, I ripped the handle out of her cold fingers, shuddering at how solid she felt, and before I could question myself, before anxiety could stay my hand, I drove the blade into her stomach.

Darya just laughed. "I'm a ghost, Cat. Do you really think you can kill me?"

I faltered back, trying to keep her and Nightmare both in my line of sight, not releasing my grip on the knife. "What happened to you? You were nice, *kind,* but now that you're dead you follow Nightmare?"

"I *always* followed Nightmare," she said, her smirk transforming her into a whole other person. "It's not my fault you're so desperate for affection you fell for the friendship routine."

But—there were no signs. Darya had been friendly and accepting and *kind.*

"You can't even accept it now, can you?" Darya shook her head, making a lunge for the knife.

I twisted aside, only adrenaline and panic keeping me out of her range. She was a ghost; couldn't she just float and grab it back?

"My mother and my mother's mother were followers of Nightmare," she informed me. "Proud followers. I willingly gave myself to her so that Nightmare could receive power from my death."

Wait. I faltered, confused. "You *chose* to die? What the fuck?"

Darya decided that was enough talking because she

came at me again, grabbing my wrist in a grip so tight I cried out. A ghost's touch shouldn't have hurt.

"Enough, Cat stay where you are, let Darya take the knife."

Nightmare's voice hit me like a whip's crack and I went deadly still. Paralysed. From this angle I could see Byron turn to Nightmare, heard him plead with her to stop this. The truth hit me like a bullet. Darya was going to kill me, like I killed her. My death would give Nightmare even more power.

"Please," Byron begged. "Leave Cat out of this."

"Don't worry," Nightmare replied gently, "I will. Cai, take the knife and kill Byron."

Her words hung in the cold air for a moment, until meaning struck.

My heart hurtled at my ribs in a violent thump. *No.* I tried to shake my head, tried to throw myself at Miz, to catch him, stop him. Cai—that's what she called him earlier. And now she ordered him to kill my best friend?

"You may speak, Cat," Nightmare said with unhidden pleasure, wind ruffling her long hair.

"Don't," I blurted, my voice choked. "Miz, *please.* Don't hurt him."

Misery strode past me, his face unchanging, but those eyes reached through skin, muscle, and bone and pierced my heart.

"You're a death god," I cried, trying to move my arms, to pick up my feet so I could reach him. "You can fight her. Please. *Please* don't do this."

But he took the knife from Darya's spectral hand, and tears fell from my eyes as he brushed past me again.

"You might want to run, Byron," Nightmare suggested.

"No," he replied, his throat bobbing. He looked past Miz and locked eyes with me. "I'm so sorry, Cat. You're right about all of it. I should have told you and Honey. Deep down, I just wanted to stay your friend, the guy you knew and loved. I didn't want you to know what I was really like. Don't remember me like this, yeah? Remember the guy I was before we ever came to Ford."

I wanted to shake my head, wanted to run to him, wanted to body slam Miz to the ground so he couldn't do this. A horrible roaring noise started inside my head.

"Miz, *please,*" I screamed when he strode within a few paces of Byron, the knife gripped between white-knuckled fingers. Oh god, oh god. *"Byron, run!"*

Byron smiled, a tiny, defiant thing. "I'm sick and tired of doing what Nightmare commands, so no, I won't run. I love you, Cat. You and Honey are the best friends I could ever ask—"

Miz drove the knife under his ribs and into his heart before the last word could leave Byron's lips, and part of me died right there with him.

My scream was deafening and raw.

CHAPTER FORTY-NINE

CAT

$\mathcal{N}$ightmare released me enough to let me drop to the ground, and my knees hit hard-packed dirt and grass, dew soaking through the ragged hem of my dress. I didn't care about the cold or the damp. I didn't care about anything. Byron was dead.

"Ah, here comes the cavalry," Nightmare said cheerfully. *Pay close attention, my terror.* Her voice flowed through my mind like smoke, wisps reaching even the deepest recesses. I flinched, digging my fingers into the dirt, and realised I was still screaming.

She took a step forward, the train of her black lace skirt sliding over the grass. "You can go now, Darya. You've been very helpful."

"Happy to serve my goddess," Darya murmured, sounding thoroughly brainwashed.

My scream died, a horrible silence filling its void. I stared across the moor to where Byron had fallen, the blade sticking out of his gut. I couldn't look away even when cold, dark shadows glided across the grass like a river flooding its banks. I didn't look away even when Tor rasped, "Miz? Cat? What's going on?"

He killed my best friend. I didn't bother saying it; one look and they'd know what happened. Miz's hands were covered in blood. *Byron's* blood. My best friend's blood. My best friend was *dead.* Dead, and a murderer, a liar, a traitor, and I was screaming again.

Grass rustled as Death knelt beside me, throwing up a veil of darkness between us and Nightmare.

"It's okay, it's okay," he soothed.

"Liar," I cried, pulling away from him. Cold rushed into my side but I didn't care. "It's not okay. Byron is *dead.*"

"Miz, come here," Tor said in a strange tone. Something like blind terror shone on his face when I glanced up, another wave of tears spilling from my eyes at the motion. "Come here."

I laughed bitterly. "He won't answer you."

Tor's face twisted with anguish as he looked at Misery, standing a little too close to Nightmare, then at me. I didn't bother getting to my feet. Didn't lean closer to Death.

"She's right," Nightmare said amiably. "He won't answer you until I tell him too."

"You took control of him again," Death growled, his voice unsettling and deep, the air vibrating around him until all my hairs stood on end. I swore the temperature dropped.

"Again?" Nightmare's soft laugh was a whisper on the air. She was enjoying this immensely. "Oh no, I never lost control of him. I've been speaking to him this whole time. I simply commanded him to forget our little conversations."

"Did you never wonder why all your plans never quite worked? Why books and weapons went missing? Cat, you must have wondered who trashed your room, who planted the cameras I used to monitor your every movement." She lifted her hand to Miz's tense shoulder but a lash of darkness from Tor snapped her hand away.

She'd been watching me? Because *Miz* planted cameras? Oh god, he was there when I found my room open and all my things ransacked, wrecked. The room he ushered me into with promises that I'd be safe... bugged, watched at every moment. All the times I'd been with Miz, with Tor, with Death, she'd *watched.*

I twisted aside and vomited the contents of my stomach into the grass.

Death rose slowly to his feet, power vibrating around him, his rage palpable. "Release your hold on him. This is your only warning."

Nightmare snorted. "No. And this is *your* only warning. If you take so much as a single step towards my first disciple, I will end everything you hold dear."

"Miz," Tor said quietly. "Fight this."

Words I'd said to him, right before he killed Byron. I looked at my friend, laying cold and still in the grass, his blue eyes open and unseeing. Miz did that. Miz who—who I was falling for. I covered my mouth with my hands, choking back a sob and tasting bile.

Tor took a step. Nightmare smiled.

My stomach roiled harder when a ripple of magic went through the air like a heartbeat, like a pulse. I'd felt it before, in Ford House.

"What did you do?" Death demanded of Nightmare, rushing to Tor, grabbing his shoulder to keep him in place. "What the fuck did you do?"

"That," the goddess said with a smile pinned on Death, "was a blanket of power cloaking the island. No one will find their way on or *off* the island until the blanket falls. Fun, isn't it?"

"To what end?" Death demanded.

"She's not done," I muttered, but I was. I was done with these liars, these scheming assholes who knew Nightmare did all this, targeted Ford students, all to get back at *Death*. Everything that happened was because of him. "This is just the first phase of her plan."

"Correct, darling," Nightmare said, beaming as I got to my feet and turned away. "Now we enter phase two."

I turned my back on them, not caring right now if Nightmare struck me. Byron was dead. Miz killed him. They all lied to me, every last one.

Oh, Cat. Nightmare's voice was sing-song and taunting, and I only realised it was inside my head when none of the others reacted. *Don't you want to know about Virgil?*

I froze. Turned back to her.

Not a word out loud, my terror, or I'll be forced to murder him. She locked eyes with me. *Not by my own hand, of course. But I think Cai here would love to draw more blood, don't you?*

She had my brother.

I do, she confirmed, her eyes gleaming. Death snapped something at her; she ignored him, fixed on me.

"Let her go," Tor snarled. "Cat has nothing to do with this."

"Oh, I think your bride has *everything* to do with this," Nightmare taunted. In the sanctum of my mind she whispered, *One false move and Virgil meets the same fate as Byron.*

I thought of the missed calls, the ignored messages. I knew I hadn't been paranoid worrying about him. I *knew* something was wrong. How fucking stupid could I have been to brush off my worries?

What do you want? I asked, testing communicating with her by thought. I didn't know if it would work, if she'd even hear me, but a corner of her mouth curled into a pleased smile.

Nothing much.

"Miz," Tor whispered. "Come here. Please."

"What do you want, Nightmare?" Death demanded, echoing my words again, sending a shiver down my spine. "To release him, to undo your curse on Cat—what do you *want?*"

"Hmm." Nightmare tapped her bottom lip with a long fingernail. "Why don't we start with you kneeling?"

I clenched my jaw when Death's knees hit the grass instantly, and no matter how furious and upset I was, I *hated* the sight of him kneeling before Nightmare.

Stop it, I snapped.

What will you give me, Cat? To release your precious Misery, to undo the curse, if that's what you truly want.

Yes, I said quickly. To have the shadow of her curse lifted from my soul, to never be terrified she'd make me kill again, to finally be able to scrub the makeup off my face... yes. I wanted to reply that I'd give her anything, but that was too dangerous.

"I'll lift the curse," Nightmare said aloud to me, to Death, "but are you so sure of their affections without it, Cat? Are *you* so sure of her affections without the curse binding you, Death?"

"Just release her," Death snapped. As if it made no difference to him either way. That was fine. Byron was dead. Miz killed him. They all lied to me. It was fine.

Nightmare's smile grew as she strode forward a step, batting aside the darkness hurled at her to rest a hand on Misery's shoulder. "Say the magic word, Death, and it's done."

"Please," he said through gritted , almost instantly a ripple of dense, oily magic spread across Ford's End, clinging to my skin like a layer of dirt until I gagged. When the magic seeped away, I felt off balance. I remembered feeling the same when the curse first took me, that I'd been taken apart and put back together wrong, and I felt the same way now. I'd gotten so used to the weight and poison of the curse that I staggered now, gasping for air.

Death was at my side in an instant. The comfort of his hands on my face, turning it up so he could scan my eyes, made tears drip from the corners of my eyes.

"It's going to be alright, Cat. I promise you."

"You lied," I said, my voice ragged. I couldn't stand eye contact; I ripped my gaze away. "You lied to me. She only cursed me to get back at you. I killed Darya because of you, and this—this revenge—"

"It wasn't malicious, little bride. We're just so early in this relationship—"

Nightmare scoffed. "Relationship. How much of a relationship is it now, without the curse?" Her mismatched eyes speared me, making my heart pulse. "Do you still care for Death, Cat?"

Say yes, or Virgil dies.

I jumped. Swallowed. Said, "Yes."

Death released a breath I didn't know he was holding, his hands dropping to my waist and squeezing tight. "We're going to get out of here," he promised me quietly.

I froze when Nightmare spoke again, a chill going through me. "And do you still care for Torment and Misery?"

I opened my mouth, not entirely sure what I'd reply. Miz had killed Byron. But her smoky voice slid through my mind before I could get a word out.

Say no, or I'll carve Virgil into a hundred different pieces and leave a new one for you to find every day.

My breath caught.

"Cat?" Tor asked, turning with a frown. He wore his heart on his sleeve, hurt and pleading hope in his eyes, and I wanted to scream.

Tell him you feel nothing.

My mouth was dry as I met his eyes. "I feel nothing for you."

And Misery.

"And Misery," I breathed, choking back tears. My heart was already broken by Byron's death, but now the shard crushed into dust. "I'm so sorry."

"You only—" Tor staggered back, surprise bleeding into devastation. "You only wanted me because of the curse."

I pictured Virgil's face and nodded, tears dripping over my lips until I tasted salt. Death let go of me to step back, staring at me.

"I'm sorry," I said again, my hands shaking, and I understood how Nightmare had kept Byron under her thumb. She didn't even need a curse to control me when she had Virgil.

Nightmare's voice slid like smoke through my mind, and I said the final damning words.

"I only wanted you and Misery because of the curse, but what Death and I have is real. Why would I want you when I have Death?"

THANK YOU SO MUCH FOR READING CAT'S FIRST BOOK AND joining me in a new series. I hope you loved this spooky, steamy, murdery little book. I have so much more planned for Cat and her death gods. You can already preorder the next book, All Hallows Game.

Or get a foiled, signed All Hallows Night paperback in my store.

And while you wait for book 2, check out these complete twisted, psycho series where the FMC doesn't have to choose:

Killers and Kings (Demons, psychos, serial killer FMC, fated mates)

Rebels and Psychos (Vamps, wolves, serial killer FMC, fated mates)

Kissed by Brimstone (Demons, mythology, possessive men, fated mates, complete in June 2024)

Happy reading!

Leigh x

THANK YOU FOR READING!

Need the next book ASAP? Let me know – the more demand for a series, the more likely I am to bump the next book to the top of my list! To stay updated with what I'm working on next, come join me in my Paranormal Den on Facebook, or sign up to my fortnightly newsletter! (Links on the next pages, so keep reading, loves.)

If this is your first Leigh Kelsey book, I have lots more books for you to sink your teeth into, and three completed series. I've got vampires, wolves, shifters, angels, and demons - and of course plenty of growly alpha males with tragic backstories.

Reviews make the world go 'round - or at least they do in my world. If you loved this book and you can spare a minute, please leave a review on Amazon or wherever else you like to review. Even the smallest, one-line review has an impact, and helps me reach new readers like you awesome people.

Thank you to everyone who's already reviewed. Your words mean I can keep writing the books you love!

LEIGH KELSEY

WHERE THE MEN ARE *PSYCHO* BUT THE WOMEN ARE *WICKED*

SIGNED, FOILED PAPERBACK!

STANDARD PAPERBACK

FOILED, SIGNED EXCLUSIVE

AVAILABLE AT AMAZON

ONLY ON SNARKYSTABBYBOOKS

You can find all my available print copies in my online book store, plus books from my cowrites and pen-names, **and all orders come with swag and a dedication from yours truly.**

https://payhip.com/snarkystabbybooks

FREE VAMPIRE ROMANCE STORY!

Hybrid's Curse is a stand-alone paranormal romance.

As a vampire-witch hybrid who can never be killed, Emilio is used to pain and suffering. But when Aislin, an innocent faerie healer, is kidnapped because of him, Emilio will do anything to stop her suffering too. Especially because she's been dreaming of him for seven years, and claims to be his mate.

If you love romantic stories with a healthy dose of suspense, and pairings of dark, gloomy men and sunny, optimistic women, you'll enjoy this happily-ever-after story.

JOIN MY MAILING LIST FOR YOUR FREE STORY

A TWISTED PARANORMAL RH SERIES

I just dug myself out of a not-so-shallow grave to find myself not-so-dead

Must be a day ending in Y

A hundred years ago, a monster of abusive proportions killed my fated mates. And me. But if I've been reincarnated, they have too. And someone thought it was a good idea to keep me from the men I love…

READ FREE IN KINDLE UNLIMITED

JOIN MY READER GROUP!

Join my reader group for news, giveaways, and exclusives!

To get news about upcoming releases before anywhere else, and early access to my books, come join my Leigh Kelsey's Paranormal Den group over on Facebook!

ABOUT LEIGH KELSEY

Leigh Kelsey writes about psychos with questionable morals and addictions to shiny, stabby objects, but she's perfectly harmless, she swears. She can be found in Yorkshire, England listening to K-Pop, watching serial killer documentaries, and writing as much spicy paranormal romance as she possibly can in a day.

LEIGH KELSEY

WHERE THE MEN ARE *PSYCHO* BUT THE WOMEN ARE *WICKED*

FIND THESE OTHER PSYCHOS BY LEIGH KELSEY!

Feared by Monsters: A stand-alone twisted paranormal romance

Killers and Kings series
(Complete Twisted Paranormal Demon RH)
Crazed Candy
Sweet Violence
Sugar Rush

Kissed By Brimstone series
(Twisted Paranormal Demon RH)
Hellborn Angel
Midnight Descent
Eternal Night
Cursed Dawn
Shadow Fall: Part 1
Shadow Fall: Part 2

Rebels and Psychos Duet
(Complete Twisted Paranormal RH)
Complete Series Box Set
Killer Crescent
Blood Wolf

Sick and Twisted series
(Twisted Death Gods RH)
All Hallows Night

Broken Alphas series

(Complete Rejected Mates Dark Paranormal RH)

Complete series Box Set

The Omega's Wolves

The Omega's Mates

NOTES

CHAPTER 1

1. Please, I beg of you, do *not* ask my full name. Mine makes *Zoltan* look ordinary and unremarkable.
2. God, what if Ford's End didn't *have* popcorn? Or iced latte and bubble tea?] My family was well-off and we didn't hide our wealth, but Ford was a whole different level of rich. Would we have truffle on toast for breakfast? Caviar blinis for lunch?
3. I had boobs though, but as appealing as that was for others, it had proven disastrous for my posture. Please spare a thought for my poor spine.

CHAPTER 4

1. How did she *do* that? She kept collecting people like trading cards, and the whole process was baffling to me. Did she bribe them with food? Threaten them with dismemberment unless they followed her around?

CHAPTER 5

1. I'd drawn the line at the veil. The dress was already overkill, as I'd realised immediately upon trying it on.

CHAPTER 7

1. Unless I got very stressed and very horny. I was at med school, and I was human after all...
2. Official name.
3. Best film in the history of cinema, and if you disagree you can fight me.

311

CHAPTER 8

1. Or eggplant emoji for the discerning Americans out there.

CHAPTER 12

1. If Ford's End didn't have a bookstore, I was burning this entire island to the ground.

CHAPTER 15

1. Inflicting it on the guilty was fun, though. Their eyes sometimes bled. Sometimes they pointed a damning finger at me, as if they'd find revenge in death. Cute. I ruled death. I was literally best buds with the big D.

CHAPTER 16

1. God, no, anything but my book!
2. Uh, I mean *scary* intensity...
3. But he thought I was *cute...?*

CHAPTER 17

1. Well, I guess it could have been worse than Misery and Torment. At least they weren't called Betrayal and Body Odour.
2. I wish I meant pussy cat, I really did.

CHAPTER 20

1. And apparently I cared about being sexy when there was a man between my thighs
2. Okay, maybe not emotionally but *physically...*

CHAPTER 21

1. Insanely good, eye-roll-inducing oral.

CHAPTER 22

1. Not a thought I ever imagined I'd have

CHAPTER 23

1. Presumably, he'd had a cane in the seventies and it had been taken off him by the dean of Ford...

CHAPTER 27

1. Not that I was complaining. I had anxiety but I wasn't insane.

CHAPTER 29

1. Even if I hadn't been married to three death gods, I would have known gods were real with a single bite of a Pop-Tart.

CHAPTER 32

1. Parts that had been awake since I choked him, but I was in firm denial about that.
2. I hadn't known I could scream. The more you fucking know.

CHAPTER 36

1. If I was going to be terrified, I could at least do it caffeinated.

CHAPTER 37

1. It wasn't my best look. I wouldn't be winning a beauty pageant sash any time soon.

CHAPTER 39

1. Though I'd die before ever pointing out her favourite pyjamas had a smear on them. Even if the way her cheeks flushed with embarrass-

ment made me want to fuck her into oblivion—the bruise her skin, stain her sheets, break her bed kind of oblivion.

CHAPTER 40

1. A name somehow worse than mine, Zoltan's and Virgil's put together.
2. Hell fucking no

CHAPTER 45

1. I still hadn't worked out why a med school needed *two* fountains.
2. With effort, because storming across grass in heels took serious determination.
3. Like an intellectual, I knew he was megawatt hot, but Honey was stubborn.

CHAPTER 48

1. Oh god, oh god, oh fucking god. If I found out a spirit had ogled my boobs, I was quitting this planet forever.

www.ingramcontent.com/pod-product-compliance
Lightning Source LLC
Chambersburg PA
CBHW030606180626
46816CB00005B/1693